MOVING ON

MARCIE STEELE

For Alison, Caroline, Imogen, Talli, Louise and Sharon. My tribe.

THIRTY-FOUR YEARS AGO

'One day I'm going to have my own roller skates, like you, Sal.' Maria pushed a pair of bright-green leg warmers over her borrowed white ones from the roller rink.

'You could have some now,' Sal replied. 'You'd only have to save the money from your Saturday job for about three weeks.'

'But when would I get the chance to use them?' Maria stood up, resting on the stoppers while she waited for Sal to do the same. 'I won't be able to wear them enough. You can go out more than me.'

'I suppose.' Sal nudged her as she spotted someone in the distance.

Maria saw Jim Wilshaw and his friends walking towards them. A swirl of butterflies circled her tummy, and her face broke out into the widest of smiles. She was glad now she'd worn make-up. Her eyes were easily her best point. Sal often said with smoky eyeshadow she had come-to-bed eyes without even trying.

That wasn't the impression she wanted to make now, though.

'Act as if you don't care,' Sal whispered and moved away slowly.

Maria wanted to follow but found herself rooted to the spot. Jim had caught her eye and smiled, so she wasn't about to ignore him.

Sal had gone no more than three metres when she turned back, tutting light-heartedly. The group were level with Maria now. She returned, sporting a grin.

'Hi, Maria.' Jim wiped his floppy fringe away from his face. 'Fancy seeing you here.'

'Yeah right.' Sal rolled her eyes. 'As if you don't know we come here most Saturdays.'

Maria smiled back at him. It was true. Whenever she could get away, you'd find her here with Sal. It was her one taste of freedom every weekend, a chance to be a normal teenager. A chance she wasn't going to waste.

'Hi, Jim.' She pointed to his feet, where he wore his own boots, too. 'Nice skates.'

'Ta. Want to skate with me?'

'Sure.'

She took the hand he offered, looking to her best friend for approval. Behind them, Sal was giving her the thumbs-up.

The music was loud so there was barely any need for conversation, which was good because Maria already felt tongue-tied. She had dreamed about this moment for a few weeks. Recently, Jim Wilshaw had invaded her every thought. They went to the same school and bumped into each other often.

Last Saturday, they'd merged as a group, although she and Jim had been on its periphery. They'd chatted together for most of it. Maria had been disappointed when they'd done nothing more than say goodnight to each other at the end of the evening. But in school on Monday, Jim had made a beeline for her, and they'd spent a lot of their breaks hanging out.

The music was loud once they were on the rink, disco lights on the floor as they skated round. They were both naturals, having practised since the roller rink opened a few months ago.

'I love this song,' Jim shouted to her, pulling her closer. 'What music do you like?'

'Most things as long as it's not heavy metal,' she shouted back.

'I hate that, too. Do you like Madonna?'

'Everyone likes Madonna!'

The music changed to another song, and they raced around, dancing along to the beat. Maria wasn't sure if it was skating in circles that was making her feel dizzy or the feelings running through her body as Jim held on to her hand. She hadn't been with many boys, just the odd date here and there. So this was all new to her, and she was loving it.

Sal was skating with Paul. Racing ahead, they flung each other forward one at a time. But then the music changed, and a slow melody came on. The DJ played one every now and then during the evening, and the kids who were in couples would go to the middle of the floor for a kiss.

Maria glanced shyly at Jim who seemed oblivious to the music, but just as her disappointment hit rock bottom, he slowed down and pulled her into his arms once they came to a stop. He bent his head, his hand at the back of her neck, and his lips found hers. They were tender at first, a little unsure, but then he kissed her properly.

Maria now knew what it was like to be one of the kids in the middle, who everyone envied as they skated around. The music, the lights, the feel of Jim so close to her. It was pure teenage fantasy. And she didn't want it to end.

Alas, after one record, the music switched to upbeat again. Jim smiled and pointed to the side. 'Let's grab a drink.'

They spent the rest of the evening together, with Sal and Paul every now and then, but mostly on their own. Maria longed to feel Jim's lips on hers, but it didn't happen. She could tell he wanted to, though.

Afterwards, they caught the bus home, she and Sal sharing a seat opposite the boys. Their last stop was in Somerley High Street.

'Can I walk you home?' Jim offered once they'd all got off the bus. 'Seeing as Sal and Paul are busy.'

Maria saw her friend necking with Paul.

When she heard her name, Sal came up for air. 'Don't mind us,' she said. 'Paul will see me home, won't you?'

'I will.' Paul nodded before his lips returned to hers.

Jim smirked and reached for Maria's hand again. 'Let's leave the lovebirds to it.'

The walk home only took ten minutes, but it was one of the best moments of her life. It had been a balmy sunny day, the heat barely dying down, so there were a lot of people about. It was almost like a Sunday afternoon. But then it went quieter the further out of the town they went.

At her gate, they stopped.

'This is me,' she said, trying to hide her embarrassment. It wasn't because she lived in a council house. It was on account of the front garden and hedges being overgrown and untidy. Every year, she tried her best to keep it under control, but the only gardening equipment they had was a dodgy lawnmower that left behind more than it cut and a set of hand shears. It often proved too much.

'I've had a great time getting to know you,' Jim said. 'Can I see you again, perhaps in the week?'

'I'll have to check with my mum, but I'd like that.'

'Your mum?' Jim frowned.

'Oh, it's nothing funny. She's ill and sometimes needs me with her.'

'What's wrong with her?'

The front door opened, and Maria jumped.

'I have to go,' she said.

'Ah, okay. I'll see you on Monday, then?'

She nodded, waves of disappointment crashing through her. She wanted to kiss Jim again, but it was too late. She rushed up the path to her mum who was waiting for her.

No sooner had Maria closed the door, she started on her.

'Where have you been?' she seethed.

'I told you, to the roller rink. It's half past ten. I'm not late.'

'You left me, and I needed you.'

'Oh, are you okay? What can I get—'

'Nothing now! I wanted help earlier, when you should have been here for me.'

'I'm sorry.' She went past her mum towards the kitchen. 'Shall I make a cup of tea?'

'You only ever think of yourself, Maria Clifton. What about me? I've been in the worst pain of my life, and you've been out with a boy. I saw you, with him. I suppose he wants to go on anther date with you.'

It was said so vindictively that Maria crumbled. Usually, her mum's words didn't hurt her, but every now and then, they cracked through her toughened shell, preying on her vulnerability. There was so much she could say to bite back, but she never did. Instead, while her mum ranted at her, she rushed up to her room, threw herself on the bed, and sobbed into her pillow.

Why couldn't she have a normal life, like Sal, and most of her friends? All she asked for was one night a week, away from the cooking and the cleaning, the ironing, and the constant caring. It was draining her. She was a teenager; she wanted a life.

It was no use. Mum wouldn't allow her to go out in the week to see Jim. She'd be better off forgetting all about him. It wouldn't work. Not while her mum was so poorly.

CHAPTER ONE

It wasn't on Maria Wilshaw's to-do list that morning to spill coffee down the front of her blouse after she'd only been wearing it for ten minutes.

'Oh, Delilah,' she groaned.

The little terrier jumping around her feet was the reason it had gone everywhere. Maria had turned to grab the slice of toast that had pinged out of the toaster and almost tripped over her. Luckily, the drink wasn't hot enough to scald.

She knew rubbing at it with a cloth wouldn't make any difference, but still she tried.

'I suppose you think this is funny.' She couldn't help smiling at the dog sitting sweetly next to her, with shiny brown eyes that seemed to say: but I haven't been fed in months. 'You're not having anything else. Your bowl is full, cheeky monkey.'

Maria ruffled the dog's fur underneath her chin before dashing upstairs to change, undoing the buttons as she took each step. She threw the blouse into the washing basket, chose another one to wear, wriggled into it and went back downstairs. At least she couldn't be late for work, seeing as it was her own business.

Fifteen minutes later, she parked across the road from Wilshaw Estate Agents. She held on to the car door, a gust of biting-cold wind trying its best to wrench it from her grip. Locking it quickly, she dashed across the road in between the flow of steady morning traffic.

Maria was hoping for a quieter time this week after the post-Christmas rush had lasted nearly two months so far. January had been as busy as expected, February, too, and they needed to get ready for the spring bonanza. She could never tell from one year to the next how sales were going. Sometimes prospective buyers were pulling in their belts and weren't buying much at all. Other times, people, on seeing the start of a new year, would want to sell and move on. A new beginning for all those hopes and possibilities.

Maria unlocked the door, greeted by the beep of the alarm which she deactivated quickly. Then she moved around in a sequence she knew so well, flicking off small lights and turning on brighter ones. Finally, she set the office machinery to work, the computers, the printers; the photocopier, the coffee machine.

Once that was all done, she settled at her desk and sat quietly for a moment. Her office was a small space she'd partitioned off from the main one, with large glass walls. She'd designed it that way as it gave her a sense of being in the thrust of things, her door mostly open. But it was also used to give clients privacy when required, too.

Maria cherished those first few minutes before anyone arrived, the phones began to ring, and her stress levels rocketed. She gazed out onto Somerley High Street, watching a few people walking by. During the day, it had a lot of passing trade, but come evening it became quiet again.

Her husband, Jim, owned a builders merchants, a mile out

of town. Both businesses over the years had become well-known, and successful. The only problem was they were so busy running them, they hardly got any time to spend together.

Maria couldn't stop thinking about how life was running away with her. It was her fiftieth birthday tomorrow, and she was dreading it more than looking forward to the day itself. How had she become so old, when she felt like she was twenty years younger? It just didn't seem right.

She sighed dramatically in the still of the room. There was so much pressure to enjoy the milestone itself that it took the shine away from it when she felt so advanced in her years.

She sipped her drink, casting her eyes around the office. On her desk, a photo of her and her husband, Jim, took pride of place in a silver frame. They were at home in the garden, taking advantage of the weather last summer, when it had been extremely hot for several weeks. As a result they were tanned, giving them both a healthy glow. For once, they seemed relaxed and at ease.

The Wilshaws had dark-brown hair, Jim having the least of it now. At one time he had a full head of it but, once it started to recede, he'd kept it short. His eyes were brown, too, laughing as much as his smile, crinkled skin at each corner showing his years. He wore long cream shorts and Maria's favourite white polo T-shirt. She smiled fondly. He'd weathered well, had her old man.

She had met Jim when they were in high school, and they'd become a little more than friends. But Maria's circumstances meant she'd barely had time to herself, so they hadn't seen much of each other after that, the relationship fizzling out on her part. A rare night out for her office Christmas party when she was eighteen had them reuniting again and, since then, Jim had changed her life for the better.

Married at twenty, they'd gone through the death of his

parents, the drama of what had happened to her mum, the terrible time she'd had carrying her first daughter, Lucy, and then breezing through everything the second time when Clara came along two years later.

Life had been busy, with nearly thirty years of marriage, not to mention running a business apiece and raising two daughters, easily their greatest achievement. Nothing had slowed them down.

Maria wasn't entirely sure whether that was a good thing or not.

CHAPTER TWO

Clara Churchill was desperate to leave her bad mood at home as she arrived at work, but she was finding it difficult to shake off. She and her husband, Alex, had been arguing again that morning. It seemed anything started them off nowadays, but apparently it had been her fault that he couldn't find his work ID pass. She hadn't moved it, but he'd complained she had. He hadn't even apologised when it had turned up in his laptop bag.

The atmosphere had been much lighter once he'd slammed the front door in his hurry to get away, saying he would be late home that evening as he had something on.

Something on had been his response for several weeks now. He didn't even have the decency to tell Clara where he was going. Well, if he expected her to stay in on her own again, that wasn't what she'd be doing. She and her sister and Sal, Mum's oldest friend, were taking Mum out for a meal that evening.

Wilshaws Estate Agents was at the edge of a thriving community in the market town of Somerley. The double-fronted establishment had a bay window either side of its entrance, its interior decorated in soothing colours. Clara crossed the high street, almost flying into the office when a gust of wind took her legs and made her run.

'Blimey, it's blowing a gale out there.' She ran a hand through her shoulder-length hair after closing the door. 'I had a style five minutes ago.'

'Morning, love.' Maria smiled. 'I have the perfect thing for you.' She pointed to the mug of coffee waiting for her.

'Lifesaver.'

Clara removed her coat, hung it up, and plonked herself down at her desk, opposite where Lucy sat. Clara had worked with her mum for over six years now. On leaving school, she'd gone to sixth form and then to university and found herself far more interested in the internet and online marketing aspect of her business degree.

After a chat with her parents, and a trial period of three months to prove to them she could do it, she became the marketing manager at both the estate agency and her dad's business. She had thrived while learning everything she could to improve sales and grow their customer base.

Now, between the two businesses, their newsletters had over twenty thousand subscribers, and an alert system that often meant properties were sold before they'd been advertised to the general public, and sales on surplus building materials hardly ever piled up in the yard.

Working with her mum hadn't been as hard as she'd expected. Clara was the baby of the family, which had as many disadvantages as advantages. Lucy called her Clueless Clara, but she didn't mind because it was said with affection – well, mostly. Occasionally, they got on each other's nerves, so when they were bickering, she'd retaliate by calling her Lousy Lucy, knowing that she hated it.

Thankful for any job while her marriage was going to the wall, Clara was grateful to get the time to switch off. As well as this morning, she and Alex had done nothing but argue all weekend, and it was getting her down. She'd hoped a new year would improve things, but it was nearing the end of February, and nothing had changed. She sensed it never would, which left them with some talking to do.

'Have you decided what you're wearing tonight?' she asked her mum, knowing she would already be panicking about it.

'I think I'm going for my black trousers and that red top I bought last month to wear over Christmas but never did.'

'Ooh, diva-esque.'

'Precisely. Because if I can't do it at fifty, when can I do it?'

'You're not *quite* fifty yet, though.'

'I know. Only a few more hours. I can't believe over half my life has gone already.'

'Don't be so morbid!'

'Well, you never know, do you? I could get run over tomorrow and—'

'Me and Lucy would take over the business and live happily ever after.'

'Point taken. I hope I can get in my trousers, though.' Maria prodded herself in the stomach and gave a huge sigh. 'You'd think I'd be a right skinny Minnie with the amount of running around I do each day. The menopause has a lot to answer for.'

'Mum,' Clara replied, a hint of a sigh. 'We keep telling you that you're beautiful as you are.'

'Flabby at fifty was not my intention. My mind says I'm twenty, but my body is a wreck. I feel as if I'm in my seventies.'

'Don't worry, we'll cheer you up this evening. We'll have a lovely time.' Clara sorted through the mail that had come in. 'You do look tired, though.'

'Insomnia struck at half past three, and I couldn't stop

thinking about work. This place will be the death of me if I don't get a break soon.'

'Why don't you and Dad go away for a week? Somewhere hot, just the two of you?'

'And have to wear a swimsuit, with sweat gathering between my thighs as I walk around?' Maria shuddered. 'No, thank you.'

Clara giggled at the sight that came to mind with her mother's description of herself. 'Where is Polly Positive this morning?'

'I fear she's still tucked up in bed, catching up on her sleep. It's hormones, I'm telling you. They play havoc with you once you get to a certain age. You and Lucy have all this to come, but I wouldn't wish it on anyone. When you're young, you don't give it a second thought.' Maria flapped the bottom of her blouse in the hope of getting a cool breeze to her skin. 'Honestly, hot flashes are coming at me in their droves. I'm afraid I'm going to be *that* woman soon.' She wrinkled up her face. 'You know, the one who wears layers, easily removable when it gets too sweaty.'

Clara couldn't help but chuckle.

'It's not funny, I tell you.' Maria was laughing, though.

As she did most mornings, Clara clicked onto a rival estate agent's website to see if there was anything new on their books. The trouble with matching first-time buyers with starter properties, or sellers ready for a move up or down, was that it made her constantly think about how unhappy she was in her own home. Even though she loved it, it had the atmosphere of a shell right now.

Perhaps she and Alex should think about moving to somewhere new, putting their mark on another property. Maybe that would jumpstart their marriage, bring it back to life. Because they couldn't go on like this for much longer. It wasn't healthy for them to fall out so much.

When you had parents who had been married for nearly thirty years as role models, Clara's five-year marriage seemed as if it was over before it had begun. She didn't want to be a failure.

The office phone rang beside her, and she gladly reached for it. At least it was something to take her mind off things before the tears burning in her eyes fell.

CHAPTER THREE

Lucy Wilshaw stooped to her daughter's level and laid a hand on either side of her pretty face. She had the same button nose and bright-blue eyes as the rest of the Wilshaw women, but Ellie's usual smile was missing at the moment. She didn't want to go to school today.

'I'm sure you'll have an exciting day.' Lucy gave her a reassuring hug. 'It will be home time before you know it. Oh, isn't that Alexis over there?'

Ellie turned, her face breaking out into a smile at last, and she wriggled away from Lucy's embrace.

'Bye, Mummy,' she shouted as she ran to join her friend.

Lucy pulled herself back to full height with a grin. Most mornings when she'd been that age, she'd disliked school, too. Mum would often reminisce about her doing anything to get out of walking through the gates. Fake a tummy ache; cry until she made herself ill. She had even sat next to the radiator before, saying she was feeling hot.

Yet when she got there, she'd enjoyed it for the most part, especially high school. There, she was quite a hit with the boys, even though she hadn't fooled around until she'd left, much to their dismay. And if it wasn't for Simon Minshall breaking her heart when she was twenty-three, she might have stayed the sweet Lucy of old.

Getting pregnant with Ellie, and then Simon not wanting to know, had been a wake-up call, and she'd become a single mum. Still, things had improved when she'd met her partner, Aaron. Lucy and Aaron had been together three years, since Ellie's second birthday. Aaron's daughter, Saskia, from his first marriage, lived with them, too. She'd just turned thirteen.

Once she'd seen Ellie into her classroom, Lucy hotfooted it along the high street, wrapping her scarf tightly around her neck against the bitter wind. She passed Somerley Square with its large oak tree at its middle and crossed the road to where Wilshaw Estate Agents stood proudly at the end of the main row of shops. Lucy worked there for five hours every weekday and the odd Saturday until midday.

'Morning,' she greeted, bustling in.

Maria was on the phone and gave her a wave. Regan, their apprentice, smiled shyly as she sat at the small reception desk.

Clara was searching around in the stationery cupboard and turned when she heard her sister's voice. 'Bit nippy out there, isn't it? Did Ellie go to school okay?'

'She had a tummy ache, but it disappeared when she arrived at the gates and spotted Alexis. How was your weekend?'

Clara's face dropped. 'The usual. Argue, not speak. Argue, not speak.'

'That doesn't sound like much fun.'

'Believe me, it wasn't.' Clara rolled her eyes.

In the staffroom, Lucy made their usual drinks in their usual mugs, even knowing they had recently had one. She wondered what had gone on between Alex and Clara this time. She'd sensed an atmosphere since Christmas Day, when

Alex had got tipsy and started having a go at Clara in front of everyone. Aaron had calmed him down, and Alex had apologised. But there was only so much making up the couple could do before they reached the decision to split up.

Lucy could clearly see the damage they were doing to each other. It wasn't healthy. In her opinion, they either needed to have a go at making things right or call it a day, as painful as that might be. Watching them work it out was distressing, but she would always be there with a shoulder to cry on or an ear to bend.

Both she and Clara wanted long relationships, like their parents. Yet, being brought up in a stable and loving environment, they sometimes talked about the pressure they felt to get things right. Mum often told them how hard her childhood had been after her father walked out. Dad's parents had been in their late thirties when they'd had him and had died when she and Clara were young. It was the reason Mum cited for always wanting family around them.

Lucy took the drinks through, handed them out, and settled at her desk. 'So what have you been arguing about?' She kept her voice low, the door to her mum's office open. She wasn't sure if Clara wanted her to know or not.

'Just the usual. Alex wants to go out with his friends more than he wants to spend time with me.'

It was the same most weekends. Lucy found Alex quite selfish, causing an atmosphere on the one Sunday a month they had lunch as a family at their parents' home. Frequently the meal was spoiled by the tension they caused, Alex miserable to be there and Clara trying to overcompensate by being too loud and funny.

Secretly, Lucy knew her sister could do better. Lucy and Aaron were happy, planning a future together. She couldn't recall Clara mentioning anything she and Alex were looking forward to.

'I know, I know.' Clara sighed. 'I think we have to do something about it.'

'Like what?'

'Sit down to talk would be a good idea. Instead, we never seem to do anything but sling insults at each other.'

Lucy, now on the way to the photocopier, leaned forward and flung her arms around her sister's neck as she walked past. 'It'll all turn out good, one way or another.' She kissed Clara's cheek. 'Whatever happens, we'll be here for you.'

Clara turned to her with a frown. 'What do you mean, whatever happens?'

For a moment, Lucy was stumped, wondering whether to say more. She didn't want to upset Clara, so she went with the easy option. 'You *know* what I mean.'

Clara's eyes brimmed with tears, and Lucy's heart went out to her. She gave her shoulder a quick squeeze before moving away. If only Clara had the courage to do something about it.

Lucy hated to see her suffering so much.

Maria came out of her office.

'Ooh, I have something to show you,' Clara said, reaching for her phone. 'My dress for the wedding.'

Lucy admired her sister's resilience to throw the scent off her melancholic mood. Clara was going to be a matron of honour in April at her friend Stacey's wedding. Alex was going to be the best man. Not Lucy's choice of wording for the idiot, but still.

'Oh, that's beautiful!' Maria said. 'It's going to be lovely on you. Nice colouring for you, too.'

'Do you think? I was worried about it.'

'Let me see.' Lucy doubled back. 'Good work, sis,' she whispered, winking at her. The Wilshaw women were made of strong stuff when it came to character strength – and diversion tactics.

CHAPTER FOUR

Maria gave herself the customary once-over before heading out that evening. She turned to the side, not seeing her flowing dark hair that had an amazing shine, or the chestnut brown of her eyes. She only saw wrinkles and strands of greying hair where the dye had grown out at the roots. Even having it touched up every five weeks didn't stop it showing now.

She took a deep breath, holding in her stomach for a few seconds: she didn't look *too* bad. At least she'd managed to squeeze into the black trousers, although she prayed the waistband wouldn't dig in too much after she'd eaten. She wanted to wear them as she felt so elegant, and dare she say it, a little bit sexy, along with her new red top. She'd got them both from Jazz Fashions on the high street and teamed them with a pair of black strappy heels from Chandler's Shoes.

Was she too old for the top, she wondered? She'd loved it when she'd first tried it on. Now it felt as if she was trying too hard, like the proverbial mutton dressed as lamb.

'Oh, get over yourself,' she muttered, grabbing her bag

and going downstairs before she could change her mind and put on something more appropriate, like a sack.

From the hall, she stepped inside their home office.

'I'm off now, love.'

Jim popped his head up and treated her to a smile. 'Have a good evening.'

She noted how tired he seemed. 'Don't work too late.'

'I won't.' He was already back staring at the monitor.

'But don't wait up either. I intend on getting very drunk to drown my sorrows.'

'Fifty is the new forty!'

'Forty was the new thirty and yet I didn't feel any younger then.'

He chuckled. 'Send my love to Sal. Tell her I'll be around at the weekend to sort out the dodgy door for her.'

Maria gave a faint smile. Jim was such a thoughtful man. At times she knew she didn't deserve him, and he'd put up with a lot from her. Having said that, there were many times when she could easily have throttled him, too.

Maria and Sal had met at school, forming a friendship that had lasted throughout the years. Sal was a mortgage broker, working from home on a freelance basis, and Wilshaw Estate Agents was her biggest client.

Delilah came strolling in. She stopped for a stretch, first the front legs and then the back, and sidled over to Maria for a fuss.

Delilah had been an unexpected part of their family for seven years now, just after they'd moved into Lilac Grove. Jim had spotted her cowering in the footwell of the passenger seat of a Transit van. He believed the driver was going to strike her and had made his feelings known. The driver had picked Delilah up by the scruff of her neck and hurled her through the window at Jim.

'Have her if you think so much of her.'

She had landed on his chest with a yelp. Jim was too shocked to say anything, and before he'd come to his senses after comforting the pup, the driver had gone, never to be seen again. Jim had brought the timid creature home, and the family had fallen in love with her. Luckily for them, Delilah had turned out to be such a loving dog.

'I won't be long.' Maria bent to stroke her. 'Keep an eye on your dad for me.'

A horn beeped outside, and she shouted goodbye again before leaving. Clara was picking everyone up, and Maria was the last stop.

'Hiya!' Maria grinned and buckled up her seatbelt. 'Let's get this show on the road!

They arrived at The Golden Spoon restaurant and were shown to a table at the far end of the room. Silver and white balloons were tied to the back of each chair with purple ribbon, the colour scheme flowing through the tablecloth, crockery, and napkins. A personalised banner saying "Happy 50th birthday, Maria" had been fixed across the wall behind it.

Maria blushed at all the attention she was getting and, once everyone had congratulated her, they settled ready to enjoy three courses of food, accompanied by wine and good conversation.

'Did you see that article in the *Somerley News* yesterday?' Maria asked. 'It was about things beginning with the letter M that affect a woman. You know, marriage, men, money, the bloody menopause.'

'Misery, murder,' Sal quipped as they all laughed.

Maria wasn't too sure that Sal was talking metaphorically. Sal had split up with her husband two years ago. Ronnie had left her for a woman half her age, breaking up a friendship the four of them had treasured. It had been a total shock to her, and Jim, and she knew Sal hadn't recovered fully from it yet.

'The menopause is no fun,' Maria went on. 'I'm either too hot to sleep or wide awake with insomnia. I can't win. And don't talk to me about mood swings.'

'Really?' Lucy smirked. 'I thought that was usual for you.'

'Oi, watch it,' Maria chastised. 'Apart from the hot flushes, the lack of sleep and the brain fog, your sex drive is non-existent, you can gain weight by breathing on food, and your foof becomes so dry that you don't want anything near it, never mind inside it.' She leaned back in her chair and pinched an inch around her waist. 'I never had love handles until last year. One moment I was a healthy range for my size; the next I'd put on a stone in a few months, and no amount of dieting will shift it. It's all around my middle.'

'Your boobs are enormous now, Mum,' Clara quipped.

Maria looked down at her chest, as if noticing them for the first time. 'So they are!'

'Your mum's not the only one who's going through hell,' Sal piped up. 'My nether regions stopped pulsing a long time ago, too. I'm left with teenage spots clustered on my chin, a raging temper that flares up at the slightest thing, *and* a ton of body fat I can't shift around my middle. I don't have one tyre. I have at least two and I wobble everywhere when I jog to the bathroom. Because I'm peeing every twenty minutes as well.'

Clara wiped tears from her eyes. 'Stop it, you two!'

'If only it were a farce and not true life.' Sal rolled her eyes in jest.

By the time coffee and mints arrived, Clara and Lucy were talking to each other, leaving Sal and Maria to do the same. Sal reached to squeeze Maria's hand.

'Jim loves you just as you are.' She spoke so only Maria could hear her.

'I can't see how, Sal. When we first started dating, I was eight stone and now look at me.'

Sal stared at her.

'What?'

'We were *all* eight stone years ago! At least you're growing old gracefully and with the love of the most incredible man. Besides, you're amazing for fifty. Now, come on, less of the gloomy face.'

Maria smiled, but inside she was sinking fast. Here she was on a night out with her best friend and her daughters, everyone enjoying themselves, and yet all she could think about was why she wasn't attractive to Jim anymore. She felt past her prime, on the scrapheap, and any other analogy she could think of.

'I love Jim, but I don't know how he puts up with the new me.' She twirled the stem of her glass with her fingers. 'It's like I've been taken over by an alien. I want to find the old Maria but I'm afraid she's gone for good.'

'Oh, love, it's so sad to see you like this. I do understand, though. Life is flying past us both. Still, I'm going to make the most of it.' Sal raised her glass in a toast again. 'Here's to the fabulous fifties, my friend.'

Maria smiled, determined to enjoy the rest of the evening. 'Here's to growing old *ungracefully*!'

CHAPTER FIVE

Maria and Sal were waiting at the front of the restaurant for Clara to bring the car around. The evening had been a huge success, but Maria was shattered and ready for bed. The street was fairly quiet, except for a takeaway a few doors down. There was drizzle in the air, and large puddles on the road, reflecting the lights in the restaurant window. The wind had died down, but it was still desperately cold.

'Why doesn't Jim find me attractive anymore?' Maria said to Sal, linking arms with her.

'He does,' Sal protested. 'He worships you; any fool can see that.'

'Do you think?' Maria stepped to one side, then swayed, a slight slur to her words. 'Some days I don't think he even notices I exist. I hate getting old.'

'I hate getting incontinent.' Sal wriggled about. 'I'm dying for a pee. I bet I won't hold all of it in until I get home!'

They were still laughing as Clara pulled up in front of them. Maria followed Sal into the back seat, hooting loudly after banging her head on the roof of the car.

'How did I become so tipsy?' she said to Sal.

'Must be the champagne we've swigged between us.'

'Some of us are sober,' Clara exclaimed.

'Thank *you*.' Maria patted Clara on the shoulder. 'The most perfect chauffeur.'

Within what seemed to be a whoosh in time, they were outside Maria's home.

Maria gave Sal a hug. 'Thanks for paying for the meal. It was a lovely thought.' No amount of arguing had stopped her from paying it in full.

'It was my pleasure. And it was a thank you to the girls, who helped me with the banner and table decorations.' Sal shooed her away. 'Now, go and jump on Jim when you get in. I know I would if I had the chance.'

'Euw,' Clara complained.

Lucy grimaced. 'Too much information.'

Maria laughed and turned back to Sal. 'You'd jump on my Jim if you had the chance?' she teased.

'Noooo.' Sal shook her head vehemently. 'That would be like sleeping with my brother.'

'Please!' Clara protested in jest.

Raucous laughter erupted again.

Maria slammed the car door, almost knocking herself off her feet. 'I'll see you all tomorrow. That's if I'm in any fit state. Bye!'

She waved until the car was out of sight and then went in, shushing herself and managing to close the front door a little quieter. It was half past eleven, and she wasn't expecting Jim to be awake. He was always up with the lark so often went to bed early.

Delilah came to greet her, all tail and waggly bum.

'Hello, my lovely, have you missed me?' Maria removed her heels rather than clatter across the tiles in the hall and tiptoed into the kitchen. There, she guzzled down a large glass of water, praying it would ease the inevitable hangover for tomorrow.

Her eyes caught the clock on the wall. In a few minutes, she would be fifty years old. Fifty! Her shoulders dropped as she stood staring at the image reflected by the window. What was she so frightened of? It was just another day. Nothing would change, really.

She giggled then, recalling some of the things they had talked about that evening. There was nothing better than being in female company and having a good laugh.

Upstairs, she crept across the landing and into the bedroom. She could see Jim underneath the duvet but wasn't sure if he was awake or not. Wriggling out of her clothes, she lost her balance and fell forward onto him.

Jim groaned.

'Sorry!' she whispered loudly.

'I take it you had a good evening?'

'I did! And it isn't over yet.' Maria decided to be bold. 'Come here, you big lump.'

'If that's your idea of a come-on, I'll take a pass.'

'Wouldn't you like a bit of rumpy-pumpy?'

'Not when you're in that state.'

'What state? I'm fine.'

'Go to sleep.'

'But I'm fifty soon.'

'And?'

'It's my birthday. You should do as I say.'

'It isn't your birthday yet.'

'It's past midnight.'

She undressed and got into bed. Jim had his back to her. She wondered whether to cuddle up to him but decided against it. If he wanted to be amorous, he would have turned over to face her.

She lay in the dark, her mind whirring and a constant buzzing in her ears.

'You don't like me much nowadays, do you, Jim?' she questioned after a moment.

'You're drunk.'

Maria pulled the covers up to her neck. 'It's fine. I know when I'm not wanted.'

'Go to *sleep*.'

Even though his voice was gentle, Maria huffed. 'G'night to you, too.' In a matter of moments, she was out like a light.

It was three a.m. when she was wide awake again. What was it with her inability to stay asleep for longer than three or four hours, even with too much champagne and wine?

There was nothing worse than lying in bed, unable to nod off again, watching the clock going round, while wondering if she should get up and make a cup of tea or stay where she was and ride it out.

She had far too much to think about work wise, and that was enough to ensure she didn't drop off again. As well, Sal's words were playing on her mind. Did Jim love her just the way she was?

Maria had a real love-hate relationship with the phrase "looking good for your age". It was hard having two beautiful daughters who were the image of her twenty years ago. She wasn't into having fillers and lifts, or getting pouty lips like a lot of women did, so it was no wonder she had an inferiority complex. It was like seeing her former self all the time.

She *did* want to grow old gracefully. She just didn't want to see someone past their prime staring back at her every time she glanced in the mirror. She wanted to feel like Lucy, or Clara, again, without the aching muscles the minute she did anything strenuous.

And now thinking of her daughters meant she'd never get to sleep. She wished she didn't worry about them so much.

She knew something was wrong with Clara and Alex, and Lucy, who was trying for a baby, hadn't been successful yet. Their pain was hers. She was far too sensitive, but they were her children.

All she wanted was for everyone to be happy, for life to be perfect. It wasn't too much to ask, surely?

She fluffed the pillow and turned over.

'For the love of Peter Kay, will you go to sleep?' Jim pulled the duvet up around his neck.

'Love you, too,' she muttered.

Perhaps she should count sheep. Did that even work? She sighed, eyes wide. She might as well get up now and go to the bathroom. She wouldn't settle until she had.

CHAPTER SIX

Alex had still been up when Clara arrived home after dropping everyone off. He was in the living room, playing a game on the TV. His thumbs were going nineteen to the dozen as he tried to negotiate a group of zombies. Honestly, he acted as if he was five, not twenty-eight.

She stood in the doorway, trying to get his attention. 'Hey.'

'Hey. Did you have a good time?'

'Yes, thanks.' She glanced at two scrunched-up crisp packets, an empty chocolate wrapper, and a can of Stella beside him on the carpet. 'When did you get home?'

'What time is it now?'

She sighed, checking her watch. 'Nearly midnight.'

'About half an hour ago. I had a couple of pints with Ben, seeing as you wouldn't be in.'

She almost sniped at him then. He made it sound as if she went out a lot when in effect, it was the other way round.

'I won't be able to make it to your mum's tomorrow,' he added, not even looking at her. 'I have to work.'

'You can't miss it!' she snapped. 'You know she'll expect you.'

'I'll try to get there but I can't promise. We have some contracts that need ironing out.' Still his eyes were glued to the game.

'And you're only telling me this now?' She'd had a feeling he would pull a stunt like this, regardless.

'Sorry, it can't be helped.'

Clara was too tired to argue with him. What would be the point anyway? Alex always did what he wanted. It was her mum she felt sorry for. It wasn't fair on her.

'Are you coming up to bed?' she asked, after standing in silence for a few seconds.

'Soon.'

Clara muttered. That meant sometime never. Knowing Alex, he'd probably play for another hour or so before sneaking under the duvet. If only he paid *her* the same attention with his hands.

She took the stairs slowly, the first signs of a headache appearing. For once, she wished she was coming home to someone who would ask her how her evening had been and actually mean it; want to know if she'd had fun. Go to sleep with his arm tucked around her waist.

Earlier, she'd dropped Lucy off, and Aaron had opened the front door almost as soon as Lucy had got out of the car. He'd given her a kiss, and they'd waited on the step, arm in arm, waving as Clara had driven away.

Even seeing that little show of emotion between them reminded her of all she missed with Alex. They had been like that at one time, and now, even though they'd only been married for five years, she already spent more time on her own than with him.

Something was coming to a head, although she didn't want to be the one to admit it. Often as she was alone when

Alex was out, she'd find herself wishing things were different. That she had the courage to leave and start again.

Thinking back to New Year's Eve, after the dreadful row they'd had, she had to admit things had gone downhill rapidly. She and Alex had been invited to let the New Year in at a neighbour's home, two doors down. Alex had practically ignored her for the best part of the evening, choosing to hole up with the men in the kitchen. Obviously, he preferred being part of a gang sharing anecdotes and tales of one-upmanship.

Shortly after midnight, she'd told him she was leaving, and he'd let her go. There had been a huge row when he'd eventually rolled in at half past two. He'd complained she was a party pooper. She'd accused him of not loving her anymore. When he hadn't denied it, she'd burst into tears and taken herself off to the spare room. Since then, they'd barely spoken to each other, except to be polite.

She and Alex had met when they were eighteen. They'd been in Rembrandt's, a nightclub in the next town, Hedworth. Back then, it had five decent nightclubs and numerous wine bars and restaurants. They'd got chatting and, eventually, arranged a date for the following evening.

Their wedding two years later had brought concerns from both sets of parents that they hadn't been together long enough and should wait a while, but they hadn't listened. They knew better, were in love, and couldn't wait to buy their own home.

When their house came on the market, the deal was sealed. For the first two years, it had been good. But then they began to spend more time alone, each having their own friends. The sex became infrequent, and there were times she could recall being in tears after their latest argument, where she had sat and worked out whether she could survive on her own financially if they split up. But she'd never had the courage to leave.

Now, Lucy's vague comments earlier that day sprang to mind. How much could other people see, sense, guess at? And, how much of that was actually true?

Did Alex still love her? Was he waiting for her to make the first move to finish things? Because if so, he'd be waiting forever. Clara was a firm believer in making things work. Her parents were tantamount to that.

So she was thankful for her mum's birthday tomorrow. At least she'd be with people who wanted to be with her, too.

CHAPTER SEVEN

Lucy climbed into bed next to Aaron. He was sitting up, scrolling on his iPad.

'You smell nice.' She cuddled up to him. 'I'm glad the girls have been okay.'

He kissed her forehead. 'So you had a good time?'

'Yes, it was fun. Mum was talking about the menopause again. She and Sal are obsessed with it. Although, it's quite frightening to imagine going through it myself when I get to their age. You should hear the tales they told us – the horrors of hot sweats, insomnia, lack of libido. Not sure I want to get like that, ever.'

'The only dead cert about life is taking what it throws at you.' Aaron set the screen into home mode and slid the iPad onto the bedside table. He moved down the bed, his hand coming over Lucy's shoulder so she could snuggle into his chest.

'Do you think some men fancy younger women because older ones *are* past their prime when they've reached that stage of their lives?' she asked.

'What on earth are you talking about? You're twenty-nine

and have no need to worry about the menopause for twenty years or so.'

'Not necessarily. Women can go on the change earlier than fifty. It's quite an individual thing.'

'On the change? What does that really mean?'

'We turn into angry bitches overnight, start crying at the sight of a puppy, want to punch out at everyone and everything, and our boobs hit our bellies.'

'Really? Not sure I'm ready for that either.'

Lucy slapped his chest playfully. 'It makes me sad that some women feel like they're no longer attractive. Mum thinks that she and Dad have lost their sparkle, whereas I see them deeply in love after thirty years. Staying together for that long nowadays shows commitment. Surely you have to at least like the person you're with enough to do that?'

'I would say so. It's one of the reasons it didn't work out with Melissa.' Aaron snorted. 'There's no point in trying to make a marriage work when it's gone too wrong to patch up.'

'Plus you never would have found me!'

His laughter warmed her.

Being with Aaron had grounded Lucy. When her daughter, Ellie, had come along, once she'd spent a few months with her parents, they'd moved into a small flat. Life then became all about Ellie and the need to do right by her. Aaron had appeared one night when she'd needed an electrician. The joke of her lighting him up on first sight was one that would never get old.

Aaron had his own home, just behind Somerley Church. His ex-wife had gone when Saskia was six. Aaron often told Lucy it wouldn't have been so bad if she'd left him, but to leave Saskia behind and not want any contact was something he could never forgive.

Lucy couldn't understand it either. As far as she was concerned, she and Ellie were an item, never to be separated until her daughter was old enough to make the choice for herself.

Melissa hadn't been in contact now for over six years. It wasn't as if Aaron had been a bad husband. Melissa was an alcoholic. She begged, borrowed, and eventually stole, to keep her habit going. If she had no money, Aaron said she would probably have sold her kidney for another drink

Many times Aaron had received phone calls from Saskia's primary school saying no one had been to collect her. He'd go rushing to pick her up and then get home to find Melissa passed out on the settee, unaware of what day it was, never mind the time.

The situation went too far one afternoon when she'd left cheese on toast under the grill and fallen asleep. Aaron and Saskia had come home to a house full of black smoke, a sheepish-looking Melissa trying her best to rid the kitchen of the damage she'd caused. Aaron had told her enough was enough and that she had to quit the booze or leave.

Melissa was gone the following morning. The only contact they'd had since had been through the post, when divorce papers came to be signed.

Life got hard for Aaron for a while, but he and Saskia soon settled into a routine. When Lucy met him, Melissa had been gone for three years, Aaron was getting on great with Saskia, and she and Ellie slotted into their life as if they'd always been part of it.

Okay, it wasn't easy at times having a stroppy teenager and a five-year-old in the same household, and even so, for the past twelve months, they'd been trying to extend their family further. Lucy dreamed about having another baby. She wouldn't mind either sex, but a boy would be a bonus. Aaron wasn't fussed at all, but deep down she suspected he'd prefer a boy, especially in their family of girls.

'At least you have Saskia,' she told him.

'And you have Ellie,' Aaron replied.

'But I've never been married.'

'If you're after a proposal, I'd ask you again, but you've turned me down several times. A man's ego can only take so much rejection.'

'I know, sorry. I'm just not ready for it yet. But you'll be the first to know.'

'I hope so.' He laughed. 'Although I might not wait around forever. I could even find a younger model and run off with her.'

'That's disgusting,' she teased.

'I mean someone in their early twenties, nothing else!'

She laughed then. 'I wonder how older men cope with younger women. I bet they'd need a lot of energy.'

'Well, you're younger than me, and I'm up for it, if you are.'

She rolled over on top of him as he slipped his hands inside her pyjama top.

Lucy had only got as far as bowing her head to meet Aaron's when the bedroom door opened. Ellie appeared in the doorway.

'Mummy, I can't sleep.'

Lucy kissed Aaron lightly. 'Hold that thought, cowboy,' she said before climbing off him. She lifted her daughter into her arms. 'Come on, poppet. Let's get you back to bed.'

CHAPTER EIGHT

'Happy Birthday, love,' Jim said, right next to Maria's ear. 'Mwah.'

'It's only half past seven!' Maria pushed him away firmly.

'But it's your big day, and the family are coming round.'

'I'd much prefer to lounge in bed.'

'You were as drunk as a skunk last night,' he remarked.

'I was not.' She turned her head towards him slightly. 'I only had a couple.'

'Of drinks or bottles?'

She smirked. 'You *do* like to exaggerate.'

'You *do* like to throw yourself at me. You were after some rumpy-pumpy.'

'I never said that!' She frowned. 'Did I?'

'Those very words.'

'Noooo!' Maria hid her face with her hands for a moment, although wishing she could go back in time to when she and Jim were in their twenties, young and supple, with no lumps and bumps and wrinkles galore. Back then she'd had no need to hold her tummy in to fit into some of her clothes and would have jumped on him in seconds.

'When I was younger, you used to call me a racing horse as I was sleek and fit,' she mused. 'I'm more like a wooden rocking horse now.'

Jim roared with laughter. 'Old age comes to us all, there's never a surer thing. Doesn't mean I think any less of you, my love. Except for when you're drunk. And snoring so loud.'

'I do not snore.'

Jim drew back the covers and got out of bed. She watched him walk across the room. Why was it men were never embarrassed by their bodies the way women were? Jim had love handles and wrinkles, but it didn't seem to bother him. So why did she think he wouldn't accept her the way she was now?

'Fancy a bacon buttie?' he asked.

'Oh, I do!' Stuff the diet, she mused, glad too that she'd made the decision to close the estate agent's that morning so she could enjoy two full days off. She was about to eat her own body weight in cake and drink a barrel load of champagne again. Besides, she would be watching her weight once more come Monday. After all, everyone knew that was the day diets officially started. It was the law.

'Don't be long then.' Jim removed his pyjama trousers from the crack of his bum and burped loudly.

'Disgusting!' she teased.

'You wouldn't have me any other way.' He blew her a kiss before leaving the room.

She smiled. She and Jim were okay. They didn't cuddle up anymore when watching the TV, but they sat on either end of the same settee, streaming box sets and watching reruns of *Vera* and *Midsomer Murders* when they couldn't find anything interesting. They mostly enjoyed the same foods, pigged out on wine and chocolate every Saturday evening, and shared belly laughs over the silliest of things. The passion had dried up, but they were still solid, not complacent and boring.

Eventually, she pulled herself out of bed and made it to the bathroom. Like she did most mornings, she stepped on the scales, squeezed her eyes shut before she dared look, and then sighed when she saw the needle had gone up a kilo. Of course she knew all about weight fluctuations and that it was best to weigh herself once a week at the same time to get an average reading, but still she was a slave to the scales.

If she had lost a quarter kilo, woohoo. If she had gained, then woe was her. It always affected her mood either way, and yet she couldn't help letting it dictate her life.

She was always turning down treats saying she was being good and then scoffing twice as many calories in stolen "just the one" chocolate biscuits throughout the day.

She often wondered if she ate what she wanted, would she take in less calories? Perhaps she wouldn't pig out on things she was craving all the time then. Because it was as if the minute she said she was cutting down on something, it invaded her every waking thought.

But if she didn't watch her weight, it would rise slowly, and then she'd end up heavier after a couple of months. She couldn't win.

The scent of shower gel was all around the room. Maria breathed it in, enjoying the manliness of it. It was Jim's signature. He always used the same one. It reminded her of, well... Jim.

Mind you, Jim always smelled of something delicious. He was one of those men who wasn't dressed until he'd added a few squirts of aftershave, always took two showers each day, and kept himself impeccable. She never had to worry about what he'd be going out in, his dress sense was stylish, even through the ages. He was wearing more classics now, but he always added a dash of fashion to them. She called him her last-chance trendy.

She climbed back into bed, relishing being alone. The

smell of bacon wafted up the stairs now, and she sat, plumping her pillow, and rested back. She and Jim were always up by six each morning, so she never got the chance to be in bed by herself and just… be still. It was nice.

Fifteen minutes later, Jim was back, and she beamed at him as he set a tray down on her outstretched legs.

'Tea and a bacon bap as promised, and two magazines,' he announced as if he were a butler. 'I'm told one is a weekly gossip fest, the other is interior design and homes.'

She smiled and opened her mouth to say thank you.

'The girls chose them for you,' he said first.

'You kinda spoilt the moment then.' She grinned.

'Believe me, I had to have their help with a lot of things that will be happening today.'

Maria pouted, wondering what was in store for her.

Jim leaned down and kissed her cheek. The stubble on his chin tickled her and brought back lovely memories. She glanced at him as he stood upright again, wondering if she had the same effect on him. Did she make him feel all warm inside, or was it more about companionship now they'd been together for so long?

'Penny for them?' He interrupted her thoughts.

'It's nothing, really.' She shook her head. 'Just wondering how I got to be fifty when I actually feel about twenty-five.'

Jim laughed, walking towards the door. 'Take your time. Enjoy the quiet before the girls arrive. I expect there will be a lot of noise.'

'From the big girls or the little ones?'

'Both, I expect.'

Maria took a bite of her breakfast bap and gave a huge sigh of satisfaction. If she got treated this well each time, perhaps birthdays weren't so bad after all.

CHAPTER NINE

An hour later Maria was still in bed, feeling a tad fragile. That was another thing about getting older. Hangovers took far too much time to recover from. It almost didn't seem worth a few hours of fun for the three days of agony that followed.

There she went again, moaning about her age. Being fifty wasn't the most depressing thing she could think of. Her health was good, her family was great. She had all her own teeth. She snorted. What more could a girl want?

Before everyone arrived, Jim had come back upstairs with a few gifts for her. She ran a finger across the face of the silver locket. It really was beautiful, something she'd cherish, and she was already thinking of which photograph of her and Jim to put inside it.

Jim was downstairs again now; said he'd gone to prepare things. There was a commotion, and Delilah barked. Maria braced herself to get up, but it was too late. Two little people burst into the room and threw themselves on her bed.

'Happy birthday, Granny!' Ellie and Saskia spoke in unison.

If you didn't know they weren't sisters, you'd be hard

placed to tell. Both girls had long, dark hair and the cheekiest of smiles. Whereas Saskia was growing into a young woman before their eyes, Ellie had yet to fill out and feel confident with her gangly legs and thin body. Yet, in some ways, Ellie was becoming a mini version of Saskia. She copied her, often following her round like a shadow.

For the most part, Saskia was accommodating, but still, they often fought because of it. Yet, Maria saw a side to Saskia where she could tell the teenager loved fussing around and looking after Ellie. They'd called each other sisters for a couple of years now. Due to her age when they'd met, Ellie had called Aaron Dad almost straightaway, but Saskia always used Lucy's first name.

Maria put a hand to her chest. 'My, you gave me a fright!'

'We have presents!' Saskia handed her a box wrapped in silver paper.

Ellie had one, too, but smaller.

She opened Saskia's first. It was all heavily taped down, so she tore it off frantically, much to the girls' delight. Inside was a pair of purple strappy shoes. Not too high, just the way she preferred.

'Saskia, these are lovely,' she said, holding one up.

'Riley picked them out for me,' she explained.

Riley was the manager of Chandler's Shoes on the high street. Maria recalled the flash mob she had set up on the high street, the video of it going viral. The owner was threatening closure if business didn't pick up, so as a publicity stunt, Riley told everyone in Somerley to be around at two p.m. Out of curiosity, Maria and Sal had stayed behind once the office was shut for the weekend.

It had brightened up their day to see a group of dancers invade their little square, including Riley and the staff from the shoe shop.

'Thank you.' Maria pulled Saskia into her arms and gave

her a kiss, loving how the teenager had become part of their family as if she were their own flesh and blood.

'Mine now!' Ellie squealed.

Maria ripped the paper off that one to find a leather purse, a silver letter M on the clasp.

'It's gorgeous. Thanks, my brilliant girl.'

The door opened again, and in came Lucy, followed by Clara.

'Right, terrors,' Lucy said to the girls. 'Your granddad wants you downstairs. He says he needs help with some secret things.' She tapped the side of her nose twice.

Both children jumped off the bed and tore downstairs in a fit of giggles and shrieks.

'Happy birthday, Mum.' Clara kissed her and sat on the bed.

'Happy birthday, Mum.' Lucy did the same on the opposite side of Maria.

'Thank you!' Maria exclaimed. 'But I'll never get out of my jarmies at this rate.'

'Before we give you your main presents, we have something from the two of us.' Lucy nodded to her sister, who nipped out of the room for a second and came back with a large brown envelope.

Maria frowned.

Clara sat back in the space she'd vacated. 'What's this?'

'Let's just say you're in for a treat.'

'Ooh, is it a week on a cruise ship? Or ten days in New York?' Maria queried, wanting to rip the envelope open immediately to see. Patience had never been her virtue.

'Nothing like that. They're only a bit of fun,' Clara added quickly.

'They? Now, I'm curious.' Maria pointed to the envelope. 'Pass it over, then.'

Clara handed it to her.

Maria grinned as she tore it open, only to find several smaller envelopes inside. She tipped them out onto the bed. There were five of them, each numbered. 'Do I need to open them all now?'

'No, only on the dates written on the back,' Clara explained.

Maria narrowed her eyes. 'What are you two up to?'

'We've paid for you and Dad to go on five nostalgic dates!'

Maria's gaze travelled between them. She couldn't believe how happy her daughters looked right now and yet she didn't understand. It instantly made Maria nervous. What did they mean by nostalgic dates?

'We think you and dad work too hard,' Lucy said, ever the practical one. 'You never seem to get a break.'

'We're tired of you saying you don't have time to do anything,' Clara went on. 'And that we're the ones who should be going out and having fun.'

'And you're only fifty once,' Lucy added, 'so we thought you could relive a few of your memories when you and Dad first met each other.'

Maria was perplexed. 'Does your dad know about this?'

'He does now. We told him this morning.'

'And what did he say?'

'That he wants you to be happy!' Lucy sounded exasperated. 'What else did you think he'd say?'

She left the room, and for a few seconds, Maria thought she'd upset her. But, like her younger sister moments earlier, she was back in seconds, this time with a white-and-silver box. She passed it to her.

'We want you to bring back keepsakes.' Clara clapped with glee. 'It can be anything – a photo, a fridge magnet. A postcard, a ticket.'

'Something that will remind you of each date,' Lucy said.

Maria wasn't sure she could keep the fake smile in place

for much longer. It was hard when the people you love were happy about something that you weren't too keen on, and unlike her girls to act so spontaneously. She and Jim didn't have time to fritter on something like this. They both had businesses to run.

Still, they'd clearly put a lot of effort into thinking of things for her and their dad to do, so there wasn't any point making a big deal about it. Especially now.

She drew both girls into her arms for a hug.

'Well, at least I have a few surprises in store.' Maria smiled. 'Thank you, girls.'

'And you get to open the first one right now,' Clara told her.

'Oh. Right.' Maria sorted through the envelopes for the one she needed.

CHAPTER TEN

Happy birthday, Mum!

For the next few weeks, you and Dad are going on a journey of nostalgia, remembering when you met, what fun you had falling in love, and a few other things besides.

It's time for you to make new memories.

On Monday at 2 p.m., afternoon tea is booked for you at The Coffee Stop.

We hope you enjoy it.

Love Lucy and Clara. xx

'Oh!' Maria couldn't help feeling deflated. She wasn't sure what she was expecting, but it certainly wasn't that. She looked at Lucy and Clara with another painted-on smile.

'It's all sorted, Mum,' Lucy told her. 'Dad has said it's okay.'

'But—'

'But nothing!' Clara broke in. 'You've done so much for us, so we wanted to do something special for you.'

'But—'

'Something that would mean a lot to us as well as you.'

They stared at her.

'We know you love us all, but you should enjoy time with Dad, too.' Lucy's smile dropped a little.

'Will you let me speak! I'm trying to say that it's a lovely thought. I hope I can persuade your dad to skive off work for a couple of hours.'

'We've told him he doesn't have a choice. We said it's for you, not him.'

Maria scoffed. 'Sometimes I think he doesn't want to spend time alone with me.'

'Don't be daft, Mum. He loves you to the moon and back.'

'Of course he does.' Maria hugged her daughters again, keeping her thoughts to herself this time. She and Jim might very well love each other, but it would be wonderful to be *in* love again, feel the first throes of passion. She laughed inwardly. They'd never get that back during five nostalgic dates.

Once alone again, Maria thought about what Lucy and Clara had done. Depending on what was in the rest of those envelopes, it had probably cost a lot of money, as well as time, to organise this for her. She was happy that they'd thought of this. But she hoped there were five good things in those envelopes as workaholic Jim would probably be fed up by number three.

With everyone out of her way and downstairs again, she rang Sal.

'Happy birthday, my friend,' Sal greeted her. 'How does it feel to be so old?'

'Depressing.'

Laughter down the line. 'Is everyone there?'

'Yes, what time are you coming over?'

'I'll be with you in half an hour.'

'Good, because I need you here.' Maria told her what had happened.

'What's a nostalgic date? A pie and pea supper? A go on the waltzers at the fair?'

'I don't know!' Maria pinched the bridge of her nose. 'I can't get my head around it either.'

'And they haven't told you what else you can expect, apart from afternoon tea?'

'Not even a hint.'

'That sounds fun.' Sal sniggered. 'It will be like a dating app, never knowing what to expect.'

'Joking aside, Sal, and I know it's going to be hard to find the time, but it is lovely of them to go to so much trouble. I wonder how involved Jim would have been for them to come up with five places to go. I was just thinking about when we were teenagers. I'm not sure we ever went for afternoon tea.'

'Well, there's always a first time for everything.'

'I can't begin to think what else we'll have to do.'

'Cast your mind back to when you were young, if you can.'

'Ha ha.' Maria's voice was laced with sarcasm.

'You obviously used to talk about going for tea and cake with Jim. What else have you mentioned to the girls, about when you were courting?'

'*Courting?*' It was Maria's turn to laugh. 'That makes me feel so old.'

'You *are* old, woman. You're the big five-o.'

Maria thought for a moment, recalling her memories. 'We went roller skating, didn't we? Dear God, I hope they didn't get us tickets to do that. I'll break my bloody neck, never mind Jim.'

Sal chuckled. 'You went away for a few cheeky weekends, too.'

'Yes, but we can't leave the businesses for any length of time to do that now.'

'Why not?'

'Because there's always so much to do.'

'Oh, come on! When was the last time you went on holiday together?'

'We went to Tenerife last summer.'

'Lucy and her tribe were with you. I mean, just you and Jim?'

'We went for a night in Manchester, I think it was the year before.'

'Exactly. You do need to get a life. Hey, maybe I should sign up to a dating app. I could meet someone every time you and Jim go out. We can compare notes afterwards.'

'We most certainly cannot! You'd get wined and dined, and maybe have fabulous, inhibited sex, and what would I get? Probably a walk in the park or half a pint in the Hope and Anchor. Because that's all Jim and I did when we were *courting*.'

'Oh, behave. You can use your imagination. Go wild, why don't you?'

'You know I don't do wild.'

'But you do beautiful, inside and out. You need to remember that.'

The phone conversation played on a loop in her head as Maria finally got dressed. How could Sal say she was beautiful? Clara had said the same thing yesterday. But Maria was at least three stone heavier than when she was in her twenties, although that wasn't an uncommon thing for women of a certain age.

There she went again. *Women of a certain age.*

Perhaps she could have fun on those dates with Jim, and it did mean they'd get to spend a little time together for a change. They had lost so much of themselves recently with one thing or another.

But Maria felt far from beautiful. More than that, she expected Jim had stuck around with her for so long through complacency rather than love.

And there wasn't anything pretty about that.

CHAPTER ELEVEN

In her parents' kitchen, Clara sat at the table in the middle of Tyler and his mum, Sal. Across from her was Lucy and Ellie, and Aaron and Saskia. Clara's mum and dad were at either end of the table. Thankfully, the space for the extra place setting had been utilised to make it less noticeable.

Despite Clara complaining to him again that morning, Alex insisted he had to go to work. Eventually, Clara had stormed out in a mood, screeching off in her car.

Now, she'd made excuses for him, again, and she was feeling terrible about it. Even Tyler, who could usually make her laugh, was finding it hard to raise a smile from her.

She and Tyler had always been close and saw each other just as much now as ever. Luckily, Alex and Tyler got along. Alex had never been jealous of the time she and Tyler spent together, which, she supposed, was hardly much compared to when he was out with his friends all the time. In fact, Alex openly encouraged them to meet up. Now Clara wondered if he did that deliberately, so she could spend time away from him.

Tyler was regaling them with one of his work anecdotes.

Tyler was a postman and had so many tales to tell. This time it was about a delivery to a couple who'd shouted at him to go through to the garden where he'd found them in the hot tub, half naked.

'I tell you, I didn't know where to put my eyes. It's brass monkeys outside, and there they were, in the hot tub. It wasn't a sight I'd want to see again. And get this.' Tyler leaned forward as if he was about to tell them a secret. 'I was sure they wanted me to join in. She's always making a beeline for me whenever I see her.'

'That's because you're such a hunk!' Sal cried, glancing at her son with pride.

It was true. Tyler was the epitome of tall, dark, and handsome. He was six foot two, with a broad chest and a strong build. His hair was thick, mussed up; his blue eyes twinkled but smouldered when required. He'd had many a one-night stand after his two-year relationship ended a year ago but he was now ready to settle down.

'Well, she obviously has good taste.' Tyler grinned. 'Most of the time she comes to the door half-dressed, hoping to cause me embarrassment.'

'Or to show you her wares.' Jim guffawed.

'Believe me, I saw more than my fair share of those when she was in that hot tub. And he was just as bad. Although he was showing off an enormous beer belly.'

'I bet she's the type to go nude on the beach.' Aaron shuddered at the thought.

'I do the knock-and-run trick now and call back a few minutes later. If the parcel is still on the step, I take it back to the depot. If it's gone, I know someone is in and I've had a lucky escape seeing her, if she took it in.'

'Oh, Tyler, you are so funny,' Maria cried.

Clara tried hard to join in, but all she could manage was a weak smile.

Maria was about to get up, but Jim raised his glass in a toast.

'Happy birthday to my old doll!'

'Cheeky,' Maria laughed.

'Happy birthday, Maria!'

'Happy birthday, Mum!'

'Happy birthday, Granny!'

When Maria began to clear the plates, Clara offered to help. Anything to get out of the room.

'Is everything really all right with Alex?' Maria asked as they loaded the dishwasher together.

'He's got a new boss and he's trying to make a clean sweep of things, upsetting the apple cart as they say, by making them work more weekends.' Clara tried to keep her tone jovial because if her mum could see through her act, then they all would. 'Alex didn't want to go in today, but he was making it really awkward.'

'As long as that's all it is. I'm always here if you want to talk.' Maria looked at her pointedly.

'I know you are, Mum, thanks.' Clara gave her a hug. She hoped to hide the blush heating up her skin. 'But everything's fine. He's just a bit stressed because of it, that's all.'

After their bellies had been filled with as much food as they could eat, Lucy and Aaron made their way home with the girls. They'd left the car behind so they could both have wine with their lunch. Despite trying for a baby, Lucy was allowing herself the odd drink. Who knew how long it might take for them to conceive? At this rate, Ellie would be well in her teens.

'That seems a bit weird about Alex, doesn't it?' she said as they walked out of Lilac Grove and onto the high street, Saskia and Ellie running ahead of them.

'Yes,' Aaron agreed. 'I wouldn't have thought anything of it if Clara hadn't gone the colour of a ripe tomato. It gave the game away that she was fibbing, but I wonder why.'

'I'll try and talk to her about it at work, if I can get her alone.' Lucy slipped her arm through his.

'Are you okay?' he asked after a moment.

'Hmm?' She smiled at him. 'I'm fine. Why?'

'I mean because it's your time of the month and you haven't mentioned anything.'

'Ah.' She looked at him sheepishly. 'I'm a bit late but I've been here before, so I don't want to take a test yet. I'm scared of it coming back negative.'

Aaron stopped for a minute. 'But that's good news, isn't it?'

'It might be.'

'Do you feel different?'

'What do you mean?'

'Are your boobs tender? Want me to investigate?'

'In the middle of the street?'

His hand wandered upwards, and she slapped it away playfully.

'My boobs are fine, although they are a tad achy. But...'

'In the meantime we keep practising like mad.'

She grinned, knowing he was trying to change the subject for her. 'Sex, sex, sex. That's all you're interested in.'

'Er, I think you'll find it's the best way to make babies.' He winked at her.

'Did you just wink at me, Aaron Foxley?'

'I did!' He drew her near and kissed her on the nose.

'Come on, Mummy!' Ellie shouted to them. 'Stop dawdling and hurry up!'

'Dawdling? I'm sure that girl is twenty-five,' Lucy muttered. 'Where has she learned that?'

'I have no idea.'

Saskia and Ellie waited for them to catch up, Ellie complaining her legs were tired. Aaron lifted her onto his shoulders.

'Oh my! You're getting too old for this,' he teased. 'You weigh more than a sack of potatoes.'

'I do not.' Ellie giggled. 'Mummy, I can see for miles and miles.'

'Hold on tight, darling!'

'Can we call into Somerley Stores to get some sweets, please?' Saskia asked when they drew level with the doorway.

'After all that trifle you scoffed?' Aaron said in disbelief.

'You had more than me!' Saskia giggled, looking at her dad in particular.

Their laughter warmed Lucy's heart. All she'd ever wanted was a family of her own. And a baby would complete their little group. Mentally, she crossed her fingers and hoped for the best.

After cooking for the family, Maria was having a well-earned break. She and Jim had cleared the table, loaded the rest of the crockery in the dishwasher, and were now having coffee.

'That went well,' Jim said as he flopped on the settee next to her in the conservatory.

'It did. Thanks for making it so special.'

'It isn't every day your wife gets to fifty years of age,' he joked.

'Hey.' She thumped him playfully. 'I don't feel any different, though. I just feel… old.'

'You are.'

'That's not helping.' She sighed. 'I'm worried about Clara and Alex. Did you sense there was something wrong?'

'Yes, but that's nothing new.'

'Maybe, but it really shouldn't be happening so often. We

all have arguments, but they seem to be miserable each time we see them. I tried to talk to her about it in the kitchen, but she insisted everything was fine.'

'Then that's how it is.'

'I could tell she wasn't being truthful.'

'And until she *wants* to say more, you should stay quiet.'

'I'm only trying to help.'

'I know, but you'd be better off leaving them to it.' He stood suddenly, marking the close of the conversation. 'Now, I know we've eaten a mountain of food today, but I fancy another slice of your birthday cake.'

She sighed inwardly. Jim always thought she worried too much when it came to the girls, but it was imperative to her own happiness. Everything had to be perfect. And that's what she'd always continue to strive for.

CHAPTER TWELVE

Clara could barely look at Alex when he arrived home from work late that afternoon, apart from to see that he seemed quite fresh if he'd been grafting. He'd changed out of his suit and into jeans and a hoody, too. Why did he feel the need to shower there, rather than at home?

'Good day?' she asked, her voice laced with sarcasm.

'I was working. I'd hardly call that good.'

'Really? You don't seem like you've had a harrowing day.'

'What's up with you?' he asked, when she'd banged enough things around in the kitchen.

'Nothing.'

'I suppose you want to sit down and discuss things again. Well, I'm not in the mood.'

'You never want to talk, though, do you?' she cried. 'You're always far too busy.'

'Lots of couples argue. We're no different.'

She scowled. How could he not see that things needed to change? Their marriage was dying.

'You can't really believe—'

'Actually, there is something. I'm tired of spending so much time with your family. It's getting boring.'

Clara turned to gaze out of the kitchen window. Choosing to alienate her by not seeing her family wasn't on. And how was she supposed to explain that to them, her mum in particular, when she loved their get-togethers?

'You used to say that you loved being part of my family,' she taunted.

'I did until it became every weekend.'

'Don't exaggerate. We have lunch together once a month. And it's Mum's fiftieth birthday! I had to make excuses as to why you were so determined to go into work.'

'It was important.'

'Was it really?'

Alex shrugged like a petulant child.

Clara groaned. 'Sometimes I wonder why I bother.'

'Why you bother with what?'

'You!' She pointed at him and then herself. 'Us.'

A lengthy silence grew between them. He didn't defend himself, didn't put up a fight to say they were worth making an effort for. Instead, he made a huge show of checking the time on his watch.

'I have to go soon or else I'll be late for Dan. I'm meeting him for a drink later.'

Clara groaned. He was unbelievable. He really didn't want to spend time with her. Something inside her made her see red.

'That's right, off you go.' She made a shooing motion with her hand. 'Mustn't leave Dan waiting instead of being with your wife.'

'We'll talk some more later. You're too angry now.'

'It's how you make me feel! You treat me like a housekeeper. I'm not here just to do your washing and ironing. I'm not here just to clean up after you, cook for you, *when* you're here, that is. Because that seems to be less and less over the past few weeks. You're always going out with someone or doing something that doesn't involve me.'

'Clara.' Alex pinched the bridge of his nose. 'Let's not do this now.'

'I'll get my phone, shall I, so we can schedule a time for when you *can* do it? What is it with you lately? It's as if you don't want to be with me at all.'

The look he gave her brought tears to her eyes. They burned as she tried to hold them in. It had only been for a fraction of a second, but she'd seen it. The desire to leave. Was their marriage over before it had really begun?

'Perhaps we could go out for Sunday lunch together, rather than spend it with your relatives.'

Alex couldn't have hurt her more. Family was everything to Clara, and yet it seemed as if he really was giving her an ultimatum. She couldn't choose between the two. She *wouldn't* choose. It was absurd.

Before she'd had time to compose a reply, he'd gone. She pulled out a chair at the table and sat down, her hands covering her face. What was happening to them?

Unable to contemplate an evening alone with her thoughts, she reached for her phone and dialled Tyler's number. As soon as she heard his voice, her tears spilled over.

'Want me to pop round?' he asked when she hadn't been able to stop sobbing long enough to tell him the whole sorry story.

'Don't you have anything to do this evening?'

'Not really. I'm still too full to move from lunch. Get the kettle on.'

She smiled through her tears. Tyler always knew exactly what to do.

He was there within fifteen minutes. Tea was made and

the mugs out on the coffee table. Now, he was sitting beside her.

'If you want the honest truth,' Tyler said. 'I think this has been brewing for far too long.'

'What, the tea?' She smirked.

'I'm being serious! I know I'm your friend, and I know we talk about this often, and it's not really my place to speak about Alex out of turn *all* of the time. But neither of you are happy. It's getting obvious when we're all together. And remember your summer holiday?'

Clara shuddered at the memory. They'd gone to Majorca for a week in July, and it had been torture for them both. They barely had a word to say to each other, and as for the sex they usually caught up on? Alex had always been tired after a day of walking while she read by the pool, or too drunk after a night in the bar. There had been holidays before that they'd been at it like rabbits, catching up on what they missed with busy lives leaving them apart more than they'd liked.

She'd come back to Somerley really unhappy and thought things might have been over then. But Alex bounced back to his normal self once they were home, and she'd enjoyed his company again. Until just before Christmas, when things changed. She couldn't pinpoint why.

'Something is wrong, but he won't tell me,' she said. 'You don't think he has another woman, do you?'

'What? No. Why would he want anyone else when he has you?'

'Well played, mister.' Clara smiled. 'Tell me about you,' she said, feeling happy enough to move on from moping about Alex. 'What's going on in Tyler's world?'

His sigh was dramatic. 'Not a lot, I'm afraid. The love of my life is still out there. I've yet to find her.'

'You need to go out more for that to happen. When was the last time you had a night on the town?'

'Can't remember.'

'We should rectify that then. Let's do a Friday, when we both don't have to work the next day.'

'Are you sure? What about Alex?'

'Stuff him. If he can go out with his friends, then so can I.'

Tyler smiled. 'It's a date!'

Sometimes Clara wished she *could* go on a date with Tyler. At least he would make her feel worthy.

CHAPTER THIRTEEN

On Monday, at ten minutes to two, Maria was at work when she glanced up to see Jim coming through the door. He'd been home and changed, casual in jeans, a checked shirt, and a thick jacket. A red scarf she'd bought him for Christmas was knotted around his neck.

She cursed under her breath: she wasn't ready to leave yet.

'Ooh,' Lucy trilled. 'Your date has arrived, Mum.'

'I'm glad you changed out of your overalls,' Clara added.

'Don't poke fun at your old man.' Jim threw them a mock-stern look. 'I know I have style.'

Everyone burst out laughing as he tried to appear offended.

'I won't be a minute, Jim,' Maria shouted through from her office. 'I just need to finish something off.'

Jim plonked himself on the end of Clara's desk while he waited. He reached for a brochure. 'Your mum was showing me this property last night. It's quite a show stopper.'

'I thought she would have taken you to see it before now.'

'We're not moving again! My old back won't take it.'

'I'm sure she'll use her persuasive charms on you. You'll be packing boxes in no time.'

'No, we won't. I'm putting my foot down now, with a firm hand.' He laughed at his joke. 'I'm settled where we are. I don't want to move.'

Maria stopped to listen to the conversation. She had been disappointed last night when Jim hadn't really wanted to view any properties online. She thought she'd sold it well to him, but now he was saying he was happy staying put? It was annoying, to say the least.

'I can't wait to get a bigger house,' Lucy said. 'It's so cramped in Aaron's little place.' She paused. 'And yet, it feels so homely that I don't want to leave. Does that even make sense?'

'It does,' Jim said. 'Home is where the heart is.'

'My old dad being a romantic.' Clara sighed.

Jim stood up and went to the door of Maria's office. 'Come on, love, work can wait.'

'Okay, okay!' Maria pulled on her coat. 'We won't be long, girls. If Mrs Rubenstein calls before I get back, tell her I'll ring her on my return. And the sale board needs to go up on the house in Broad Street. Oh, and—'

'Mum, stop!' Lucy pushed her towards the front door. 'Go and have fun.'

'And bring us back some chocolate brownies,' Clara added. 'They're the best from The Coffee Stop.'

'Is this my treat or yours?' Maria teased before sticking her tongue out at them.

Once they were across the road, she turned to Jim. 'I still don't really know what this is all about, do you?'

'Well, I—'

'I mean, it's a bit weird asking us to do five things we used to do when we were teenagers,' she continued before she'd given him the chance to finish. 'And speaking bluntly, I can't recall a time when we had afternoon tea!'

'No, but I can remember when we had coffee and cake after the first time we'd made love. We were all smiles and giggles, and we couldn't keep our hands off each other. You asked me if anyone could tell what we'd been up to, and I said probably.'

Maria glanced at Jim, surprised he'd remembered something so vividly. She hadn't, but he'd brought it back to her in multi-colours. She smiled as she linked an arm through his.

'Can you believe that was over thirty years ago? We're getting old and wrinkly together.'

'Exactly how it should be.'

The Coffee Stop was a modern establishment, all lilacs and silvers, chrome seats at tables and leather settees to lounge on in a large bay window. The noise of the steamer was the first thing to hit them, above the chatter of people. A bar at the far end of the room was where Maria spotted Chloe. She waved, rushing over to them as soon as she could.

Chloe and Kate had owned the business for a few years now, since the previous proprietor had died. They'd done a fantastic job of improving trade, introducing a takeaway service and a wide selection of coffees and cakes. Eventually, they'd brought in locally sourced sandwiches, and no end of delicious snacks, to give them more time to be on hand. There was always something new to seek out on the menu each month.

To Maria's right, The Book Stop had been created in the next shop along, double doors joining each establishment for ease and temptation. Kate's husband, Will, owned the whole row of buildings, and there was talk of a further area being created for a space for the kids to play, and a bar upstairs for private functions after hours.

'Welcome, you two!' Chloe pointed to a table at the back

of the room. It had been set out with a tablecloth and a red rose in a stem vase. Several balloons were bobbing up and down from the vase, too.

Maria was a tad embarrassed at all the fuss. She walked quickly as some of the other customers stared at her.

'Special occasion, is it?' an elderly lady asked as they passed her table.

'My birthday,' Maria replied.

'Not just any birthday.' Chloe came up behind her. 'She was fifty on Saturday, and she doesn't look a day over forty, does she, Irene?'

Irene shook her head. 'I wish I was your age again, love. Happy birthday.'

'Thank you.' Maria sat down.

Jim sat opposite her. When she caught his eye, he was grinning.

'What's up with you?'

'You're blushing.'

'It's warm in here.'

He placed his hand over hers. 'Relax and enjoy yourself.'

'I can't.'

'Why on earth not?'

'Because.' She stopped. Did Jim really want to know how much of a faff she thought this was? If they were going to go out for a treat, she would much prefer to be wined and dined.

And truth be told, she couldn't really spare the time in the middle of the day. In her mind, she was still at her desk, running through what price to value the property she'd viewed that morning. The customer wanted a quick sale and, even so, Maria was determined to get her a decent price.

She groaned inwardly. She was such a control freak. Why couldn't she switch off? But with her woolly brain letting her down so much, she felt unable to do so. She needed to stay on top of everything.

Jim let out the most enormous sigh. 'Lucy and Clara wanted to do this for you, so the least you can do is enjoy it and stop moaning.'

Maria was mortified at the hurt in his sharp tone. 'I know, I'm sorry.'

He relented. 'I'm told the carrot cake is delicious.'

'Let's have some. I've forgotten how lovely this coffee shop is. We usually only get takeaway.'

'There's a lot we miss out on, isn't there?' Jim sat forward a little. 'Perhaps we could do more together?'

'As if we'd ever find the time.'

'Maybe we could take a day off every now and then during the week.'

'It's impossible. Our phone hasn't stopped ringing and—'

Jim reached for her hand. 'You have to agree, this is nice, just you and me.'

Maria gave him a faint smile. Even if this was a treat, it seemed false. It felt as if they were trying too hard to enjoy it. She couldn't recall the last time she and Jim had sat down together like this outside of their home. It was sad, really. So the gesture from Lucy and Clara was a good one. She might as well sit back and enjoy it.

Chloe came over with a cake tray full of scones and cream, sandwiches, and mini cakes. She popped them down in the middle of the table. In a few seconds, she was back with a bottle of Prosecco.

'Happy birthday from me and Kate.' She smiled.

Maria saw Kate waving from behind the counter. She waved back.

'Thank you,' she said, fearing she was sounding like a parrot. But everyone was being so nice. Tears pricked at her eyes, and she burst into tears.

Jim handed her a napkin.

'Bloody hormones.' She laughed, even though she was crying. 'Let's tuck in.

CHAPTER FOURTEEN

At home later that week, Maria was taking a moment before she left for work, leaning with her back to the kitchen worktop. The late-winter sun was streaming in through the window at her side. It was her favourite room in the house, where she and Jim spent most of their spare time.

Maria loved its spaciousness. A row of navy-blue bespoke units lined two walls in an L-shape, and in front of her was a huge island with a white marble top that also served as a breakfast bar. But to Maria's mind it was the colourful display of drawings from Ellie, held on with magnets, and stickers from Saskia spread all over the fridge that stole the show.

Behind that was a settee next to a dining area. A bank of doors covered the far wall, overlooking the garden. Through the years, the large dining table had seen birthday parties, Sunday lunches, Christmas banquets, a christening, and was the hub of the home. This was their fifth house, they'd been in it for seven years, and it was the second longest they'd stayed in any property.

With Maria being an estate agent, one of the perks of the job was getting to see properties before anyone else did.

Maria always got first dibs. There had been many an argument, or sharp word, between her and Jim over the past few years when she'd spied a property she loved, and he was reluctant to move again.

But, like he'd said earlier in the week, Jim was settled there. He didn't want to go through the rigmarole again, whereas Maria always seemed to have itchy feet. She was insistent on there being a better place on the market for them and got cross when Jim said she'd probably never be fully happy anywhere due to her lousy childhood.

'Sometimes, all you change by moving is your address,' he'd told her when she'd shown him that last property she'd coveted the other evening. 'You don't need to keep getting bigger and better to prove that you're good enough.'

Even though it had stung, she knew he was right. Having come from a broken home, she was always overcompensating. Which was why she was so proud that she'd run her own business for so long. It had been a struggle at times, but with Jim by her side, and loyal staff before Sal had come on board as well, it had been worth all the hard work, and something of a dream come true.

It was during a walk on a balmy summer's evening that she and Jim had noticed the for-sale sign over the old estate agent's door. At that time, Maria managed the office and admin staff for Jim and had been moaning about being bored. Building supplies weren't exactly thrilling, and she'd wanted her own business to run alongside his. Lucy and Clara were fourteen and twelve, capable of looking after themselves to a certain extent. The timing seemed right.

They'd stopped to peep inside the first bay window, and her stomach had flipped as she'd stared past the houses on offer and imagined herself sitting at the desk inside, showing a client details of a property they could make into a home. It seemed an ideal choice of profession for her.

'I could do something like this,' she'd said, glancing at Jim.

'It's certainly something to think about,' Jim had replied. 'Especially after what we've done to our last few homes, plus your flair for interior design.'

Maria had loved him more from that moment, when he hadn't laughed at her, or put her down for not having the right qualifications. To her, it was about getting people their forever home, ensuring they felt safe and secure. Their haven.

She'd thought about it a little more until it had taken over her every waking hour and she'd gone to find out further details. The previous owner, who was retiring through ill health, had been wonderfully accommodating, staying on for four months to train her into office manager. She'd kept one of the staff on – Sue was a qualified estate agent – until she'd taken the required exams herself. So, when Sue handed her notice in, retiring to live in Spain, Maria had bitten the bullet and taken on the role. The business had gone from strength to strength.

It had been strange not to work with Jim, but it had also been quite freeing. It didn't give them any more to talk about than business and the kids, but that was her and Jim. Business first from the get-go.

As well as running the estate agency, Maria would often take houses on her books that she would then give a makeover to ensure they sold quickly. Over the years, she'd gained a reputation as being able to sell nearly everything. It had won her several industry awards, too.

And at least being her own boss meant it was okay to have hot sweats, and brain fog days, without feeling inadequate. It made her blood boil to think how some women weren't able to talk about menopause symptoms because they were too ashamed or fearful of losing their jobs. Half the working population was pushed aside for something that could be worked at to make it better. Imagine how many wonderful women left their careers because of how it had made them feel.

She could still recall watching the Davina McCall documentaries, in tears because she had felt understood. As much as her body had changed when she'd had the children, the menopause was a whole new ballgame.

Finally ready to start the day, she collected everything she needed. Purse, phone, handbag, house sale promotion folder with keys. Before leaving, she stooped to say goodbye to Delilah who was now curled up in her basket.

'Bye, my honey bunny,' she spoke quietly to her, stroking her ears. The dog looked up in ecstasy. 'I'll be back before you know it, but I'll leave the radio on.'

She laughed to herself as she left the house, wondering if every pet owner did the same. Said goodbye to their pets, telling them to behave and that they wouldn't be long. She even changed the channel on the radio to something she assumed Delilah would like.

The weather was damp and grey, another miserable day forecast. She waved at her neighbour who was getting into his car across the way. There were only ten homes in Lilac Grove, with large gardens, set in a quiet cul-de-sac. As neighbours went, they'd been very lucky here, having no problems at all.

So it begged the question. Why *couldn't* it be her forever home?

CHAPTER FIFTEEN

Harper Road was just behind Somerley Church, a quiet row of terraced cottages, on the next street to where Lucy lived with Aaron. Maria managed to squeeze her car into the smallest of spaces a few houses along from the property she was showing. There was a slight drizzle in the air, and it was still bitterly cold. In the far distance, a postman pushed his trolley along the pavement, delivering the morning's post.

A tabby cat was curled up on a car bonnet, and she smiled as she went past it. When she and Jim had bought their first property together, they only had a small van. Really, they didn't have much need for anything else until Jim's business was established, and she'd then had her own little run-around to ferry herself and the kids in.

Maria tutted, stepping off the pavement and straight inside number twenty-two. The place was a tip, having been rented out to a family who had trashed it. Some of the doors had holes kicked in them, a built-in TV corner unit had been gnawed by dogs, and there was wallpaper torn off in the living room. The kitchen was practically non-existent, and don't even mention the state of the tiny bathroom.

But it was all cosmetics. It had huge potential for anyone who could see past its issues. The sale price reflected its condition, and everyone liked a fixer-upper for their first property, surely? There was nothing better than arguing over putting together flat-pack kitchens, wallpapering uneven walls, and sanding skirting boards before layering them with several coats of paint to get rid of yellow stains. She could remember it well.

If it weren't for a local couple coming to look at the cottage, most likely it would be snapped up by a builder who would rip the heart out of it and put it back on sale for double the money when it was finished. It priced so many first-time buyers out of the market.

Even she couldn't shift everything, though.

Maria got rid of the negative talk immediately. She *would* sell it. She excelled in that type of thing.

A few minutes later, there was a knock at the door, and she rushed to open it. A young couple stood on the pavement. Maria knew both sets of parents, having moved them once or twice. Lewis and Nicole Ramsey had grown up in Somerley and were first-time buyers. Lewis was extremely tall with glasses and unruly spiked hair. Nicole was a lot shorter than him, with a heart-shaped face and short blonde bob. Both of them were wearing long coats and scarfs, noses red due to the cold.

'Lewis, Nicole!' Maria beckoned them forward. 'Come on in. What a nasty day.'

They stepped through a small vestibule that Maria could just about turn around in, and into a hallway not much bigger, stairs to the first floor straight ahead. To their left was a door, which she pointed at.

'Now, you've seen photos online, so you know what to expect, but I happen to think that you only get the feel for a property when you see it first-hand.' She paused for dramatic effect.

Lewis and Nicole glanced at each other, then back at her.

'Picture it when it's all finished to your taste,' she went on. 'You have to look past what's here and envisage it with everything you want to do to it, how it will be when you are sitting on the settee, watching a film on Netflix, or cooking supper in the plush, new kitchen. You can choose everything you want from the start, rather than live with someone else's choice.'

'I love that idea,' Nicole said.

'It's certainly going to be a labour of love,' Lewis joked.

'And something you can be proud of once it's finished.' Maria took Nicole's arm. 'Let me show you the kitchen area first. It's quite a good size, and there's even room to add an island or a table for eight. Plus it opens straight out onto the garden. Very handy for all the entertaining you're going to do.'

Despite the condition of the property, the viewing had gone well. Maria had known from the moment Lewis and Nicole took their time walking around the rooms by themselves after she'd given them the guided tour. They had made an offer there and then. It was five thousand pounds below the asking price, but she'd rung the owner and said she could get a couple more for them. Another phone call had Lewis and Nicole sealing the deal. Property sold!

No matter what the price, there was a buyer for everything. Maria hated all the gazumping that went on; she wasn't in the business of crushing dreams. Hers had been built on trust and integrity. Indeed, she'd had to let a few staff go when she'd heard they'd been pushing clients to pay more.

Now, locking up, she sighed with satisfaction. It was time for Lewis and Nicole to make memories of their own.

Coming full circle, she was back in Lilac Grove in half an hour. Seeing her own home again, the immense sense of achievement overwhelmed her. Every room had been done to her taste, lots of cream and gold, dashes of orange and caramel colours. Jim always said she had a good eye and left it to her. So far, even with some of the bold moves she'd made, she'd met his approval.

Even though she kept on wishing the years could roll back until she was in her twenties again, she was so proud of what she and Jim had achieved. Being fifty wasn't that frightening now she'd got the day over and done with. She would attack her next decade with vigour, making it the best one yet. So what if she wasn't as agile or as thin? She was healthy, and so was her family. There was a lot to be said for that alone.

THIRTY YEARS AGO - 17 GARRETT STREET

As there was no one living in the property and there was nothing of value, Jim had been able to collect the keys from the estate agent's on his way home from work, so they could view it on their own. The house had been repossessed because someone had defaulted on their payments, so it was a "sold as seen" purchase.

It didn't take Maria and Jim long to walk around the five rooms. The living room had bare floorboards and a picture rail that had seen better days. There was a hole on the chimney breast where a fire had been removed. The hearth had gone, too.

The kitchen, if you could call it that, was a room with a sink unit, an eye-level gas cooker, and a metre-long worktop with a gap underneath it, below the tiniest of windows that let in a little light. A hideous brick archway had been erected to separate it into a dining room. The ceiling was missing, electric wires hanging down and water pipes on display.

Upstairs, there were two bedrooms, and a bathroom with a burgundy suite. The grout in between the tiles was almost black in places, and there was mould growing on the corner by the roof.

'What do you think?' Jim asked once they came back downstairs.

Maria grimaced, noticing again the peeling chip-wood wallpaper and the damp patch on the ceiling. There wasn't even a fireplace. The bay window was stunning, but the single-glazed windows looked as if they would fall out if they were pushed, the wooden frames so rotten.

'It's a bit nasty,' she admitted.

Jim grasped her from behind and rested his chin on her shoulder. 'Close your eyes.'

'Why?'

'Just close them.'

With a sigh, she did as he'd asked.

'Now, picture this. Those floorboards sanded down or covered in Axminster carpet if you prefer. New sash windows with Roman blinds, letting in the sun.' He shuffled with her, so she faced the other way. 'An Adam fireplace with a living flame gas fire. Chrome wall lights with a soft glow. Larger skirting boards to reflect the character of the house. Better doors, too. Can you see it, Maria? Can you picture our new home?'

Goosebumps coursed over her body as she imagined all that and more. 'A pink Dralon three-piece, with curtains and cushions that match. A pine corner unit for the TV. And our wedding photo hanging above the fireplace.' She opened her eyes and turned to him.

'It's going to be our first home, I can feel it.' Jim kissed her. 'We'll make it into a palace. What do you say?'

She nodded, her excitement mirroring his.

'I say, let's do it. Let's put in an offer.'

CHAPTER SIXTEEN

Lucy lay in bed that morning, relishing the final twenty minutes before the alarm went off. After a long and deep sleep, she was exhausted but had to get the girls ready and out for school. Aaron had left an hour earlier, stubbing his toe on the bed in his quest to sneak out quietly. He was working near Manchester so had an early start.

She rested a hand on her stomach, wondering if she was brave enough to do what she'd set out to do today. It had been another week, and there was no sign of her period. She was having lots of the symptoms that she'd had when she was pregnant with Ellie. She felt really emotional and snappy, constantly running to the loo, and her stomach was bloating no matter what she ate. Heartburn was unbearable, too.

Having tried for another baby for so long, she was in a dilemma. She needed to know if the hope she was feeling was rightly placed, yet she didn't want to find out if she wasn't pregnant as she would be distraught.

Most of her spare thoughts had been consumed by babies since they'd decided to try for one of their own. It had been something they'd discussed in late autumn, and she'd come off the pill straightaway. It was exciting thinking about what was to come.

When they conceived, both she and Aaron didn't want to know the sex before it was born. Choosing baby names with him was what she was really looking forward to. She couldn't wait to get to that stage, where their child would be growing inside her, getting bigger every week.

Pushing the things she'd hated about being pregnant aside, she laughed. Everything her mum had told her about the struggles of pregnancy and then the birth had materialised, yet most of it was forgotten the minute she'd held Ellie in her arms. The rush of love she'd felt for the little person she'd created, despite being a single mum at the time, was like nothing she had ever experienced. She couldn't wait to do it all over again.

And after all, it was only nine months of her life that she had to give over, not forever. Once she'd had the baby, she hoped she'd get herself back into shape fairly quickly. Well, if history repeated itself, she would. She'd barely put any weight on when she'd been having Ellie.

The alarm went off, bringing her out of her lovely daydream. She leaned over and switched it off, pulling back the covers. Time to start the day.

She crossed the landing to Ellie's room, the door ajar. Ellie was still asleep. Lucy sighed at the sight of her mop of dark hair, the rest of her deep under the covers.

'Morning, sleepyhead.' She opened the curtains. As it was a grey and damp morning, she switched on the lamp by the side of the bed.

Ellie rolled over onto her back, yawned, and stretched her arms above her head. 'Is it a school day?' she asked.

'It sure is. What would you like for breakfast?'

'Can I have cornflakes… please?'

'You sure can.' Lucy smiled at her child's manners being a slight afterthought.

She left her to it for a moment. Ellie's uniform had been laid out on a chair the night before. She was at the age where she wanted to dress herself, and was capable of doing it, only occasionally doing the buttons on her shirt or cardigan up wrong.

Knowing better than to walk into Saskia's bedroom, she gave a sharp rap on the door.

'Time to get up, Saskia,' she said. 'Are you awake?'

A grunt was all that came back at her.

Lucy shook her head. At least she'd got a reply.

She had a quick shower before going down to make breakfast. When she joined the girls in the kitchen, Saskia was helping Ellie to pour out her cereal.

Lucy's heart melted at the sight. It hadn't always been like this, and indeed it wasn't always that way now. When she and Lucy had first moved in, Saskia had been quite hostile towards Ellie. The age gap of almost eight years was a lot for a young girl to deal with, plus having to share her dad with another woman. So it was at times like this she relished the older girl helping the younger. It certainly made her day easier.

'Have you eaten?' Lucy noticed Saskia hadn't got anything of her own.

'I'm not hungry.' Saskia poured milk into Ellie's bowl. 'Say when.'

'I'm not sending you to school on an empty stomach. Why don't you have some cornflakes, too?'

'I said I'm not—'

Ellie put up her hand. 'When.'

'What do you say, Ellie?' Lucy chastised.

'Thank you, Saskia.'

'Good girl. Now, your turn.' Lucy pushed a bowl over to

Saskia. 'It's either cornflakes or a slice of toast. Which is it to be?'

'I don't want either.'

Lucy folded her arms and stared at her.

Saskia caved in. 'Fine,' she snapped, reaching for the cereal box.

Lucy smiled. That wasn't too hard.

'It's like being a baby,' Saskia muttered.

'What was that?' Lucy turned back.

'Nothing.'

There were no more dramas and, once she'd dropped Ellie off at school, Lucy headed to work, calling in at the chemist on the way. If Fiona, behind the counter, noticed, she never said anything. She just smiled at Lucy and passed the time of day with small talk. Lucy liked her for that. It was hard having only the one chemist in Somerley. There were two supermarkets on the retail park a few miles away, but she'd have to make a trip purposely.

Then she scolded herself. Fiona wouldn't care about her buying pregnancy tests. She probably had way more important things in her life to worry about than whether Lucy Wilshaw was about to become a mum again.

Lucy shoved her purchase into her bag, and with the flip of her stomach at the thought of what might be, she set off for work.

CHAPTER SEVENTEEN

Date number two, Mum!

On Thursday, you have a trip to the cinema. Dad told us the first film you went to watch together, so we suggest you choose something similar as it's your treat. We hope you have fun – not too much snogging on the back row, mind!

Maria and Jim had driven over to Hedworth to the cinema complex which housed seven screens. Maria couldn't remember the last time she'd come to see a film during the day without Ellie and Saskia in tow, viewing something age appropriate for them. There was no reason why, just life taking over and things being easier to stream on the TV in the comfort of your own home.

As it was her treat, Maria had been contemplating getting tickets for a romantic comedy. Sometimes Jim enjoyed them, but she knew he preferred action movies, all blood, guts, and gore. So, if they were to sit in those seats for nearly two hours, she'd have to watch something that would keep his attention.

'What did you choose?' Jim asked as they went inside the foyer.

'Wait and see.'

'Screen two,' the usher said once he'd checked their tickets.

They walked towards the entrance, and Jim turned to her when he saw what was above the door.

'*Top Gun: Maverick*!' His smile was wide. 'Oh, you wonderful woman. I've been wanting to see this for ages.'

'If we have to endure five of these dates, the least I can do is not make them too tedious for you.'

'*Endure?*' Jim's smile dropped in an instant.

'Did I say that? I meant *enjoy*. Now, pass me that popcorn, while I lock and load.'

'Yeehar.' Jim grinned. 'You can be my wing woman anytime.'

Maria hoped he'd never lose that look, the one that showed her how happy he was. Maybe this cheap date reminiscing thing would turn out to be fun after all.

'This is more like it,' Jim said as they settled into their seats.

'I hope I don't have to run to the loo too often.' She groaned.

'Well, if you do, make a cup of tea while you're there. I'm not sure I can sit through a whole film with my dodgy back.'

Maria giggled, but then she sighed.

'They could have chosen a better time than mid-afternoon, though. I have a mountain of work I haven't finished. I'll need to do some of it this evening when we get home.'

'You said the W word.' Jim gasped. 'When we first went to the cinema, I bet we never worried about anything.'

'Life hadn't happened to us then. We were young and in love.' She turned to him. 'Why did so much change us, Jim?'

'I don't think it did. We've had a great life compared to lots of people.'

'I know but—'

'We had so much energy back then, no aches and pains. No money worries, no worries at all, come to think of it.'

'You'll be calling it the good old days soon.' She laughed.

'They *were* the good old days. When we hadn't got a care in the world. When we were wrapped up in each other.'

'When I hadn't got a double chin and three spare tyres around my middle. And two kids to take care of, worry about all the time.'

They went quiet for a moment, watching a young couple settle down a few rows in front of them.

Maria turned back to Jim, keeping her voice low. 'Can you remember what we went to watch, our first time?'

'Can I ever. It was *Ghost*. You never shut up about Patrick Swayze for days. Put me right off. Talk about an inferiority complex.'

'I wasn't that bad!' She nudged him. 'And you were just the same, drooling all over Demi Moore.'

'She was quite fit when I was eighteen.'

'You see!'

A dark cloud came over Maria as she thought about her past. Her mum had been at her worst then. Maria was almost taking care of her full time when she wasn't at work, so it had been a rare treat to go to the cinema with Jim.

Two years later, Maria had let herself into the house to find her mum lying on the settee. At first, she'd thought she was asleep, but then she'd noticed the blue tinge around her lips. It had been a fortnight before she and Jim were due to be married.

'Back then, we used to call it the pictures, not the cinema,' Jim said, bringing her out of her thoughts.

'The flicks!' Maria cried excitedly, glad of the distraction. 'We used to go often at one time.'

'This is like déjà vu.' Jim reached for her hand. 'I almost feel eighteen again.'

'I wish I could go back to that age. I'd have stayed on one long diet so that I could be slim forever. Weight really ages a person, and I—'

'Maria, for once I wish you wouldn't go on about your appearance and see yourself through my eyes. You're still as gorgeous to me now as you were when we first met.'

Maria balked. Was he being truthful? Did he really think that?

The lights went down, and the screen lit up with several short trailers of the films to come. She sipped at her drink, glancing surreptitiously at Jim. He really was quite handsome still, so, why couldn't she be happy with what she had, rather than pick fault with herself all the time?

Was it a woman thing, or a Maria thing? Either way, it was definitely a thing she wished she didn't have. She was really great at making other people feel good about themselves, but when it came to herself, she had zero confidence.

She tried to concentrate on the film, settling back into the reclining seat, and it was okay for a while. But, forty minutes in, once the nostalgic scenes had been done, she wasn't all that keen. The effects were outstanding, but where was the chemistry like it had been between Maverick and Kelly McGillis? In her opinion, it was what made the first film such a hit. Who wouldn't want to be pushed up against a wall and ravished by a young Tom Cruise?

She glanced at Jim, his smile wide, his eyes on the screen. He seemed to be in his element, repeatedly turning to her with a huge grin. She couldn't spoil his fun.

She might as well lay her head on his shoulder for a moment. Close her eyes for a little while.

CHAPTER EIGHTEEN

Clara was at home relaxing on the settee. She'd just finished talking to Tyler on the phone. They'd been speaking for nearly an hour, *Coronation Street* long since come and gone.

Tyler had been telling her about a woman he'd had a date with, and it had made her feel melancholic. Clara wanted to be happy for Tyler, and she hoped he hadn't guessed how despondent she was feeling. But their conversation certainly shone a spotlight on her marriage.

Just after ten p.m., she heard Alex pull up in the drive, his key in the door shortly afterwards. He'd been to the gym straight from work, which always meant having a drink in the bar before coming home. He wasn't usually this late, though, and she wondered if she was cross or not concerned either way.

He came into the room, his face unreadable, and unable to meet her eye.

'Hey,' he said, sitting across from her on the armchair in the window.

'Hey. You're late.'

'Yeah, sorry. Lost track of time.'

A silence fell between them, and Clara was glad the TV was on for background noise. She wanted to talk but knew it would end up in a row so late in the evening, so decided against it. But when Alex got up, leaving the room without saying another word, and went upstairs, she knew something had to be said. She pushed herself from the settee and went through to the kitchen, flicking on the kettle to make coffee for them both.

She was pouring boiled water in the mugs when he reappeared, for some reason loitering in the doorway. Her gaze landed on the overnight bag he was carrying, and she frowned.

Alex's face was devoid of emotion. 'I'm going to stay at my parents'.'

'But I'm making coffee.' Clara realised as soon as she'd said it how silly it sounded, shock taking over. 'Why?'

'I'm leaving, Clara. This isn't working for me.'

'I don't understand.' She did, perfectly well, but she didn't want to acknowledge what was going to happen.

'We're not a couple anymore, we haven't been for a long time, and we want different things.'

Alex said nothing else, almost willing Clara to understand what he was saying, to fill in the gaps that he didn't want to. But she wasn't going to do that.

She couldn't.

'I've got a few things in here.' He raised the bag in the air. 'I'll arrange to come and get the rest of my stuff soon.'

He was at the front door before she shouted at him.

'Alex, wait!'

He turned abruptly. 'I have to go.'

'Can't we at least talk things through?'

'There's nothing to say.'

'Well, I'd like to know why you're leaving.'

'I've just told you.'

He opened the front door, and she shut it with a bang before he could go through it.

Alex groaned. 'Please don't do this.'

'You can't just go. We should talk about it.'

They stared at each other for what felt like forever. She took in his face, the small scar on his top lip where he'd gone over the handlebars on his pushbike after braking too hard when he was ten. The way his eyelashes curled more than hers. His blue eyes that turned indigo the more upset he got.

'I'll call you later in the week,' he said.

'Will you be gone just for a few days?'

'No, I... I'll call you.'

This time she let him open the door and leave. What was the point in arguing? He didn't want to be with her at the moment.

At the sound of his car reversing out of the drive, her legs buckled, and she sat down on the stairs. She burst into tears, snotty big gulps. How could he do this to her? They were married, a partnership. They had a beautiful home and everything they wanted. He couldn't end that.

It was just a blip, wasn't it? All Alex needed was a bit of space.

The more she sat and thought about it, the more she realised she should see this as a positive opportunity. Maybe it would do her good to be away from him, too. If they saw how much they missed each other, they could try again, and be more optimistic about things.

He'd be back soon and, once he'd calmed down, they could talk things through properly this time.

CHAPTER NINETEEN

Despite Lucy's best intentions to take the pregnancy test the other day, she hadn't been able to do it. Now, however, she was at the stage where she *had* to know, not to mention Aaron was badgering her to find out, too.

She was in the bathroom at home, sitting on the side of the bath. She stared at the stick in her hand.

PREGNANT

Lucy gave a little squeak, not wanting to wake the girls, but it was all she could do to contain the rush of exhilaration.

She was pregnant?

She was pregnant!

How was it possible to feel dizzy, elated, scared, and shocked all at the same time?

She dashed to her phone to call Aaron but stopped. Should she wait and tell him this evening? It might be nice to allow the news to sink in first.

She placed a hand on her stomach. 'Hello, little one,' she whispered. 'I'm going to be your new mummy.'

She gasped out loud at the words. She had been waiting so long for this moment, and now it was here. She took a photo of the test. But still, she couldn't send it to Aaron. She wanted to see his face when she told him.

She checked her watch. Better get a wriggle on or else they'd all be late. A warm glow would follow her wherever she went today. She had a secret. Hopefully she'd be able to keep the news to herself.

Getting the girls ready that morning had been tiring but, finally, they were through the door. Luckily, Mum had gone straight out to three appointments, and it was Regan's day at college, so there was only Clara there when she arrived at the office after dropping Ellie off. She shook the water from her umbrella.

'It's raining cats and dogs out there. Roll on summer.'

Clara glanced up, catching her eye and giving a faint smile.

'Oh, Cee, I hate to see you so sad,' she said, noticing her sister's eyes were puffy.

That was all it took for Clara to burst into tears. 'He's gone to stay with his parents for a few days.'

Lucy grabbed a handful of tissues from a box and rushed over to her side. She sat close while Clara told her what had happened the night before.

'Why didn't you call me?' she said afterwards.

'It was late, and I was too upset to tell you.'

'And he gave no explanation other than it wasn't working for him?'

Clara shook her head.

'When did he say he'd be in touch?'

'He didn't.'

'Has he rung this morning?'

'No. I'm glad really. I don't want to tell Mum yet in case he comes back. I'm praying it's all a storm in a teacup.'

Lucy hoped it was the opposite. She didn't want to see that lowlife back in her sister's life, although she kept that thought to herself.

'If I get my hands on him, I'll rip off his balls and shove them down his throat,' she said. 'How dare he walk out like that. He hasn't even given you a chance to put right the wrong.' Lucy grimaced. 'I meant he should have talked things through with you. Not... this.'

Clara shook her head and burst into tears again.

Lucy hugged her, shushing her like a baby. 'Everything will sort itself out, you'll see,' she soothed. 'I know this will hurt now, but it won't be forever. He doesn't know a good thing when it's staring him in the face. What an idiot.'

The morning flew past in a flurry as they went about their work. With Regan missing, they manned the phones and covered reception, as well as helped people who came in without an appointment.

Before they knew it, Maria was back. Lucy was on her own, and the office was quiet again.

'Has Clara gone to lunch?' Maria asked.

'Yes, she's nipped to Somerley Stores for some sandwiches. She's getting you the usual.'

'Fabulous. I'm famished.'

'How did the viewing go?'

'It was a lovely house, but the interior was awful. There was so much colour in each room, and none of it matched. I'm sure it will sell, although not for as much as they hope.'

Clara came through the door as if on the tail of a whirlwind.

'Hi, Mum, how did your second date go?' She reached in her bag and handed her a sandwich and a chocolate bar.

'I was just going to ask about that.' Lucy cursed herself inwardly, taking the sandwich she was offered. In her excitement that morning, she'd forgotten all about it.

'I'm not sure, really.' Maria gnawed her bottom lip before speaking again. 'I fell asleep.'

'You didn't!' Lucy giggled.

'The film was so long *and* in the middle of the afternoon. I needed a nanna nap.' Maria raised both hands in the air and sighed. 'It was a lovely gesture, though, thank you, and it was nice to spend the afternoon with your dad. He really enjoyed it.' She pointed at her desk. 'Although, the in-tray fairy didn't do their job. I have so much to do, I'll have to stay late this evening to catch up.'

'Anything we can help with?' Lucy wanted to know.

'Not really. I'll get through it all eventually. Are you okay, Clara?'

'Hmm? Sorry, I was miles away. Yes, all good.'

Lucy glanced at her sister surreptitiously, giving her a reassuring smile. They each had a secret they were trying to keep from Mum, both praying she wouldn't guess. Thankfully, the young couple who had just walked into the office would keep her busy for now.

CHAPTER TWENTY

The noise of the traffic came in with the couple for a moment. They were in their mid-twenties, the woman proudly sporting a tiny pregnancy bump.

Lucy tried to stop her face erupting into a huge smile, sure she would give away her secret. It was going to be hard enough for her mum not to guess straightaway, and she was dying to tell her family, but not until she'd spoken to Aaron.

'Hello there.' Maria greeted them as she was the only one not eating her sandwich yet. 'What can we do for you?'

'We've seen a house we'd like to view,' the man said. 'Twenty-seven Knight Street.'

'Ooh, that's a lovely property,' Maria chirped. 'There's been quite a bit of interest in it. I have two viewings lined up for later in the week.'

Lucy smiled at hearing her mum's sales patter. She watched the woman glance at the man. Lucy knew that look. It said, "I can't let anyone else have that property as I've fallen in love with it. And it would be perfect for us to start a family in."

Family.

A baby.

Lucy almost choked on her sandwich. She covered it up with a cough.

'Would you like me to arrange a viewing for you?' Maria went on. 'I can do tomorrow morning if that suits.'

'Yes, please. We have a hospital appointment first thing, but we could make the afternoon.'

'Excellent, I'm sure you'll love it even more then.' Maria showed them into her office to make the arrangements.

'What's up with you?' Clara whispered to her.

Lucy turned to her sharply. 'What do you mean?'

'You're acting all weird.'

'Oh, I don't mean to.' Lucy shot out of her seat and nipped to the bathroom. There, she took some deep breaths to calm herself. She was dying to tell Clara and her mum the news, but she wasn't sure how long Aaron would want to keep it between the two of them once he found out. She must only be a few weeks gone. It was going to be risky for a while.

She went back to her desk, but the office was empty.

'Mum has gone to do a valuation,' Clara explained. 'She's going straight home afterwards.'

Lucy sat down, thankful for the reprieve. She only had an hour and a half to go before she could leave for the day. Surely, she could contain her excitement until then?

A few minutes later, she saw Clara staring at her.

'What's going on?' Clara narrowed her eyes.

'Nothing.'

'You're practically fizzing with excitement.'

'I—'

'Look, I may be feeling low because of what's happening with Alex, but if you have good news, please don't think you'll upset me.'

Lucy paused and then reached in her handbag for the test. She held it up for Clara to see.

'Pregnant? Oh, Lucy!' Clara's face brightened as she embraced her. 'That's wonderful news. I'm so pleased for you. I bet Aaron is over the moon.'

'He doesn't know yet. I only found out this morning. My period is a fortnight late, but I didn't want to take the test, you know? I didn't want it to be negative, even though I had a feeling it wouldn't be. And now it isn't, I want to tell him in person. So I have to wait until I see him after work. Please don't tell Mum.'

'I won't! I promise.'

'I shouldn't have told you really, I need to let Aaron know first, but I was bursting!'

'I'll act surprised.' Clara ran an imaginary zip across her mouth. 'Oh, Lucy, this really is the best news!'

The clock went slowly round to finishing time. Aaron was collecting Ellie from school, so Lucy went straight home as soon as she'd finished.

She was in the kitchen when they got in. Saskia would be in soon, so Lucy knew she didn't have much time.

'Hi, Mummy!' Ellie flicked off her shoes and removed her coat, leaving them on the floor.

'Hello, munchkin.' Lucy refrained from chastising her this once. She hung Ellie's coat on the peg, which they'd put lower down purposely for her to use, and tidied away her shoes. 'Did you have a good day at school?'

'It was okay. I had art. I like art. Can I have a biscuit, please? I'm really hungry.'

'Just the one until your tea. Then pop upstairs and change out of your uniform.'

She was gone in seconds, her feet banging on each step as she went to her room.

Aaron came to her and gave her a kiss. 'Have you had a good day?'

'It's not been too bad.' She wrapped her arms around his waist. 'We have about two minutes.'

Aaron laughed. 'I'm quick, but not *that* quick.'

'No, you big idiot. Before Saskia gets in and while young madam is missing, I have something for you.' Lucy pulled the pregnancy test from the back pocket of her jeans and handed it to him.

'Oh!'

Aaron's face was a picture she never wanted to forget, his expression changing from shock to disbelief to amazement and then to absolute joy in a matter of seconds.

'Really, we're going to have a baby? This is the best news ever.' He took her face in his hands and kissed her. 'Have you made an appointment to see the doctor?'

She nodded, then hearing footsteps upstairs, she popped the test in the drawer, out of sight at the back. She'd dispose of it later, once small children weren't around.

'I don't want to tell the girls until I'm a bit further along,' she told him.

'Okay.'

'I don't really want to tell anyone but I'm sure my mum will guess, and I'd hate for her to find out that way. Or if I blurt it out due to my excitement.'

'I think we should go round later, tell them together.'

'How are we going to do that, with the girls there, too?'

'I'm sure we can lure them into the kitchen, for chocolate or something, and quickly tell your mum and dad. It's the only way really.' Aaron drew her into his arms again.

Lucy sank her head into his chest. 'I can't believe it, Aaron. We're going to have a baby!'

CHAPTER TWENTY-ONE

Maria pulled her scarf tighter around her neck as she got out of her car ready to do her first viewing of the day. Even without the threat of her usual insomnia hanging over her, she'd hardly had any sleep the night before after finding out she was going to be a grandmother again.

Aaron and Lucy had popped round after texting them to say they were on their way. As soon as they'd sat down, Lucy had told Saskia and Ellie that there was a treat for them in her handbag that she'd left in the kitchen. While they'd gone off to find it, she and Aaron had quickly told them their news.

It had been wonderful to hear, with tears all round being wiped away before Ellie and Saskia's return. Maria would have liked more time to celebrate, but she was glad to be told straightaway. Once she was further along, Lucy would be bursting to tell everyone. So she could understand why they didn't want anyone to know yet.

Twenty-seven Knight Street was in a quiet cul-de-sac, the last of a set of four houses, and had its own parking area. Maria walked down the path, mentally rehearsing what she was going to say. Room for parking was an added bonus, but so too was the small garden at the front. There weren't many townhouses, or terraced cottages in the middle of Somerley who boasted this and, if the new owners wanted to, they could easily remove it to make room for further off-road parking.

Inside the house, she quickly waltzed through each room again, mentally noting things she wanted to point out and making sure nothing was out of place or needed to be hidden from view until her clients had gone.

People wouldn't believe some of the things she'd been greeted with and had to clear before a viewing over the years. She'd washed breakfast dishes and opened windows wide to get rid of ominous odours. She'd shoved toys into boxes and those boxes into the bottom of wardrobes. One day, there'd been a pair of women's knickers on the sofa, all curled up as if they'd been peeled off in haste! She'd used a paper tissue to pick them up and hide them – in the bin.

Everything inside was laid out so homely. The owners had taken all her suggestions to heart. Fresh flowers in the living room. A full fruit bowl, a bottle of wine and two glasses on the table. Upstairs, the landing smelled of lavender and vanilla. The bathroom window had been left open, to let out any odours, so she quickly closed it.

Since the couple came into the office yesterday, she had a feeling they'd be perfect for this house. Maria loved her job of matching homes to new owners. It was a special skill she'd harnessed, knowing in seconds whether someone was interested in the property or not.

She wouldn't have to do too much to sell this one. Since she'd made the appointment for today, she'd had several more enquiries, so the property would go soon, one way or another. But she hoped Ade and Rebecca liked it.

Finally satisfied, she went downstairs to wait for the

couple to arrive. She checked her emails on her phone as she waited, delighted to see two more viewings come in for another hot property and three potential clients who had asked for valuations. If the year went on as well as the past couple of months, she'd have her new kitchen in no time. If she couldn't persuade Jim to move, then that would be the other alternative. Maria didn't like standing still for too long.

A car door slammed outside, alerting her to the arrival of her clients. She rushed to the door and flung it open.

'Welcome, Ade and Rebecca, and the bump,' Maria beamed, ushering them in.

She showed them each room, pointing out special features and things of importance; telling them where the light flooded in at the front and where the sun would be at its best in the rear garden.

Once they were back in the living room, she left them to look around on their own. She liked this most, when she could instinctively sense if the house was sold. Nine times out of ten she came up with the right outcome.

Despite the excited whispering and stifled giggles, she could tell immediately from the couple's body language that they loved the property, and it was a joy to see Rebecca rubbing a hand over her tummy after they'd entered each room. She was sure they'd be putting in an offer later that day.

They came downstairs, but before she had time to go into her sales spiel, Ade spoke.

'We want it,' he said. 'If we offer the full price, will the owners take it off the market?'

'I can certainly ask.' It wasn't something Maria liked doing, but the choice wasn't hers. 'You have a mortgage in place?'

'Yes, we have an offer in principle.'

'Well, in that case, I think we can say it's safe to move on with this sale.'

Once the couple had left, and she was locking up the property, Maria smiled, recalling how her second home had looked once it was finished. Like their first, she and Jim had chosen everything themselves, making their mark on it from day one. There was no living with someone else's choice of kitchen units, or rust stains on the bath from a dripping, decrepit tap, but they had been living in the equivalent of a building site for a while.

It had taken them seven months to finish. Most of the jobs they'd tackled themselves, after learning from trial and error in Garrett Street. Back then, there were no YouTube how-to videos. A lot of them would have come in handy, yet learning on the job had proved to be a bonus for the properties they'd also bought in the future.

And even though it had been hard at times, feeling never-ending on some occasions, the sense of pride they'd felt when it was finished was overwhelming. Now she remembered a bottle of champagne, curtains closed on a dark night, and making love on freshly laid carpets.

Maria hoped Ade and Rebecca would be as happy as she and Jim had been then.

TWENTY-EIGHT YEARS AGO - 5 COPELAND AVENUE

Maria was on all fours, her head in the sink unit. She wasn't impressed by what she could see.

'What do you think?' Jim asked her, walking back into the kitchen.

'There's a water leak, and a large damp patch.'

'I mean about the house. That won't matter, because we'll be ripping this tatty kitchen out and starting again.'

'But I won't be able to help you as much if I get pregnant, and you know how much I had to do with you in Garrett Street.'

'When would having another baby ever stop you? Knowing you, you'll be eight months gone and still hanging wallpaper, getting Lucy to help you clean up!'

She laughed at that. 'She's only one!'

Jim walked towards her, bending to peer in the sink unit. He rubbed a hand across his chin. 'I bet we can get a bit knocked off the price if we make out the leak is a bigger issue than it is.'

'You're ruthless, James Wilshaw.'

'I'm actually being shrewd!'

'I suppose so.' Maria laughed. 'I'll be fine. I can't believe how much we learned doing up our first house.'

'Nor how much profit we made.'

'I'm looking forward to doing it again.' Maria wrapped her arms around his waist and rested her cheek on his chest. 'Do you really think we can afford this, and do it up as well? It means a bigger mortgage, and with Lucy growing out of everything the minute I put it on her, and—'

'I'm sure we can,' Jim interrupted her. 'Although, it will be tough to live in while we do it up, especially with Lucy.'

Maria shuddered at the thought. It would be hard, yet they'd done it once, and with great success, so they could do it again.

'We have to be sure,' he went on. 'Let's think about it?'

But Maria didn't need to. She could already see herself in the new kitchen, Lucy playing on the tiny patch of lawn in the garden. Drinks around a large dining table.

'Just think of all the extra space we'll have,' she said. 'And three bedrooms, room for the family to grow.'

They stood in silence for a moment, each contemplating. The property needed a lot of work, but it was bigger, with an extra room downstairs, too. More importantly, they couldn't have afforded it if they'd bought it already renovated to a high spec. This way they could put their style on it straightaway again, having everything they wanted from the start.

'One day we won't have to do all the jobs ourselves,' Jim said, giving her a squeeze. 'We'll be rich enough to employ someone to do it for us.'

'Oh, I quite like putting our own stamp on things.'

'Yes, it's fun, apart from erecting flat-pack furniture.'

Maria recalled the falling out and swearing they'd done the week before, putting together a TV cabinet. She'd told Jim he had the wood on the wrong way round, but he hadn't listened. It was only when he'd screwed it in tightly that he realised she was right. And then he'd cursed a lot.

She smiled. It was all short-term problems, and once it was finished, they'd have another, bigger, home to be proud of.

'Let's do it.' She nodded, her smile wide. 'Let's buy home number two.'

CHAPTER TWENTY-TWO

Although Clara had managed to cope at work each day, and also keep what was happening away from her mum, she'd hated stepping into the house she'd always thought of as her sanctuary. Even though she was used to it being empty most evenings, as more likely than not, Alex wouldn't be in from work until late, it had still been hard. She'd spent a lot of the time hoping that he'd show willing to come back and try again. They'd planned a life together. How could he walk away from that?

Finally, on Friday evening, when she'd been dreading a weekend alone, he'd messaged to say he would call round shortly. It had sent her all of a tizzy at the thought of seeing him again.

She dashed upstairs to take a shower. She took time styling her hair, applied fresh makeup, and dressed in her best slouch gear. When she went downstairs, she at least felt a little decent.

She couldn't face anything to eat so made coffee and took it through to the living room. Her hands shook, she was a bag of nerves as she waited for him to arrive, so she messaged

Tyler for a while. He mentioned coming round if she didn't want to face Alex alone, but she'd declined. This was something she had to do by herself.

Her thoughts turned to Lucy. Even though the timing was a bit off for her to be fully happy about news of the baby, she was thrilled for her and Aaron. They were in a great relationship, and she was certain they'd be married soon.

She could understand Lucy's reluctance after what the idiot who'd fathered Ellie had done, but Aaron wasn't like Simon Minshall. Aaron was kind, gentle, and so soppy at times. He wasn't scared to show his emotions, even though she loved to rib him when he cried at a Disney film.

Her stomach flipped when she heard Alex's car pull up outside the house. She didn't go to the front door, but when he stood in the living room doorway after letting himself in, she found it hard to contain her annoyance. Already, it felt like her home and not theirs.

He still had his work suit on. Why hadn't he showered at work, like before? Did that mean he wasn't planning on staying long? Or that he'd come straight from the office because he couldn't wait to see her?

But then, he'd had his hair cut, and she was surprised to see how much this upset her, as his life went on without her. Nevertheless, she was determined to talk him round this evening. He wasn't going anywhere, not if she could help it.

'Hey.' He moved to sit on the settee.

Clara gave a weak smile.

'How have you been?' he asked, maintaining eye contact for as little as possible.

What a stupid thing to say. Clara was lost without him; couldn't understand why he'd left without trying to sort things out. Couldn't believe he didn't want to be with her anymore. Couldn't begin to think of life without him.

'Okay.' She voiced none of her thoughts. 'How about you?'

He shrugged, then pulled out a piece of paper from his pocket. 'I've made a list of things we need to talk about.'

'Such as?'

'The house, the savings we have. The way we want to move forward, I suppose.'

That put a dampener on things. Clara cringed at its finality.

'I just want things to go back to the way they were,' she said.

'You know I still care about you, but it could never work.'

'Why not?'

'We didn't really like each other towards the end, did we?' He looked at her then. 'It was painful for me to come home, so I expect it was the same for you.'

'*When* you came home. I was here a lot of the time on my own.'

'I know.' With no apology forthcoming, he opened out the paper. 'So what do you want to discuss first?'

'I need a glass of wine.' She got up quickly and walked towards the door. 'Would you like one, or a coffee?'

'No, thanks. I'm not staying long.'

Tears burned her eyes. So she was only worth half an hour of his time now? It wasn't as if he had anything to rush off for.

In the kitchen, she poured a glass of wine, took a large gulp, refilled the drink, and went back to him.

She sat down again. 'How have you been, staying at your parents'?'

'It's not ideal, as you can imagine.'

'I can't see why not.' Clara glowered. 'I bet your mum's loving fussing over you.'

Clara had never really got on with Alex's mum. Alex was the youngest of four children, and in every way he was the baby of the family. His dad was okay, but his mother, Sandra, was a bit of a dragon. She'd interfered so much in his sister's marriage that it had ended in a really messy divorce.

Clara suspected Sandra wouldn't have been happy with anyone Alex married either. She was always keen to point out faults, as if Clara wasn't good enough for her precious son. It was the one saving grace if this was all over, that she didn't have to see her, speak to her, or interact with her again.

Alex chose to ignore her sarcastic tone. 'We need to talk about the house.'

'The house?' Clara's voice came out as barely a squeak.

'Well, unless you can afford it on your own, we'll have to sell it.'

'Sell it?' She was aware she sounded like a parrot, but she couldn't help it. 'I love this house.'

'Then you'll have to get it valued and buy me out. And I don't want your mum doing it. I want my fair share.'

Clara bristled. 'You were quick to grab money for a deposit when it was offered by my parents, but now you think my mum will dupe you?'

'I didn't mean that. I—'

'This is my home!'

'Mine, too – well, half of it. I have to get a place of my own, so I'll need money for that.'

Clara was about to shout him down but then realised what was the point. He'd clearly made up his mind that their marriage wasn't worth saving. She wouldn't give him the satisfaction of showing him how upset that made her feel.

'I'll get Mum to do a valuation. It will be done professionally, not in my favour. Like it or lump it, but I'm not asking anyone else.'

'Two quotes are better than one. If you're not free, I can show them around.'

Unbelievable. 'Do whatever you like.'

'Yeah, I will.'

Clara could feel herself crumbling. He was over her, and she wasn't over him.

'I suppose your mum's happy to see the back of me,' she couldn't help spitting out. 'She always made it clear that I wasn't good enough for you.'

'That's not true.'

'Of course it is.'

'You're being childish now.' He ran a hand through his hair.

'I'm not the one who's walked out of our marriage, showing no commitment.'

'I think we're done.' Alex stood up. 'I'll see myself out.'

'Yeah, you do that.' She flopped back in her seat and stared at the TV.

'I am sorry it hasn't worked out, Clara.' He paused at the door, then turned back. 'Let me know when you've decided what you want to do about the house.'

She continued to stare at the screen, worried her emotions would spill over before he left.

As soon as she heard the door close behind him, she let her tears fall. She'd lost him. He wasn't even interested in working anything out. All he wanted was his money so he could start again. Without her.

And where did that leave her now? Because she hadn't thought any further than him coming back. She didn't want to lose the house, but neither did she want to stay here with all the reminders of what could have been. It would be bittersweet.

Everything she had planned for a future with Alex was over. What was she going to do now?

CHAPTER TWENTY-THREE

Date number three, Mum!

You have a game night planned! Buckaroo, KerPlunk, Frustration, Mouse Trap, Operation, Draughts, Monopoly, Connect Four. It needs to be fun. No competitive streaks are allowed.

We've compiled a music list for you to play that will remind you of the good old days!

All day Maria had thought about cancelling, or even postponing, the evening. What was the use when she wasn't in the mood? She'd been rushed off her feet at work, with several viewings and valuations back to back, so she'd have to catch up on more emails before she went to bed. It was a never-ending circle of work and home, work and home, and there weren't enough hours in the day to fit that in, let alone anything else.

So, she'd had to admit to it being a pleasant surprise to see that when she got home, the kitchen was set up in readiness. Several games had been stacked in a pile on the table. A wine cooler sat next to them, a Post-it note attached to it, announcing "white wine is in the fridge". Alongside those were several bowls of nibbles, a cheese board, crackers, and a bottle of red wine.

'Lucy must have popped in after she finished work,' Maria said as Jim came into the kitchen behind her. 'There's another note on the front of the fridge. What does it say?'

'"Eat, drink, and be merry! There's food prepared. We hope you have fun!"' Jim popped it on the worktop and reached for the wine.

Guilt flowed through Maria when she saw that he'd already had a shower, making an effort to get home early.

'What do you want to play first?' He nodded in the direction of the table. 'Or need I ask?'

'I expect you'll choose draughts because you always win.'

'You won, once. You've never let me forget. Whereas you've thrashed me several times playing Twister.'

'I wish I could still play that. I'd be in agony with my dodgy hip.' She sighed. 'I'm not much for this date, are you?'

'It is what it is. Anyway, we can make it —'

'Fun, I know. But I could have done without it this evening.'

'Got something else planned?'

'I have things to catch up on.'

'Then it's good that we're doing this. You wanted to work less, not more, when you reached fifty.'

'Yes, well, now I'm there, I prefer to keep busy.' Maria shuddered. 'I don't want my mind to go idle.'

'Get away with you.' He laughed, leaning forward to kiss her cheek. 'So, Connect Four?'

'I might be mean and choose Frustration.'

Jim groaned, much to Maria's delight. He didn't enjoy that game at all.

'It *will* be fun.' He nodded, as if to convince himself.

'It's a chance for me to whip your arse,' she taunted.

'That might be nicer.' Jim waggled his eyebrows in comical fashion.

She slapped him on the shoulder as she walked past to go upstairs.

Twenty minutes later, she was showered, changed, and back with him. The aroma of something delicious was in the air.

'Pasta bolognese,' Jim told her. 'Lucy's made it.'

'That sounds like heaven.'

'Draughts first?'

'If we must.' She sat across from him.

Jim slid over a glass of wine.

'Red counters or cream?'

'Red. Not that it will make any difference.'

He groaned. 'Would you prefer to play Connect Four?'

'I'm not in the mood for any of it.'

'Well, smile for the camera.' Jim held up his phone to take a photo. 'We can't buy a souvenir, so this will have to do.'

Maria held up her middle finger, her smile comical. She really didn't want to do this, but she could at least make an effort. 'What's on the playlist?'

'Songs from the nineties.' Jim set the music up.

The first notes of 'Vogue' instantly flipped her back to 1990. 'They really have thought of everything.'

'The night is young, even if we are getting ancient.'

Maria rolled her eyes in reply.

Forty minutes later, Maria's irritation was back. Jim had won a game of draughts and two games of Connect Four. That was *her* game to win.

'I can't believe you've beaten me again,' she cried.

'I'm on a roll,' he replied, grinning.

'You're loving this, because you always win. You're so competitive.'

'This is your choice of game, remember?'
'Which means I'm going to lose all night.'
'Do you expect me to let you win?'
'Yes!' Maria cried. 'Once or twice at least.'
Jim shook his head. 'That would be wrong.'
'It would show that you love me.'
'You know that I love you.'
'Do I? Because you never say it anymore.'
'Neither do you.'
She reached for her drink to hide behind. 'I do!'
'Name the last time you did.'

Maria thought for a moment and then glanced at him sheepishly. She couldn't remember. If she'd said it recently, she was so busy it had failed to stick in her head.

With embarrassment, she flipped up the bottom of the frame, so the remaining counters fell to the table.

'You cheat!' Jim cried.

'I'm not playing anymore.' Maria stood up. 'I'm going to dish out the food.'

She let out a silent sob as she reached for the bowl of pasta bolognese from the oven. Now she was cross with herself for being peevish.

Years ago, when they'd first started dating, and been unable to go out for an evening, she and Jim had played games for hours at her house, listening along to music. If it wasn't draughts, it was a pack of cards or a set of dominos.

But she didn't want to think about why she'd had to stay in so much then. Jim hadn't minded, but she had.

Instead, she dished out the food and put the bowls on the table, entwining her feet with his when she sat down again.

Jim looked up in surprise.

It was something else she used to do all the time. When had the tiny, intimate things gone by the wayside in their relationship?

'Eat up, and let's play again,' she said. 'And this time, I *am* going to whip your arse.'

'Oo-er, missus,' Jim said in his best *Carry On* voice. 'I hope that's a threat and not a promise.'

Another song came on which stopped her eating, fork held in mid-air. 'Wilson Phillips. I haven't heard this in years. How did they know about it?'

'I might have given them a little help on which songs to download,' Jim admitted.

'I'm impressed you remember it.'

'I can clearly recall where we were when we first heard it. You'd got a new job at Murray's Factory in the offices, and we were in The Woodman pub. You wore that blue dress I loved so much.'

'You used to say it matched the colour of my eyes.'

'That's because it did.'

She smiled, remembering. 'We ordered lager, and cheesy chips. It was soooooo delicious.'

'And then shortly afterwards, you were sick all over my shoes because you'd drunk too much.'

Maria's eyes widened, and she burst into laughter again.

'That really was a cheap date.' She reached across for his hand. '*I* was a cheap date.'

'I remember I had never loved you more.'

'When I was sick over your shoes?'

'When you were wearing that dress.' There was a twinkle in his eyes. 'I much preferred removing it, though.'

She clammed up then, her easy mood evaporating. She'd never feel happy about him seeing her naked now.

She stood and picked up the plates. 'It's late. We'd better get tidied up.'

The hurt on his face had her blushing, and she dipped her head. Why couldn't she accept the way she looked rather than miss a night of intimacy? It wasn't fair on either of them.

Had she got the courage to put that right?

The back door opened, and Clara burst into the room, her face wet with tears. Delilah was up in a flash to greet her.

Maria's stomach lurched, her heart beating rapidly at the sight of her daughter in pain.

'What's happened?' she asked, rushing over to her.

'Alex has left me.' Clara sobbed. 'Our marriage is over.'

CHAPTER TWENTY-FOUR

Clara awoke the next morning, her eyes so swollen that she struggled to open them. She snuggled underneath the duvet in her old bedroom. Mum had insisted she spent the night there, rather than go home. She'd been far too upset to leave anyway.

She glanced around the room, still the same as the day she'd moved out. It was decorated in all shades of pink. Saskia used it now, whenever she stayed over. For Clara, it felt as if she was right back where she'd started six years ago, before she'd bought the house and moved in with Alex.

As soon as she'd told her parents what had happened, her world had fallen apart. Up until she'd met with him last night, she'd been convincing herself that they would say sorry to each other and make up.

She wasn't sure how she was going to live without him. She didn't want to move on with her life as a single woman. A divorcee, even, as that would be the next step.

She'd barely eaten. What was the point of cooking meals for one when she could survive on a slice of toast? Lucky for her, she hadn't succumbed to drinking more, but she had drunk herself to sleep once.

Still, at least she wouldn't have to bump into him on a regular basis. He worked in Hedworth. It meant their paths wouldn't cross much, so she couldn't be reminded of her failure day after day. Because, all last night, she couldn't stop blaming herself for him leaving.

If she had shown him more attention, he might not have wanted to go.

If they had been able to talk through their problems, they might still be together.

If they hadn't got married so young.

Her parents' words came back to haunt her. But *they* had got married when they were just out of their teens and were still together nearly thirty years later.

And things worked both ways. If Alex had been willing to listen to her, she would have talked to him.

If he'd stayed in more often, rather than going out with his mates, they would have had more to say to each other.

If he'd put down that blasted games console when he was at home and given her the same attention, they would still be a couple.

She sniggered at her yo-yo thoughts. One minute, if Alex knocked on the door right now, saying he'd made a terrible mistake and that he still loved her, she'd have him back in a flash. It might be the wrong thing to do, but the thought of not being able to try again was crushing her.

The next she'd be feeling optimistic about getting a divorce and starting again on her own, knowing that their marriage was over well before the new year had started. She wondered which she would settle for eventually.

As well, their two closest friends were getting married in a fortnight, and this would make things awkward. Last summer, she'd been thrilled to be asked to be the matron of honour, as had Alex to be the best man. She and Stacey had been friends for years, their men meeting when they were dating, and they'd all got on.

What would happen now? It would make it really awkward as she and Alex would need to spend a lot of time together.

A door opened downstairs, and she heard her mum speak to Delilah as she let her out into the garden. It was early, just gone seven a.m. Her dad would have left for work by now.

She got up and went to see her mum.

'Morning, love, how are you feeling today?' Maria enveloped her in her arms and gave her a huge squeeze. 'I've been thinking about you for most of the night.'

'That won't help with your insomnia,' Clara joked as she moved away. 'I'm okay, Mum. I've been thinking of my options, about what to do next.'

They sat together on the settee, a mug of tea apiece. Clara pulled her legs up, and Delilah curled up beside her. She stroked the dog's fur absent-mindedly.

'I've been wondering if I could afford the house on my own,' she said. 'I've totted up the bills, everything I'd have to pay out monthly, and how much would be left of my salary afterwards. I know I could cover the cost of the mortgage if I bought Alex out, but I'm not sure that would give me money to survive on, never mind living a little, too.'

'I suppose there are three questions here,' Maria said. 'Do you really want to stay there, or start afresh somewhere else?'

'I don't know yet.'

'And do you think Alex would buy you out, if you wanted to move? Perhaps he might want to stay. How would you feel about that?'

Clara paused for thought. *Did* she really want to live in a house where there was only one part of the partnership left? Memories of the two of them in every room, thinking of things they'd done together there; how that had changed over the past year.

She needed to speak to Alex again. Maybe he would want to move back in. It would really hurt her if he did, but if it meant they had a clean break, then she would agree to it. He'd clearly made his mind up that they were over, so there was no reason really to fight it out.

In the office, she was always on the lookout for bigger properties, daydreaming about when she and Alex would move when they started a family. Now, with her plans in tatters, at least she didn't have to show too many prospective house buyers around houses on their books, like her mum. Clara only did the viewings when Maria was on holiday. She wasn't sure she'd have been able to keep her emotions in.

'Still, working in the business has its advantages,' she said.

'That's the spirit!'

'I can spot the properties coming in before anyone else has time to view them. I know all the best sites to view, plus I'm registered for new alerts. I might not be able to afford the detached home I have now, but there are some lovely terraced cottages in Somerley.' She turned to her mum. 'What am I going to do about Stacey and Craig's wedding? I can't be a part of it with Alex there, too. It will be torture.'

'I'm not sure you have any choice about that. I know it will be hard, but Stacey is your friend. Alex will be gone after that day, out of your life, but Stacey won't.' Maria stared at her pointedly. 'Not unless you let her down.'

'I can't face him, and everyone will know.'

'You need to pull on your big girl pants and take whatever the day throws at you,' Maria told her. 'You're a strong, independent woman. You can do this.'

Clara wasn't so sure.

'Have a word with Stacey, put her in the picture. Believe

me, she'll be far more interested in other things than to think about the atmosphere between you and Alex.'

'Do you think?' Clara laid her head back. 'I've been looking forward to this for months, and now he's ruined it for me.'

'Only if you let him. And you won't, because you're much better than that.'

CHAPTER TWENTY-FIVE

Maria was glad the office was only open until midday on Saturdays. She couldn't concentrate. Her mind was all of a muddle. She didn't know whether to think about last night or this morning.

The game night had mostly been fun once she'd settled into it, especially when Jim had recalled her wearing her blue dress. She had probably forgotten more things that had happened during their time together rather than remembered, so it was sweet of him to tell her about that.

Yet it hadn't seemed spontaneous to her the more she'd thought about it. She was getting the sneaky feeling that Mr Wilshaw might be involved in the nostalgic dates project after all.

Or perhaps she was overthinking things, as she had a tendency to do, and he'd just remembered how lovely she'd looked in that dress because she had been nice in it back then. She couldn't even take a compliment from him.

In her twenties she'd been so thin and shapely, thanks to three visits to the local gym every week. Back then, she'd been able to eat as much as she liked without the weight piling on, too. She sighed. Why was growing old so hard for her to take? It wasn't as if she could do anything about it. Each year brought a different problem. She was already dreading her next big birthday, even though it was ten years away. But then, the alternative was death, and she didn't want that to happen either.

Why did she feel such a mess? Why did she let it get on top of her rather than embrace the way she was? Why did she feel the need to take her pyjamas into the en suite and get ready for bed so that Jim couldn't see her? He was amorous enough to let her know that he wanted her. It was she who put him off all the time.

She straightened out a photo in the shop window that didn't need straightening. Did it hurt him, she wondered, when she wouldn't make love to him? When she was actually in the mood but didn't want him to see her latest spare tyre?

She pushed those thoughts away, but that space left her time to worry more about Clara. It was agony as a mum to see her in pain. Maria had never once thought any of her children would get divorced. It certainly didn't fit in with her plans for family perfection. But she couldn't help thinking, had she pushed Clara into trying to make something work that was never destined to stay the course?

Ever since she'd been a child, Maria had wanted a family to be part of. She had grown up in a home where she'd never felt loved. It was the reason she'd been a full-time mum until both girls started school. From then, she'd worked during term hours only, so that she was there to take them in the mornings and collect them in the afternoon. They'd often stop off at the park on nice days, and she'd make cupcakes with them on wet days. She'd sit with them while they did their homework and was always there if they were feeling unwell or needed someone to talk to.

She'd take them shopping and treat them to lots of

clothes, and then to lunch somewhere nice. She made sure they had the best of everything, giving them all the things she'd never had, plus the main one. Stability.

When she'd reconnected with Jim, it was as if they fitted together. Jim was an only child whose parents doted on him. When they were married, it was then she vowed that her children would grow up knowing both their parents loved them. Between her and Jim, she believed they'd done a great job of raising the girls.

Shortly before she closed the office for the weekend, the front door opened. Sal came in, sporting a huge smile. She held up a brown paper bag, The Coffee Stop logo on its side.

'I've finished the work I planned to do over the weekend, so I thought I'd drop it off and have coffee and cake with my bestie.'

'Ooh, you're the *best* type of friend.' Maria's eyes widened in glee as Sal dished out her treats.

'How was your date last night?' Sal asked, before she bit into her slice of carrot cake.

'It was going okay until Clara came by.' Maria reached for a napkin. 'She and Alex have split up.'

'Oh, no.' Sal paused. 'We were all expecting it, to be fair.'

'I suppose. They haven't seemed happy in a while.'

'I hope they decide to divorce. Clara deserves someone better than him.'

Maria grimaced. 'I hadn't thought as far as that.'

'It's not a crime to end a marriage. Not everything can work out as planned, Ms Perfect.'

Maria smiled. Only Sal could get away with saying that, knowing how the slightest thing set her off in a spin these days. 'So how about you? No one on the horizon yet?'

'Where am I going to meet anyone? I rarely go out.'

'You need a bit of loving every now and then.'

'Most of the time, I'm fine. But I must admit, sometimes I miss coming home and there being someone to talk to.'

Maria made soothing noises. Since Ronnie left, Sal had dated a few men, but none had led to anything serious.

She checked her watch to see it was closing time, went to the door, locked it, and turned the sign to closed.

'How about trying that dating app again?' she suggested when she rejoined her.

'I haven't logged on in months, despite continuing to pay the monthly fee. Not after meeting Disastrous Derek. He spent more time on his phone talking to his mum than he did making conversation with me. Shame, because he was good-looking *and* a year older than me – I definitely would have if the opportunity, or whatever, arose.'

Maria sniggered.

'His face was a picture when I left him to it. I must admit, it put me off trying again.'

'Well, you shouldn't bow down to idiots like him. Get out your phone.'

'What? No.'

'Come on, hand it over. Let's see if there's anyone suitable.'

Sal searched it out of her bag and brought up the app. She passed it to Maria who scrolled down it in glee.

Maria stopped and turned the screen towards Sal. There was an image of a man with a dog at his feet.

'Oh, please. He's never in his thirties! Lots of them lie about their age to get dates with younger women.' Sal shuddered. 'I'd probably end up with a seventy-year-old. What female in their right mind would want to do that? Seeing a young naked body is a treat, but a man with saggy bits? No thank you.'

They were both laughing now. Maria continued to scroll through the profiles, getting Sal to say yes and no. But minutes later, she hadn't found a single attractive man in his fifties who wanted a relationship with anyone his own age.

'It's all about the younger woman. Yet at any age, or sex for that matter, most of us come with excess baggage of exes and children.' Sal wiped her hands on her napkin. 'At least Tyler is old enough to fend for himself.'

'There were a couple you wanted to go back to,' Maria recalled. 'Message them.'

'No.'

'Go on. Take a chance.' She pointed at the photo on the screen. 'He's fifty-four and has a great head of hair. His teeth are straight and white, his profile isn't weird.' She waggled the phone in the air, inquisitive eyes imploring her to agree.

Sal gave in. 'Okay, let's see if David Martingale wants to meet.'

Maria grinned. The last half hour with Sal had at least made her realise one thing. Maybe her date with Jim hadn't been such a terrible evening after all.

CHAPTER TWENTY-SIX

Clara stared at her reflection in the full-length mirror. The dress Stacey had chosen for her was gorgeous. Pale purple in colour, it had off-the-shoulder sleeves, a tight-fitted bodice, and a slim skirt that fell to the floor. Stacey had teamed it with the most delicate of silver heels. Her hair was in an up-do, tiny flowers entwined between some of the strands.

A rush of pride rose through her. Clara felt beautiful, there was no doubt about that, the separation diet working as the dress was a little loose on her now.

The time leading up to the wedding had gone by so quickly. Even so, Alex had pulled out of his best man duties at the last minute. He'd cited he didn't want to make anyone feel uncomfortable, nor ruin the atmosphere on the day.

Clara had thought it was a cop out, especially as it had taken all her courage to turn up. If it wasn't for her mum pushing her out of her comfort zone, she would have dropped out, too. But, at least she could relax more, rather than worrying about what she'd say to him.

'You doing okay?' Stacey came up behind her, touching her arm gently.

Clara turned to the bride-to-be who was still in her dressing gown. Her hair and make-up had been done, but she hadn't wanted to put on her dress until the last minute.

'I'm holding up, thanks!' Clara's voice sounded far cheerier than she was.

Stacey handed her a glass of champagne. 'Get that down your neck. It'll make you feel much better.'

Clara took it from her, knowing it would do nothing of the sort. She glanced behind Stacey to see a gaggle of women. She had known most of them for years, yet somehow, she felt like an outsider.

Stacey reached for her free hand. 'I know how hard this is for you and I really appreciate you being here. But if you feel at any time that you want to slip away after the wedding, I'll understand.'

Tears burned her eyes, but Clara held them back. That was nice of her to say.

'Thanks,' she said quietly.

'Right, come on over. Let's get me in my dress!'

Clara picked up her bouquet and took one last glance at herself in the mirror. *You can do this*. Then she knocked back her drink and went to join in with the fun.

Lucy was lying in bed, enjoying a lazy afternoon with Aaron. His last job had finished earlier than expected, and he'd coaxed the girls into going out, seeing as the weather was dry. Saskia had taken Ellie to the park at the end of the street. So after a brief bit of couple time in case they returned quicker than planned, he'd disappeared to make a mug of tea before coming back to bed.

She rested a hand on her tummy, excited at the thought of something growing inside her again. Already she could see a slight swell. The doctor had confirmed the pregnancy and given them a due date of twenty-sixth November. They would almost have a Christmas baby! Imagine all the cute first Christmas things they could buy once it was born, not to mention her mum who would go overboard with gifts.

Lucy was glad they'd managed to conceive at last. For a time, she'd been worried she and Aaron weren't compatible. They'd both had children with other partners, so not much could be wrong with either of them. But she'd started to think that something was stopping them.

And then, just like that, the test had been positive, and it was as if those months of trying, being disappointed when she'd had a period, evaporated. Just like the pain of labour vanished once the baby was placed in your arms. Well, most of it, she giggled.

'You're going to rub that baby away if you're not careful.' Aaron came into the room, a mug in each hand. He closed the door with a nudge of his bottom.

'I still can't believe it's happened.' Lucy pulled herself up to sitting position and took her drink from him. 'Can you?'

'Yes, because you haven't shut up about it.' He grinned. 'Not that I'm complaining. It's good to see you so happy.'

'Are you saying I was miserable before?'

'Not really. But there was a sadness about you. I could tell it was taking its toll. And I know you'd blame yourself when it could have been either of us.'

'But it wasn't. It just took a while longer than we thought, that's all. And it's an anxious time going through it, before and now. You just never know.' She smiled. 'It was sweet of Saskia to take Ellie out this morning.'

'It was! It gave us some alone time, which was *very* nice.'

Lucy put down her drink and snuggled in next to him for a moment. 'Do you ever talk to her about her mum? I mean, when you get a moment together?'

'We used to, but not so much now. Of course, I'll always answer any questions, but they stopped a while ago.'

'I suppose that's good. You know I'd hate to come between you and her in any way.'

'I'm more interested in the future.'

The look Aaron gave her brought sudden tears to her eyes. He noticed immediately.

'Hormonal?' he queried.

'Yes, happy ones.' She laughed through them. 'It's been a long time coming. I'm going to enjoy every moment of it.'

'Yeah, right.' Aaron's tone was teasing. 'I'll remind you of that when you get morning sickness, when your ankles are swollen, and your belly is so big that you can't put your socks on. When you're going on about stretch marks and left with baby fat.'

'You make it sound so attractive having a baby. But it is a job.'

'For the fathers, too. We have so much cajoling to do, moaning to listen to, food we can't eat for a while because it makes you gag.'

She punched him in the arm, even though he was poking fun at her.

'Seriously,' he pulled her a little closer, 'I can't wait to see our little one. It's going to be such an amazing time. When do you think we should tell the girls? Another fortnight, perhaps?'

Lucy nodded. 'How do you think they'll react?'

'Oh, Ellie will be ecstatic, I expect, and Saskia will hate it.'

'Don't say that!'

'I mean she's at the stage where she hates anything we'd like.'

'She'll be okay about it, won't she?'

'She'll have no bloody choice.'

'Aaron!'

'I meant to say, I'm sure she will!'

Lucy nudged him. 'Stop teasing or else I'll tell *her* to punch you the next time you're annoying her.'

Joking aside, Lucy knew it was important that Saskia was okay about it, so they would have to tell the girls sooner rather than later.

CHAPTER TWENTY-SEVEN

The wedding was painful to be a part of yet fun at the same time. Stacey had opted for a church service, and once Clara had spotted her mum crying as she sat in the front pews, it had started her off, too. That was nothing new. Clara always cried at weddings, but feeling so emotional today, she had to will herself not to ugly sob.

Then came the photos, where she'd chosen to stand to one side when the bridesmaids' partners had joined them. This was followed by a small trip to a country hotel, set within hundreds of acres in the middle of the Staffordshire Moorlands. Clara had joined the party at the main table, where she'd faced *tons* of couples sitting around tables of eight.

The speeches had been fun, but afterwards, she'd decided her duties were done for the day. Half past seven found her sitting in a comfy armchair by the side of an ornate fireplace.

The venue was so extravagant, no expense had been spared for the reception. Clara couldn't help feeling cynical, hoping it wouldn't all go to waste, like it had done for her.

Even though Stacey and Craig had been a couple for eight years, there was no guarantee their joining together in matrimony would last forever.

She sipped at her drink, chastising herself for putting a downer on things. Clara thought a lot of Stacey and wished her well, it was just her miserable frame of mind doing its worst. She needed to go home once she'd finished her wine.

'Hey, you. Thought you might like some company.'

Clara looked up to see Steve, one of Alex's friends. She smiled, having always had genuine affection for him. He and Alex had worked together in their twenties and had stayed in touch ever since, although often months went by between their catch-ups now.

'Hi! How have I not seen you until now?' She touched his arm as he bent to kiss her cheek.

'I've only just arrived.'

'Are you on your own?'

'Yes, between fellas at the moment. Me and Troy split a few months ago. It wasn't worth the drama.' He rolled his eyes in exaggeration to show he wasn't at all broken-hearted. 'Anyway, enough about me. I was hoping to see you. Sorry to hear you and Alex are no longer together. How are you doing?'

'So-so,' she said truthfully. She'd never had any airs and graces with Steve before and she wasn't about to start. 'I miss him, though.'

'I'm glad he didn't come to the wedding because I would have probably punched his lights out. It was so underhand. He should have left rather than do that to you. I still—'

'What do you mean?'

Steve paused. 'I thought as much. I came to find you in case you didn't know.'

She stared blankly at him.

'I hate to be the bearer of bad news, but Alex was seeing

someone else before you separated. He moved in with her when he left you.'

A rush of cold flooded her veins, and Clara was relieved she was sitting down. It couldn't be true. But her eyes had never left Steve's, and the sincerity in his made it clear he wasn't lying.

'I thought he'd gone back to his parents' house.'

Steve shook his head. 'Her name is Kirstie.'

'Do you know where she lives?'

'Ivory Cottage, Ivory Lane. It's at the far end of Hedworth by the leisure centre.'

'That sounds a bit posh.'

'I think it's a row of ex-mining houses.' Steve shook his head. 'But they're buying a new place together when...'

Although he'd stopped talking, Clara held up a hand. She didn't want to hear anymore yet. The last time she and Alex had spoken, she'd offered to buy him out, but he hadn't been interested. He still wanted to sell the house. And even though it didn't change anything, it was galling to hear it was because he and his new piece of skirt wanted to buy one together.

'He's a snake.'

Clara's brow furrowed at his angry tone. She watched Steve's face darken, the fury coming from him.

'He's your friend,' she replied.

'Not anymore. I hate what he's done to you. He should have ended his marriage before messing around.'

Clara decided to torture herself some more. 'Do you know how long he was seeing her before he left me?'

'Yes, but I'm not going to say. It isn't fair. I've said too much to hurt you already.'

'And I'm glad you care enough to do that. I've been here for hours, and no one's said a word about it.' Clara rested her hand on his arm. 'But please. I have to know.'

'Since last July.'

Clara mentally did the sums and her mouth dropped open. Just before they'd gone on holiday. Maybe that would explain the weird mood he'd been in.

'*Nine* bloody months and I had no idea? Did everyone else know?'

'I'm not sure. I only found out by accident just before Christmas. I saw him out with her, at a work do.'

'She works with him?' Clara couldn't hide her disgust.

'No, he was at her work's do.'

'The slimy *bastard*.' She couldn't help but smile, realising she was angry more than upset.

He chuckled, seeming to relax a little. 'Did you have an idea?'

She nodded. 'I just didn't want to do anything about it, hoping we were going through a sticky patch that would be resolved.' She snorted. 'In the end, it was quite a relief when he left, even though rejection hurts like hell.' She leaned over and kissed him on the cheek. 'Thank you, for being a true friend.'

He smiled at her, patting her hand. 'I'm glad I came over now. I wasn't sure whether you'd want to know, but equally I felt you deserved to.' He stopped. 'You won't take him back, will you?'

Steve's question was straight to the point, and so was her answer.

'After what you've just told me? Hell, no. It's just... it's only been six weeks, and yet, should I be more upset after what you've just told me?' She laughed, realising how silly she was going to sound. 'I was hoping he'd be here today, to be honest. So I could see him, get him out of my system and move on. I think what I've learned has done that for me regardless.'

They sat together for a few more minutes, catching up with general chit-chat, and then Steve left to mingle.

As she finished her wine, a warm glow enveloped Clara. She was pleased he'd come to find her, glad he'd told her what he knew. Because all at once she felt good, powerful, as if she had the upper hand.

CHAPTER TWENTY-EIGHT

Dear mum

On Sunday, you and Dad are going to Sapphire Lake. I rooted out your old hiking boots, but they were good for nothing, so we've treated you to some new ones. You'll find them in a box in the utility room, in the cupboard underneath the sink. Break a leg – well, not literally, ha!

Maria sighed. It was date four, and that one was definitely going to be a challenge. She hadn't been for a hike in a long time. What on earth were Lucy and Clara thinking? Why would they assume this was a good idea? Maria was so out of condition that she'd most probably be worn out before she'd walked a kilometre.

She cast her mind back to when she and Jim had first met. Like most things on their doorstep, they hadn't been to Sapphire Lake much. They did, however, like to go walking. It had been something to do that was free, too.

But then she remembered the picnic. She was seventeen, Jim eighteen, when he'd got his first decent job. He'd been working at Taylor's DIY Store, slogging his guts out for days at a time, grabbing as many hours as he could so that they could afford a deposit for a house.

When a position had come up for assistant manager, Jim had thought he didn't stand a chance at getting it. It was only because she'd persuaded him to aim high that he'd gone for it, and he'd been successful.

He'd told her halfway through a five-mile walk, as they'd rested at the top of a hill on the sunniest of days. He'd produced a small bottle of fizzy wine, two paper cups, crisps, and sandwiches. They'd perched on a bench, looking down on the most beautiful scenery, talking about their futures.

'One day I'll have my own business,' he'd said. 'And not just a run-of-the-mill shop. I'll have a large builders merchant, and you can work with me.'

It had been the start of many dreams that had come true for them.

It wasn't quite a picnic they were going on today, but she wondered if that was what the girls were alluding to with this date. She and their dad had told the story so many times to them over the years. So, even though her body would complain bitterly tomorrow, she was going to enjoy the walk, whatever the weather.

However, Maria wasn't too keen to get out of bed when it came to it, and she'd already moved the date forward from the previous weekend.

'Can't we put it off until summer?' she protested.

'Don't be so ungrateful,' Jim chided as he got up.

'I have a ton of things to do. I could have done without a wet day by Sapphire Lake. And it's only round the corner. It's weird to go somewhere so close to home.'

Jim pulled on his trousers. 'This is supposed to be a treat, and yet here you are again—'

'If you must know, I'm getting tired of the dates already.'

He stuck out his bottom lip like a child about to cry. 'That's not a nice thing to say.'

'I don't mean I'm fed up with you, but I do think they're a faff.' She shook her head. 'At least there's only one more after this one.'

'Don't be so miserable.'

Maria kept her sigh to herself. It all seemed a little childish to her.

'Come on, get up,' he insisted. 'I'm looking forward to it.'

Maria made breakfast last as long as possible, and pretty soon there was no choice but to set off.

Sapphire Lake was less than ten miles from Somerley. They left the high street to join the dual carriageway, the skies grey, overcast, and decidedly murky. Jim had checked the weather forecast before they'd left, only seeing rain for later that evening.

She got out of the car, breathing in the air as if she hadn't been outside in months. It instantly raised her spirits. It couldn't be that bad, surely. She might even enjoy it, coming back exhausted but happy. And then she could go home and catch up on some work. Mentally, she switched off her work brain.

Jim pointed to the hill. 'I think we should take a selfie at the top of there.'

'You would.' Maria's shoulders drooped.

They walked in silence as they took in their surroundings. There were quite a few people out and about. A group of children huddled around a man, crouched on his knees, showing them something on the ground, couples of all ages walking their dogs, and a man marching along as if he were on a mission.

They settled into a leisurely pace, chatting about something and nothing for a while, and before long, they were halfway up the hill. Maria made Jim stop as she struggled to get her breath.

'Is it me or is the air up here a little fresh?'

'It's you.' Jim chuckled. 'Remember when we used to walk for ten kilometres at a time? I'd plan the routes out to end somewhere we could grab a bite to eat.'

'A bag of crisps and a drink between us was all we could afford back then,' Maria recalled. 'We used to walk and talk for hours, putting the world to rights. I wish we could do this more often.'

'We should make time. There's no substitute for the outdoors, and the feeling like you're on top of the world when you look down from a mountain you've conquered.'

She laughed. 'It's a hill!'

'That, too.' He chuckled, striding ahead. 'Come on, let's quicken our pace or we'll never get there.'

CHAPTER TWENTY-NINE

Twenty minutes later, Maria decided it *was* a mountain. Her breathing had laboured, she was sweating profusely, her face hot, and her fringe stuck to her forehead. She paused, putting a hand on each knee while she took a moment.

Jim, who was a few metres in front of her, finally turned to see where she was.

'That's right,' she cried. 'You're so far ahead of me that you didn't even notice I'd stopped.'

'Take a breather if you like,' he said. 'But we're nearly there, so it's best to keep going.'

'Best for who? I'm exhausted already.'

'Stop whining!' He headed up the path again.

Maria groaned. Where was her fighting spirit? Right, she wasn't going to let Jim win, not after he'd thrashed her at draughts. She increased her pace and raced after him.

But as she tried to keep up, she tripped over her own feet and fell forward, landing on all fours. Thankfully, it dented her pride more than anything.

Jim came rushing back to her. 'Are you okay?' He offered his hand for her to grasp.

She slapped it away with a muddy one. 'I'm fine, not that you would have noticed as you're way ahead of me. Again. I asked you not to rush off.'

'You walk too slow.'

'*You* should wait.'

He sighed, impatience clear for all to see.

'I thought this was my treat today.' She got to her feet and brushed herself down. 'You should go at my pace.'

'If we do that, we'll never get there and back before the rain comes.'

'Don't be so mean.' Maria trudged off, knowing in a few strides he'd overtake her again. That was the problem with him: he was so competitive. She was going to give her girls a piece of her mind about this *date* when she got home.

'Maria,' Jim shouted then.

'I'm coming as quick as I can.' Her feet stomped along the path in protest.

'Maria, don't move!'

'I'm not listening.' She huffed: that man.

When she finally looked up, she could see a large dog bounding along the pathway towards her. She squealed as it knocked her off her feet in its haste to get past. She landed with a thud on the grass.

'I seem to be on my arse again,' she retorted when Jim jogged back to her.

'Are you okay?' The dog's owner came running to them. 'I usually find no one around when the weather is bad, so I let her off the lead. I'm so sorry. I didn't see you until it was too late.'

'I'm fine.' Maria smiled through gritted teeth. She could have given him a mouthful, but what use would it do? At least he'd apologised. 'No harm done.'

He clipped the dog's lead into place, and she let him pass.

'I'm not meant to get to the top, am I?' she said to Jim.

'Well, seeing as it's your challenge, let's simplify it.'

'*Simplify?*' Maria glared at him. 'Are you suggesting I made that dog run at me and knock me over so that I didn't have to walk with you?'

'No, I'd never—'

Maria had had enough. She pushed past Jim to go down the hill. 'You can do the rest by yourself. I'll be in the car.'

'But what about the selfie?'

'I don't care!'

'Maria.'

'No, no.' She waved over her shoulder. 'If you're so good on your own, you go up to the top.'

She marched off. What she would do for a nice warm pub, a meal, and a glass of wine.

She thought Jim would follow her, but when she glanced behind, he'd disappeared. She stopped. Had he really gone on without her? How was that nostalgic? Her eyes brimmed with angry tears.

In the car park, she sat in the car, arms folded while she waited for him to come back. Every muscle she had was aching. She couldn't remember *that* happening when she'd been younger.

When he appeared twenty minutes later, she was in a foul mood.

'You took your time.'

'We weren't far from the top. You should have carried on. The view was amazing.'

'Well, I didn't, and I've been sitting here ages waiting for you.'

'I wasn't going to stop just because you were in a strop.'

'I was not in a strop!' She'd really had enough now. 'This is the last date I'm doing. They were supposed to be fun, not challenges. I'll tell the girls I've done enough of them now.'

'They've gone to so much trouble to do these things for you, and yet all you've done is moan about every one!'

'So I'm supposed to be grateful when I'm not enjoying myself?'

'You could at least try to have fun.'

'What's that supposed to mean?'

'Do it for them, if not me.'

'They're not your dates,' she snapped, like a petulant child. 'They're mine.'

'Then complete them.'

'What will they have us doing next?' Maria was on a roll. 'Feeding lions at the zoo? Trapeze artists? Going to the Arctic Circle?'

'You're exaggerating now.'

'Am I? If they hadn't come up with the idea, you wouldn't have spent the day with me, would you? You'd be at work, as far away from me as possible.'

'You told me you wanted to work this morning!'

'That's because I know you'd rather not spend the day with me.' It was the only thing she could say in her shock about his outburst.

'What's brought this on?' Jim was perplexed.

'You look at me at times, and I wonder what you see.'

'You're being ridiculous.'

'I'm still me, Jim.' She poked herself in the chest as tears filled her eyes. 'Nothing has changed. But I'm not sure you still want to be with me.'

Jim went quiet. 'Is that what you really think of me?'

'I *think* I want to go home. It was a stupid idea anyway.'

'Fine.' He started the engine.

The journey back was made in silence. She glanced at Jim, his eyes on the road, his face creased in anger.

Maria held in her tears, knowing she had gone too far. She

might have just turned fifty, but she was acting like a teenager, not a grown-up. Her words had been spiteful, meant to hurt him, and yet she didn't know why.

One thing was certain. It was going to be a while before she could put it all right again.

CHAPTER THIRTY

At home, Clara was sitting on the settee, the room silent as her thoughts whirred round her head. Somewhere between getting home from the wedding yesterday evening and that morning, she'd gone into maudlin mode. It was mid-afternoon, and she was still stuck in it.

Finding out that Alex had been cheating on her, and for so long, had been a huge blow. Even though she'd wanted to know everything Steve could tell her, it hadn't helped. It had just hindered. Now, she needed to see what Alex's new home looked like – what Kirstie was like. What had she got that Clara hadn't been able to give Alex anymore?

She'd picked up a cushion and covered her mouth, screaming into it loudly for a few seconds. Then she'd pummelled it, trying to rid herself of the pain.

Then, for some reason, she'd got out their photo albums from years gone by and tortured herself as she'd flicked through them. She'd deleted lots of photos from her phone, but she hadn't been able to get rid of the physical ones. It had seemed too final.

Now, she had reminders of holidays they'd been on,

parties they'd gone along to. Weddings, their own in particular. They had been so happy back then. And it had all been for nothing.

She wondered if Kirstie had known about her. Had Alex been one of those men who'd told his lover that his marriage was dead? Then he'd come home to Clara, sleep with her in all senses of the word, and then meet up with his bit on the side whenever he could.

Steve was right. Alex was a snake.

Anger coursed through her, and she raced upstairs to the box room they used as an office. She searched out a large envelope and, back downstairs, she took the photos from every album and shoved them inside it. Then she picked up her car keys and set off to Hedworth. She would search for Alex's car, post the photos through the letterbox of Ivory Cottage, and see if Kirstie really did know about her.

Following Google's directions, she found Ivory Lane quite quickly, a pleasant row of semi-detached houses. It was comforting that it was nothing like the idyllic country lane she'd imagined, all tree-lined with fields around it, rose bushes in gardens and tiny windows.

At the far end of the row, she spotted Alex's car. It was in the driveway, alongside a black Mini. Out of sight, she parked her car a little further along, picked up the envelope, and hotfooted back to the house before she could change her mind.

She was about to post the envelope through the letterbox when she heard her mum's voice in her ear. It made her stop.

"Two wrongs don't make a right, our Clara."

It *was* ill-judged, getting revenge on someone because Alex had cheated on her. Sure, it took two to do the deed, but for all Clara knew, he could have spun her a web of lies.

Alex had hurt *Clara*. It wasn't Clara's place to do the same to Kirstie.

Before she was spotted, she rushed back down the path, climbed into her car, and drove off in haste. Once she was past the house, she glanced in the rear-view mirror, half-expecting someone to come running out of the property after her, shaking their fists.

What was she thinking? Thank goodness she hadn't been spotted.

Laughter escaped her, relief evident. On impulse, she pulled into the side of the road again and took out her phone. She was going to ruin his Sunday, nonetheless.

'Nice house you've moved into,' she said when Alex answered. 'Mind you, Ivory Cottage is such a lovely name for a creep like you.'

There was quiet down the line, so she continued.

'I know that you were seeing *Kirstie* for months before we split up, and obviously you moved in with her when you left me, rather than with your parents. You bastard, how could you?'

'How did you find out?'

'Is that all you have to say? Not even sorry?'

'I—'

'Does she know about me?'

'Yes.'

'All the way through your affair?'

'Yes, but it's not—'

'Do you know what? You can stick your amicable house sale where the sun doesn't shine. You did the dirty on me, and now I'll do it back the only way I know how. You can wait for your money because I'm not selling.'

'You can't do that!'

'Maybe not, but I will drag it out for as long as I can. And that's what I intend to do. Perhaps nine months will be enough.'

She disconnected the call, having a little laugh to herself.

She hadn't meant a word of what she'd said. She wanted the house gone, and Alex out of her life, as quickly as possible now, but it wouldn't hurt to let him stew.

She waited for the tears to come, but there were none. Instead, all she felt was numbness. Nothing towards Alex at all. Not anger, nor frustration. There was definitely no love lost.

In actual fact, it didn't hurt at all. She was far better off without him. It felt as if she'd had an epiphany.

She rang Tyler. Perhaps he was around to dissect the past couple of days with her.

'Hey, how was the wedding?' he asked.

'Never mind that. Do you fancy doing a bit of house hunting with me?'

CHAPTER THIRTY-ONE

At work the following morning, Clara told her mum and Lucy what had happened yesterday. She'd spoken to them both after the wedding, but they didn't know she'd been to visit Alex until now. She filled them in on her trip to Ivory Lane.

'I can't believe he was seeing someone else for all that time.' Maria shook her head. 'I hope I don't ever bump into him again, nor any of his family. They'll get the wrath of me if I do.'

'*I* can't believe you nearly posted everything through the front door!' Lucy tittered.

'Oh, don't.' Clara hung her head in mock shame. 'I was just so angry he lied to me, and then finding out about her as well was too much. Imagine if I'd have gone through with it, though!' She laughed.

'It's good to see you smiling, love,' Maria said. 'We've missed it over the past few weeks.'

'That and your savvy go-and-get-'em, nothing-will-stop-me attitude,' Lucy piped up.

'Are you saying I've been a bit of a wimp?'

'Oh, not at all!' Lucy groaned in jest.

Clara flicked her the V sign. Then she rubbed her hands together. 'I think it's time to get my house sold.'

Lucy and Maria glanced at each other. Clara could tell they were surprised.

'I gave it a *lot* of thought yesterday and I want to do it.'

'Well, you're certainly in the right place for that to happen.' Maria beckoned them to follow her.

They went into her office. Maria sat down at her desk, waggled the mouse to boot up the computer, and clicked away.

'Operation Clara is to sell your old house and find you a new home,' she said. 'Have you spotted anything you like?'

'Not really. Tyler came over last night, and we went on a few sites. Nothing caught my eye.'

'Excellent, because I've just had this in to sell, and I think it's perfect for you.'

Maria showed them photos of a small cottage on Penley Street. It was a ten-minute walk from Somerley High Street, and the rear overlooked fields rather than the usual view of the back garden of the house in the next street.

'Ooh, now that is nice,' Lucy exclaimed. 'The kitchen is incredible.'

Clara said nothing as her mum clicked through the rest of the photos, but she, too, was impressed. It was really tastefully done, no expense spared.

'The owners have spent a lot of money on it,' Maria enthused, 'but they're now after a quick sale. The details are in draft at the moment, ready to go once I've valued it, so no one else has seen it. What do you think?'

'Our house isn't even on the market yet!'

'Since when has that stopped me?' Maria waved a hand in the air. 'It's a beautiful home. I can have that gone in a matter of days.'

'Not if Alex insists on getting an independent valuation.'

'He'll snap your hands off to use us now, especially as you have his affair as a bargaining tool.'

Clara had now seen all the photos and was clicking through them again. The property was decorated in a style she liked. She wouldn't have to do anything to it. That would be a bonus with only one salary coming in now. She swallowed. Was it all a bit too soon?

Her mood dipped as reality sank in. 'I'm not sure. Can I even afford the mortgage on my own?'

'Of course. Sal will get you the best deal.' Maria took Clara's hands in her own. 'Just come and see it with me. Then you can decide. It's definitely your style, and I think you'd be better in something new, with no reminders of the old.'

Clara knew what her mum was doing. She wanted to tell her that she couldn't fix everything but didn't want to hurt her feelings. Maria's intentions were good, even if she didn't understand what it would be like to move out of their marital home. It would rip Clara's heart out.

But she had to do it sometime, so she'd better start preparing herself.

Maria was looking at her, waiting for an answer. 'It wouldn't hurt to take a peek, surely?'

Clara nodded. 'Okay.'

'Great. I'll get the keys.'

'We're going now?'

'No time like the present!' Maria clapped with glee. 'Come on, grab your coat. Lucy, you and Regan, can you hold the fort until we're back?'

'We sure can.' Lucy grinned at Clara. 'And if you don't want it, I'll try and twist Aaron's arm so that we can have it instead.'

As soon as they pulled up in Penley Street, Clara's stomach was doing a loop-the-loop. She recognised the cottage from the photos.

'Oh, Mum, it's even nicer when you see it up close.' Clara released her seatbelt and got out of the car.

'I'm just glad there's no one home right now.' Maria jangled the keys in the air. 'They gave me these to do future viewings with, though.'

Clara took them from her and grinned.

From the moment she stepped inside, she wanted the property. The house had a good vibe about it. People had been happy here, she could sense it. Her mum could, too, although she also had a knack of spotting which client would buy which house. That was some talent to have.

Clara couldn't stop beaming as she went from room to room.

She imagined herself soaking in the bath with chrome-clawed feet, a glass of wine to hand.

She saw herself cooking a meal in the kitchen while her friends or family sat around the table in the adjoining dining room.

In the garden, she spotted a picnic bench at the far end; imagined herself reading a book in the sun.

Maria came up beside her. 'What do you think?'

'You're right, it's perfect.' Even so, Clara's bottom lip trembled. 'Do you really think I can afford it on my own?'

'I know you can. I messaged Sal before we left the office. She's just replied to say she's already found you a good deal. And just think, it will all be yours.'

Clara threw her arms around Maria. 'You are the best mum ever, do you know that?'

'I do,' Maria teased.

'No, you're the best *person* ever.'

Maria's shoulders drooped at that. 'Your dad doesn't think so at the moment.'

'Ah, you're talking about your date yesterday. Sorry it didn't work out well.'

Maria's eyes narrowed. 'How did you know?'

'Lucy asked Dad, and then she told me. Before now, you've always mentioned how they went. So we kinda guessed you were upset.'

Maria's eyes brimmed with tears.

'Oh, Mum, don't cry. Do you want to talk about it?' Clara offered.

Maria pooh-poohed the idea. 'It's hormones, darling.' She laughed it off. 'We just had a tiff. Nothing we can't sort out.'

'So you didn't get attacked by a big dog and strop off down the hill?'

Maria glared at her. 'He told you that?'

Clara nodded, her face breaking out into another grin.

'I'll kill him.' But Maria was smiling now. 'The dog bouncing all over me until its embarrassed owner dragged it away was quite funny in hindsight.'

'Never mind, Mum. You only have one more envelope to open.' Maria was quiet then, so Clara decided to plant the seed. 'Dad told us you don't want to do the final date. It's such a shame because we saved the best until last.'

CHAPTER THIRTY-TWO

Maria drove to her first viewing straight from home. She had left Jim working in his office. They were still pussyfooting around one another, but they'd get through it. They always did. Having said that, Maria must have hurt him more than she'd thought for him to react that way.

She still didn't want to do any more of those stupid dates, despite Clara jokily trying to encourage her. She was being selfish, and a little juvenile, but Jim had laughed at her, and then left her to fend for herself. If she'd known that would happen, she would never have let him drag her up that hill in the first place.

She pulled up outside Clara's house, a huge sigh escaping as she switched off the engine. She'd sent the photographer around as soon as she and Clara had got back to the office, and the sale details had been mailed out to their list before close of business yesterday. There had been three emails requesting viewings that morning. This was the first of them.

Maria had been so proud when they'd bought the house. It had been perfect for them, so to be proved wrong was bittersweet. And now she was about to show a couple with two young children around it. The price was good. Maria was certain it would be snapped up.

Her mind slipped back to when Clara and Alex were married. Both sets of parents weren't entirely happy that their children were so young. Two years didn't seem long enough to know that you wanted to be with someone forever.

Yet, Clara was always quick to tell them that she and Jim weren't much older when they were married. Maria couldn't say that it was different for them, but it had been. She and Jim had grown up alone and wanted a family.

For Clara and Alex, there didn't seem to be the same rush. However, knowing how she and Jim felt when they were married, it made them realise that young love couldn't be stopped and would either run its course, like theirs had, or fizzle out. She couldn't help but be disappointed that it was the latter, but equally, Clara's happiness was the most important thing.

The couple were waiting for Maria this time, and she cursed herself for being late. Still, in the scheme of things it didn't matter. As they'd been first to ask for a viewing via email, they'd wanted to see it immediately. Maria had moved a few things around to accommodate them.

'Mr and Mrs Danson?' She stuck out her hand for the man to shake.

'Yes, hi,' the man said. 'I'm Stuart, and this is Jane.'

The woman next to him was holding a small baby in her arms. Even though spring was here, her hair was hidden underneath a woollen hat, her smile lighting up her face.

'Pleased to meet you both.' Maria cooed at the baby. 'And this must be Charlie. What a darling.'

'Well, Charlie is his real name, but he's going by a number of rude ones at the moment as he's not sleeping well.'

'Oh dear. I remember that as if it were yesterday, and my daughters are both in their late twenties. And you have a little girl, too?' Maria mentally went through the notes she'd made while talking to them on the phone.

'Yes, Maisie,' Jane said. 'She's six. The house we've sold only had two bedrooms, so we're after something bigger now.'

'Jane had hoped to be settled in the new home in time for Charlie's arrival,' Stuart said. 'But it took a lot longer than planned to sell the old one.'

Maria wished they'd come to her for a quote, but she didn't voice it aloud. Although she couldn't profess to sell everything that came on her books, she loved a challenge and was certain she would have got them out, and into a new home, before Charlie had made his appearance. Still, at least their little bundle of joy, born three months ago now, was here and by all accounts looked very well.

'I do have to mention that this home belongs to my daughter and her husband. I have valued it myself and will have it independently valued for any buyer, but I can assure you it will come out at the same price. Also, if you prefer to have it valued to show the price is right, I'd be more than happy for you to do that, too.'

Maria watched as Stuart and Jane exchanged glances. Shaking heads and shoulder shrugging followed.

'No, we're fine as it is,' Stuart replied. 'You have a good reputation. But thanks for letting us know.'

Maria pointed to the house. 'Let's get you inside then.'

There had been no need to check this property over before setting up the viewings. Maria knew its selling points so well. A huge state-of-the-art kitchen, a conservatory added onto the living room, and the garden had recently been landscaped. Anyone could see that Clara and Alex had spent a fortune on it.

Maria had mentioned earlier that they'd had several calls

about the property as soon as it went online, so it seemed a little disingenuous to repeat it. She stepped into a large hallway, stairs leading off it, and showed them around.

When she heard them talking, Jane saying which bedrooms were suitable for each child, and Stuart fitting their furniture into the living room, she knew it was a done deal.

TWENTY-TWO YEARS AGO - 159 SOMERLEY HIGH STREET

For a few months while they sold their house in Copeland Avenue and found somewhere else more suitable for the next chapter in their story, Maria kept a mental list of her top priorities required for their next home. It had to be a larger property, with a garden this time, not a yard. She wanted a family kitchen where she could fit a table that would seat six; where her children would do their homework while she cooked their meals; where she could do her work looking out onto the garden.

The bathroom needed to be bigger than the six by six they had now, and she wanted space to park both cars side by side in the drive, rather than fight for two on the road every night when they got home. Jim would love a garage, too, even one that was falling down that he could make do with until they could replace it. Oh, and she didn't want a fixer-upper as their time was more limited nowadays.

Would this be their last property? She wasn't sure. Who knew what the future would bring.

When they eventually found it, house number three for Maria and Jim had been one that didn't need much fixing up.

Jim had spotted the "for sale" board on his way home from work. It was at the end of Somerley High Street, not too far out of town, but away from the hustle and bustle.

Across from it was a large park, several acres of greenery. Maria was already imagining her and Jim strolling along the pathways, the girls running ahead, perhaps even a dog trotting alongside it; around the lake, stopping to watch the bowls in the evening, and having coffee at the pavilion café.

They'd arranged a viewing and, with Lucy at nursery school and Clara thankfully asleep in her pushchair, the estate agent had shown them around.

'I want you to go round it again, at your leisure for a few minutes,' the woman had said. 'Open every cupboard, check in every room. Inspect the doors, the fitted wardrobes. I'll go and sit in the garden, and I'll be ready to answer any questions you have afterwards. I always find you get a feel for a property if you can look at it by yourself.'

Maria and Jim started upstairs, going from one bedroom to another.

'This seems strange, having someone showing us around,' Jim remarked. 'Up until now, we've been given a key and done it ourselves.'

'Oh, I don't know. I like that she can tell us things about it,' Maria replied. 'When we moved into Garrett Street, we had no idea how little sun the back of the house got. It would be a must to know which side the sun sets on, but at that age, I wouldn't have thought of asking about it. And I like that she's let us look around on our own, too.'

'And what are you feeling about the place, Mrs Wilshaw?' Jim drew her into his arms. 'Are you ready to make another move?'

'Yes! Are you?'

'I think so. Not only can I see our girls loving it, but I can also picture grandchildren, too.'

'Grandchildren?' She slapped Jim on the arm. 'Don't make me old before my time!'

'Knowing us, we'll probably have moved several times before they come along.'

Maria grinned at that. They had certainly got the house bug.

'So we'll put an offer in?' Jim raised an eyebrow inquisitively.

She nodded. 'Although I'd live anywhere with you.'

'Soppy sod.' Jim kissed her.

Maria gave a contented sigh. She was glad she and Jim had plans to grow old together.

CHAPTER THIRTY-THREE

Clara was exhausted when she got home from work that evening. In the past two days, she had put her house up for sale, made an offer that had been accepted on another, and signed for a mortgage in principle. Fair play to her mum and Sal who had organised it all. It never failed to amaze Clara how hard they worked, and being on the receiving end of it had been fun, if a little intense.

Tonight, Alex was coming over. She had brought with her the paperwork for the house sale, for him to sign. He hadn't wanted to come into the office, obviously not keen to show his face.

Having had lots of time to think about things over the past few weeks, Clara knew she and Alex had been simply covering over the cracks, keeping a united front with people they knew, whereas behind closed doors, there were more empty silences than conversations. They'd been civil to each other, but they were living like brother and sister. Who would want a platonic relationship at twenty-seven?

All the same, she changed into a flattering dress and redid her make-up. Wasn't it better to be looking glam and on top of the world when she saw him again? Show him how well she was surviving without him?

Yet the feelings that came crashing back when she saw him shocked her. Maybe it was because selling the house seemed so final. Or as he'd been out of sight for a while, it had been easy to fool herself.

She missed him.

No, she missed what they'd *had*.

She turned away from him at the feel of her skin heating up. 'Would you like a coffee?'

'Yes, please.' He moved into the kitchen. 'You never did say who told you about me and Kirstie.'

'It doesn't matter.' She busied herself adding water to the kettle and getting out mugs.

'It does to me.'

'There are umpteen people at the wedding that you could take a guess at.'

'I suppose, and at least you didn't throw a brick through the window before leaving.'

She turned to give him a mouthful but caught him smiling shyly. She let her anger evaporate. There was no need to fight anymore.

He took the mug she offered, and they sat down across the table from each other. The paperwork was in a file to the side.

'Ever since you rang to say you were selling the house, I've been thinking about you, about what we had,' Alex said.

Clara scoffed. 'That's more than you did before you left.'

'It's not as if I can wipe you out of my heart.'

'You did a perfectly good job of that the six months you were seeing both me *and* Kirstie.'

'That was different. I don't even know if I've made the right choice moving in with her. Everything happened so fast and... Christ, it's all such a mess. I'm really sorry, Clara.'

She dipped her eyes away from his stare, knowing that she would burst into tears if he was nice to her, and reached for the file. She still cared for him, too. It was hard not to, even after what he'd done to her.

She flipped the file open and turned it towards him. 'There are two places for your signature,' she said.

'I miss you.'

The floor almost came up and hit her in the face. Was he saying he wanted to try again? Her heart beat out a tune, and for a second it leapt with joy. Then scepticism set in, and reality, too. She didn't want this.

'Isn't it working out with Kirstie?' she wanted to know.

'Yes, but she's not you.'

'I missed you for the first month, but after that I began to get on with my life. Until I heard about Kirstie, I was doing fine. I must admit, it hurt. A lot.'

'I never meant for that to happen.'

'But you were right, it hadn't been working for a while. Are you happy with her now?'

'I think so.'

She stopped as realisation sank in. 'Did you think I wanted you back because I came to see where you live?'

'Isn't that why you did?'

Clara began to doubt herself. *Had* she done it to gauge his reaction? She'd thought it was a spur-of-the-moment thing, yet had she wanted to see him, to cement her feelings for him, rather than put their relationship to bed? Even just now, she'd thought she wasn't over him.

'No, it wasn't,' she snapped, cursing her mixed emotions.

Alex took the pen she was holding out and signed the forms.

Clara closed the file once it was done. 'That's that, then. I assume the next thing will be divorce papers. Shall I start the ball rolling with those, too?'

He nodded. 'Might as well.' He stood up to leave.

At the door, Clara felt as if she wanted to give him a goodbye hug but didn't think it was appropriate. She was glad they hadn't had children. They could at least have a complete break from each other.

But Alex took the matter into his own hands by embracing her. It felt so alien that she almost pushed him away. Yet, it was good for her, cathartic to see that he meant nothing to her now.

'Bye, Clara.' Alex stepped away. 'If you need help before the move, call me.'

'Okay. If there's anything you want to take, let me know. It's only fair we split certain things – furniture and whatnot.'

'Thanks. I'll have a think.'

Even though she'd put on a brave front, Clara was spent of emotion when she closed the door behind him. Her heart had been shattered, squeezed, and broken into so many pieces, but she was pleased she'd come out of it the other side.

And she was sure she'd had a lucky escape.

CHAPTER THIRTY-FOUR

The next day, when Aaron got in from work, Lucy was waiting to talk to him.

'How did Clara get on with Alex?' he asked.

Lucy laughed. 'You're dying to go round and sort him out, aren't you?'

'We might have been known as the A-team, but you know there was no love lost between me and Alex. I never really liked him. He was egotistic and always had to do or be better than anyone else.'

'He signed the papers for the house sale to move forward, and she's sorting out the divorce. I'm glad, to be honest.'

'Shame, because I would have liked to punch him first.'

Lucy laughed. Aaron hadn't got a fighting bone in his body. 'We may have a bigger problem than that to think about. I had a bad bout of morning sickness, and Saskia commented on it. She said there must be something wrong with me. Ellie got upset about it.'

'Has she guessed, do you think?'

'I think she has an inkling. Maybe it's best if we tell them. I was wondering how you felt about it.'

'You know I want to shout it from the rooftops, so I'm happy. As long as you don't think it's too soon.'

'It's a risk whenever we tell them, really.' She grinned. 'Let's do it tonight, after tea.'

It was shepherd's pie, a family favourite, and once they'd eaten, Aaron gave Lucy's hand a squeeze.

'Are you ready?' he asked.

Lucy nodded, excitement rippling through her.

'Girls,' Aaron said. 'We have something to tell you.'

'We're going to Disneyland!' an excited Ellie squealed.

Aaron winced at the high-pitched sound. 'No, I'm afraid not.'

'What is it?' Saskia folded her arms. 'You're not getting married, are you?'

Lucy noted a quiver of fear in her sarcastic tone.

Aaron tutted. 'No, we're not, but we will be one day. You need to get over that and stop going on about it.'

'I don't want a stepmum.'

'Lucy has been more of a mum to you than yours ever was. I can't see why you—'

'Guys,' Lucy protested. 'Not now. Because we have some special news.' She reached for Aaron's hand and looked at him. 'Shall I tell them, or will you?'

'Go ahead.' Aaron winked at her.

Lucy ignored the roll of Saskia's eyes and continued regardless. 'You're having a new brother or sister!'

Ellie squealed again, clapping excitedly. 'This is the best news ever. Alexis's mum is having a baby, too. She's having a brother. Can I have a brother?'

'I can't just ask to order, little one.' Lucy laughed. 'But I'll try my best.'

Saskia had suddenly lost her tongue.

'Saskia,' Aaron said. 'You're very quiet.'

'It's all about you, isn't it – and *her*.' She glared at Lucy before folding her arms.

Although expecting an outburst, Lucy felt her good mood evaporate slightly.

'Actually, yes, it is.' Aaron nodded. 'Lucy and I are very happy to be having a child together.'

'But there's not enough room here! It's bad enough having to share with the squirt. Where will a baby go?'

'Right in your cakehole if you don't mind your manners,' Aaron quipped. 'It's big enough.'

'Aaron,' Lucy chided. 'The baby will sleep in our room for quite some time after it's born,' she told Saskia. 'At least a year.'

'We're going to have a baby,' Ellie sang. 'We're going to have a baby.'

'You're already a baby.' Saskia sulked. 'I can't believe I don't get a say in this at all, when it affects *my* life, too.'

'I'm saving that comment for when you're eighteen, bringing boys home and I want to embarrass you,' Aaron muttered.

'We're both happy about it, Saskia,' Lucy said. 'I'm sure you will be—'

'*I* wish that you hadn't come to live with us, that it was just me and Dad.' As tears fell, Saskia scraped back her chair and ran out of the room.

'Saskia!' Aaron stood up, but Lucy put a hand on his arm.

'Leave her. She'll get used to it in her own time.'

'She shouldn't be so rude.'

'It's a shock, that's all.'

Ellie was moving back to the settee now.

'She's more than likely thinking she won't get a look-in with her dad if a new baby comes along,' Lucy added. 'She's your little girl. She's just threatened that she won't be anymore.'

'She'll always be that to me.'

'It's not how she sees things right now.'

Aaron sat down again. 'You're right. I'll talk to her later, when she's calmed down.'

'We're going to have a baby,' Ellie sang again. Then she stopped, turning to them quickly. 'You will ask nicely if I can have a brother, won't you?'

'We sure will.' Lucy couldn't help but smile. At least one of the girls was happy with their news. They would win Saskia round, she was sure.

Despite that, nothing would make her sad that evening.

CHAPTER THIRTY-FIVE

Things were still strained in the Wilshaw household the following week. It wasn't like them. They were still being polite to each other but avoiding the elephant in the room. Sadly, Maria's insomnia had worsened due to her worrying about it. As well as that, she couldn't stop thinking about Clara. Luckily, Lucy and Aaron seemed settled now with news of the baby, so that was one less thing for her to worry about.

They were in the kitchen before leaving for work and Jim was trying to get Maria to complete the nostalgic dates again.

'There's only one left to do, and the girls gave you the envelope two weeks ago,' he was saying again now. 'When are you going to open it?'

'I'm not.'

'Then you'll have to tell them. It isn't fair after all their hard work organising them.'

'It wasn't *fair* of you to laugh at me when I fell over.'

Jim groaned. 'Not that again.'

'It was spiteful.'

'Don't be so immature.'

Maria banged her mug down on the worktop. Delilah

jumped up from her slumber. 'Oh, *I'm* being childish all of a sudden?'

'I'm not the one who walked back to the car in a huff.'

'No, you're the one who left me, even though you knew I was upset.'

'Someone had to take a photo from the top of that hill.'

'Just for a souvenir? That's laughable, as I never want to be reminded of it. It's bad enough that you told the girls, and they thought it was hilarious.' She hadn't told him yet that she thought it was amusing now, too. For some reason, she seemed to be spoiling for a fight.

'It was a bit of fun, lighten up!'

'I didn't find it amusing. I think the whole idea was stupid.'

'For crying out loud, Maria, *I* asked Lucy and Clara to set the dates up for me! I wanted to do something special for your birthday. Something that we could look back on, remember with fondness, because we'd been thinking about the times when we first met.'

Maria froze. Oh, no, what was he saying? She grimaced, realising how much she would have hurt him if that were true.

'Why didn't you tell me it was you?' she asked.

'Because you wouldn't have gone on any of them.'

'What do you mean by that?'

'Well, heaven forbid you ever spend any quality time with me nowadays. When I see you, you're always going on about work. Or, if it isn't that, you're worrying about Clara and Alex getting a divorce, or the fact that Lucy isn't married yet, not that it's any business of yours.'

'They're our daughters!'

'They have their own lives and families.' He prodded his chest. 'You give Delilah more attention than me.'

'That's not fair, especially after you've been so sneaky.'

'So wanting to do something nice for you is now *sneaky*?'

'Of course not.' She tried to backpedal. 'When *were* you going to tell me?'

'The last date was going to be Sunday lunch out with the family, instead of us cooking. That's what I see our family being all about, getting together around a large table to chat, and to celebrate.'

Maria didn't know what to say. How had she got things so wrong? It had been such a nice gesture, and yet she'd been annoyed about the time it took from her work. She needed to make amends. Trouble was, Jim wouldn't listen right now. She hadn't seen him so angry in years.

'I'll do the fifth one,' she relented. 'I've just been so busy and I—'

'You're always busy. Or is that an excuse so that you don't have to spend time with me?'

'No!' Maria touched his arm, scared he might move away if she was any more intimate. 'It's not that, at all. But you know, if I feel that anything needs fixing, I have to put it right. What with Clara and Alex, and—'

'Not everything has to be perfect. It never will be. And I'm tired of being pushed aside.'

'You work long hours, too,' she objected weakly.

'I had a special present for you when we reached the top of the hill!' His fists clenched in temper. 'I had a small bottle of champagne as well, and sandwiches for a picnic.'

Maria's eyes widened in dismay. Jim had gone out of his way to make everything so special for her, and she'd ruined his surprise. She cursed inwardly.

But, equally, it was important to her that everything was running smoothly, and he knew that. That's why she worried about most things all the time. She and Jim, well, she'd thought they were solid, so she didn't need to be concerned.

Had she taken him for granted too much? Stopped giving

him love and comfort because of complacency? When she'd thought it was because he wasn't attracted to her anymore?

She gnawed at her bottom lip, trying not to see the anguish on his face that she had caused. 'We need to talk about this, don't we?' she said softly.

'*You* need to talk about it because it'll be on your,' his hands made an inverted commas sign, 'need-to-fix-to-make-perfect list now, won't it?'

'I've said I'm sorry and I—'

'Have you apologised?'

She paused: had she?

'It goes without saying,' she replied defensively.

'No. It doesn't.' Jim shook his head. 'I'm going to work. I can't be with you right now. I'll see you later.'

'Jim,' Maria cried.

He was walking out of the door but, suddenly, he turned back. 'You're such hard work at times. Don't you see that I do these things for you because I love you? When will you realise that you are safe, and your past can't hurt you? You don't need to make amends for it by making sure everything is always perfect.'

Maria jumped as the front door slammed behind him. It wasn't like Jim to leave in a mood. But his words had meant to linger, to hit the mark, and that was really hurtful.

Delilah came up to her, nudging her leg with her nose. Maria reached down to stroke her. 'I'm such an idiot at times, Delilah. What am I going to do now?'

She flopped down at the table, head in her hands. She hadn't realised until it was pointed out to her that they might actually be having problems. Jim was a placid man. He'd rather have a cup of tea than an argument. So when he blew, he often said some straight-to-the-point things. Then, he'd go silent for a few minutes, and then he'd ask if she wanted a drink. It was always his olive branch.

Of course, he'd be sorry later. As much as she was a control freak and needed everything just so, Jim didn't like there to be an atmosphere. She would have to sort it out first, as she knew it was her doing. Knowing Jim, he'd probably be feeling pretty crap already.

She wiped at the few tears that had escaped and then set off to work.

CHAPTER THIRTY-SIX

Maria tried to stay jovial that morning at work, hoping that Lucy and Clara wouldn't pick up on anything amiss. She'd have twenty questions if she wasn't careful. Luckily, the morning was busy, and she was out with clients for the most part. So it was a nice surprise to see Sal waiting for her when she got back just after one.

Sal had come to drop off the work she'd completed and to pick up what couldn't be done online. Usually, Maria loved their get-togethers. They often went out for a bite to eat afterwards to continue chatting. But today, she couldn't raise anything more than a weak smile. Which, like a true friend, Sal noticed as they sat down together.

'What's up?' she queried.

'I've screwed up.' Maria closed her office door so they could talk in private and told her what had happened.

'Oh dear.' Sal grimaced. 'But that's typical Jim.'

'What, arguing?' Maria frowned.

'No, surprising you. Your Jim is one in a million thinking of something like that. It's so romantic.'

'Jim won't be mine if I don't sort this mess out.'

'It will blow over. He loves you to bits, and he doesn't like any ill feeling. I'm surprised he hasn't rung you already.'

Maria gave a faint smile. She'd been checking her phone, just in case, but there had been no contact from him. She really must have annoyed him.

'I don't know how to make things right. I've been wanting to ring him all morning but I'm afraid to make things any worse. I thought it best to wait until this evening.' Her eyes brimmed with tears again, and she reached for a tissue, dabbing at them as secretly as she could. 'It *was* really sweet of him to do this for me, and I've been a right cow. I've probably upset the girls, too.'

'I've said to you, many times, that the pair of you need to spend more time together. You're both as bad as each other, working too hard. You only live once, Maria.'

Maria spied her chance to move the conversation away from her and Jim. 'Speaking of which, how did your latest date go? Peter, wasn't it?' Sal had been on a couple more dates since David Martingale had turned out to be a waste of space.

Sal shuddered at the mention of his name. 'It was hideous.'

'Come on, spill. I need the gory details. It might cheer me up.'

'I'm glad my love life is such a joke to you,' she teased.

'What was he like? Was he nice-looking?'

'Yes, he wasn't bad at all.'

'So what went wrong?'

'Well, I was enjoying myself with him. He's a headmaster at a junior school and he had a few funny anecdotes. At that point, I quite fancied him bossing me around like one of his pupils. Not that I think he should boss them around, but you know what I mean. But then I felt my face heating up, that familiar heat rushing to my chest. You know the one?'

'I do!'

'I hadn't even got any layers to remove, having taken off my jacket.'

'Oh dear.'

'Peter told me I'd gone awfully red, so I excused myself and then shot into the ladies. But when I went to tidy myself up in the mirror, I'd been sweating so much that my fringe was stuck to my forehead.'

Maria couldn't help but giggle. Sal was smiling, too.

'I stayed in there for as long as I could before Peter might send a search party to look for me, and then I went back to the table. He was not impressed. He asked me outright if I was going through the change.'

'He didn't!'

'Oh, it gets worse. His tone was so sharp that I snapped back in defence. "If you're talking about the menopause, then yes, I am," I told him. He screwed up his face like he'd swallowed a wasp, as if I'd said I'd got a contagious disease. I asked him if there was something he didn't like about the word. And he said it's what it does to women that he dislikes.'

'He should try being a woman for a day,' Maria sympathised.

'And then we had a row.'

Maria caught her breath. 'A row?'

'He started complaining about older women, saying their sex drive goes completely and that foreplay was out of the question as everything becomes so...dry. I wasn't sure if I was mortified or angry at his gall.'

'I'd have slung my wine over him.'

'My glass was empty, or else I would have. I could feel my cheeks reddening even more, but it had nothing to do with my body temperature this time. He was making assumptions and being quite rude about it. I wasn't having that.

'I told him whether I am menopausal or not, his attitude

wasn't appealing to me. I was about to go on when he butted in and said he wouldn't be asking me on another date anyway. Talk about making me feel inadequate.' Sal paused for dramatic effect. 'Do you know what he said then?'

Maria sat forward in anticipation.

'Who'd want to get covered in sweat when we're making love?'

'He said that to you? The creep! What did you say back? Please tell me you called him all the names under the sun at the top of your voice.'

'Not quite. I said, extremely loud, that I loved to be covered in sweat after a marathon session of good sex. But I also liked to do that with a lover who was sincere and thoughtful, not one who thinks he's going to be hard done by because he'll need to use a lubricant before he gets his fun.'

Maria burst out laughing. 'I wish I'd been there to hear that!'

'He blushed as the people on the next table stopped their conversation. So I stood up to continue. I said I wouldn't take that shit off him or anyone else. I didn't want to be with a man who had no idea how to be courteous. And then I grabbed my jacket from the back of the chair and marched from the restaurant.'

'Good for you.' Maria fist-bumped Sal. 'What a sleazebag.'

'I had to take a few deep breaths to calm myself when I got outside, I can tell you. I did overreact – stupid hormones. But I feel quite good about it now.'

'If you ask me, I think you did the right thing. He sounds —' Maria's mobile rang. It was Jim, so she held up a finger to silence Sal. 'Hey, you,' she cooed. 'Are we good?'

'Maria, it's Paul.'

There was a pause, long enough for Maria's stomach to lurch. Paul was one of Jim's supervisors. What was he doing on Jim's phone?

'Paul, what's wrong?'
'It's Jim. He's had an accident.'

CHAPTER THIRTY-SEVEN

'What's happened?' Maria was on her feet as she listened to Paul.

'He was running upstairs, and I don't know... I think he fainted.' Paul's voice cracked with emotion. 'I saw him fall backwards but I wasn't near enough to stop him. His wrist seems broken, and he hit his head and knocked himself out for a short while. He's still a bit confused, but the paramedics are with him. They're taking him to A and E.'

'I'll meet you there.' Maria disconnected the call, her hands shaking. By now, Clara and Lucy had opened the door and were standing in the doorway, concern etched on their faces. Behind them, Regan had stood up, too.

'Your dad has fallen down the stairs at work, silly sod,' she told them, trying to sound like it was something and nothing.

'Is he badly hurt?' Clara asked.

Maria shook her head and laughed, a trill sound emanating as panic set in. 'Paul's taking him to A and E,' she fibbed. 'I'm going to see him.'

Maria didn't want to share any details until she knew exactly what had happened and if Jim was all right. Clara and

Lucy would both want to see him, and she wasn't sure she could cope with that until she'd found out more. If it was necessary, she'd be straight on the phone to them, but she didn't want to think of that yet.

'I'll come with you.' Clara grabbed her jacket.

'We don't all need to go.'

'It's fine, Mum,' Lucy soothed. 'We'll take care of everything here.'

'But—'

Lucy threw Clara a warning look.

'I have appointments this afternoon,' Maria said, almost as an afterthought. 'They'll need to be cancelled.'

'I'll do that. You get on your way and let us know as soon as you can.'

'I can take you, if you like?' Sal offered.

'I don't see why I can't go if Sal is,' Clara muttered but sat down anyway.

'Honestly, I'll be fine on my own.' Maria glanced at Lucy and then at Clara before smiling convincingly at Sal. 'I'll call you as soon as I know how he is.'

Then she was out of the door, eager to get to her car and on her way. She was grateful that Lucy was trying to reassure Clara, but even so, she wasn't convinced herself.

Images of Jim lying dead on a hospital trolley after the paramedic had been unable to save him, and her too late to say goodbye, flashed through her mind.

She sobbed, pushing her fear aside. But what if it was more serious than Paul was letting on? If Jim *did* die, what was she going to do without him? There was so much they hadn't done yet, so much they had put off because they were always working. She wanted him to see the new baby growing up, as well as Saskia and Ellie. She wanted him to be there to help Clara with her new home. She wanted him to be there for her when she needed him.

She couldn't lose him.

She tried not to think of the argument they'd had that morning, nor the cross words after visiting Sapphire Lake. Why had she been so mean to him when she hadn't meant any of it?

The hospital was four miles away, on the outskirts of Hedworth. Traffic was horrendous the nearer she got. Finally, the signs came into view for the Accident and Emergency Department. Maria parked up and raced inside. She joined the queue at the admissions desk and waited as patiently as she could while bouncing from foot to foot.

'He'll be fine,' she repeated under her breath over and over. 'He'll be fine.'

It only took a few minutes to be seen, but it felt like hours before it was her turn.

The receptionist gave her a smile as she stepped forward. 'How may I help?'

'My husband, James Wilshaw, has been brought in by ambulance. He had an accident at work.'

The woman's head went down and she checked her computer screen. 'He's in cubicle fourteen.' She pointed to a door to her right. 'I'll buzz you through.'

Maria could barely breathe, walking fast along the corridor. She passed by a lady with a gash to her head, a man hooked up to a beeping monitor, his heart racing too fast. A mum was trying to cajole a toddler to let the nice lady see up his nose.

She found the bay she needed. The curtain was partly across. She could see Paul standing at the edge of the room, a hand on his chin as he looked on. To her right, she spotted Jim's feet first. Either side of the bed, two female staff in blue uniforms attended to his needs.

Maria gasped for breath. 'Jim,' she whispered.

He was sitting up, his chest bare with all sorts of wires

attached to it. A bandage had been wrapped around his head, dried blood on his face, and his left arm below the elbow was in a splint. His cheeks were flushed, and he was wearing an oxygen mask. Even from here, she could see his breathing was erratic.

But he was alive. Relief flooded through her, and she cried.

'Mrs Wilshaw?' One of the women came to her. 'I'm Susi. I know it's hard, but please try not to upset yourself. Jim is in good hands. He's stable at the moment, but we're running tests before we can deal with his minor injuries. There's a nasty cut to his head, and his wrist is broken. The main thing we are working on is trying to ascertain why he fell.'

'His heart.' It was all Maria wanted to know about. The rest could be fixed.

'We don't think anything is wrong with it. His breathing is laboured because he's a bit confused about why he's here and he's panicking. I'm sure seeing you will calm him down.'

She nodded. The woman's words were blunt but soothing at the same time.

Jim caught her eye, and then he burst into tears.

Maria went to his side. She ran a hand across his forehead and bent to kiss his cheek.

'I'm here, darling,' she whispered. 'I'm here.'

'I... I... don't know what happened.'

'You mean you can't remember?'

'No, I... where '

'Try not to talk too much, Jim,' Susi said. 'We'll get you sorted out as soon as possible. But, for now, I need you to stay still.'

'Has he lost his memory?' Maria asked, frightened to see him so muddled.

'We'll know more when he's had further tests. He's confused, but that may be due to the trauma.'

Eventually, Maria turned to Paul. He was white as a sheet, dried blood across his cheek and underneath his fingernails. The sight of it made her want to gag, but she managed to compose herself. She offered him a weak smile

'You never said he'd cut his head.'

'I didn't want to alarm you.'

'Are you okay?'

He nodded. 'I couldn't get to him in time, I'm sorry.'

'Hey, come on. You know Jim. He was born running.'

'He just fell. It was awful.' His face paled as he recalled the incident. 'Mickey rang for an ambulance while I sat with him, trying to keep him still. He kept being sick.'

'Thank you for looking after him.' She gave Paul's arm a squeeze and went to Jim's side again.

'How many times have I told you not to run up those stairs?' Maria joked, determined to keep up a happy front. She laughed through her tears, when inside her heart was beating as wild as her husband's. 'You gave me a fright.'

'We're going to take him for a CT scan in a moment,' Susi told them. 'Then we'll give you an update on his condition.'

'He's going to be okay.' Maria nodded vehemently, reaching across for Jim's hand. 'He's a Wilshaw.'

Maria said it as much for herself as Jim. Because the thought of losing him was getting too much to bear.

CHAPTER THIRTY-EIGHT

Maria woke with a start, a clatter beside her. She looked up to see a nurse tending to Jim. How had she'd fallen asleep with all the hustle and bustle around her? She assumed it was exhaustion, her emotions being pushed to their limits today.

It was half past nine. Next to her, Jim lay sleeping. He'd been moved into the corridor, the cubicle needed for someone else, and they were still waiting to be transferred to a ward. His colour had returned a little, and he'd been given more medication to ease his pain. Lucy and Clara had come to see him, staying for an hour, but when Jim was moved, Maria had sent them home.

It was a relief when the CT scan had revealed nothing wrong. Maria had talked to the consultant about the likelihood of it happening again. At the moment, with no other symptoms, it was being put down to a dip in Jim's blood pressure, causing him to faint, but they were referring him for further tests, just to be sure. The worst seemed to be over for now, however.

She'd found out from Paul that Jim had worked through his lunch. Two orders had arrived at the same time, and another had been missing. Jim had been about to chase it up when he'd fallen. When questioned further, Paul had admitted that Jim worked through quite often. Maria was going to put a stop to that.

Even after his scan, Jim had still been a little disorientated, so they wanted to monitor his condition overnight. His wrist was broken, now in a cast. She reckoned he'd have a lot of aches and pains in the morning once the painkillers wore off.

But he was safe, and he was going to be okay. That was the main thing to think about.

'Any news?' Maria asked the nurse as she was done with her checks.

Jim hadn't made a murmur.

'No beds yet, I'm afraid. But we're hoping to free one up soon. I'm so sorry.'

'There's nothing to apologise for, I know you're all stretched. We're very grateful for your help.'

Maria left her to it. A bit of fresh air plus another cup of coffee was in order to keep her going a while longer.

Clara was on the phone to Tyler, giving him an update after talking to her mum.

'He's still waiting for a bed,' she told him, curling her legs up beside her on the settee. 'He's stable, though, and asleep, Mum says.'

'Do you want me to come round?'

'No, but thanks.' It was sweet of him to offer, but she was going to bed once they'd finished the call. The emotion of the day had taken it out of her.

'I give far better sympathy hugs than Alex ever did.'

'You're so conceited, but yes, you do.'

'He was lucky to have you.'

'Who was?' Clara had lost the thread of the conversation.

'Alex.'

'Oh? Why so?'

'Because you really brighten up a place when you're around.'

Clara smiled. She loved how Tyler felt the need to cheer her up.

'He was lucky to have you because he's missing out on a great fry-up that you cook.'

'He can get his fancy bit to do that.'

'Yeah, but would she? Hmm, hmm?'

Clara smirked at that.

'Let's think.' Tyler paused. 'Actually, Cee, he was lucky to have you long enough until you realised that someone better needs you instead.'

'Smooth talker!'

'I know. Have you had anything to eat?'

'From lover vibe to parent vibe in so few words,' she teased.

'You're beginning to resemble a broom handle! I'm worried about you.'

'I've had tea and toast and about as much vending machine crap as I could handle.' She yawned. 'I need my bed. Thanks for cheering me up.'

They said goodnight, and she went around the house turning off the lights and checking the doors were locked. Then she took herself off to bed, falling asleep as soon as her head hit the pillow.

Lucy had just got off the phone when Aaron joined her in the kitchen.

'How is he?' he asked.

'Still waiting for a space on a ward. He might end up being

monitored on a trolley bed all night at this rate. But still, he's been seen and he's going to be okay.'

Aaron wrapped his arms around her.

'He seemed so vulnerable, and what if he has lasting damage with the bump to his head? You should see how big the gash is.'

'Oh, he'll be showing his scar off for years to come.' He kissed the top of her head. 'I love you.'

'I love you, too.'

'Let's go to bed.'

Lucy gave a faint smile. She *was* lucky to have found Aaron, that he had grown to love her and Ellie, too, and that Saskia accepted her without too much fuss.

Things hadn't always run smoothly because of their blended family, especially after the news of the baby, but, for the most, life was good. She couldn't wait to raise a child with Aaron, after he'd taken on Ellie as his own.

Seeing her dad in hospital had made her think about her future, too. Aaron kept asking Lucy to marry her, but she always put him off. Maybe it was the right time to make it more official.

But that wasn't a question for now.

CHAPTER THIRTY-NINE

With a heavy heart, Maria opened the door to an empty home. Delilah came rushing out of the kitchen to greet her, skidding across the hall in her haste. While she'd been at the hospital, Aaron had checked in on her twice. It had been one less thing to worry about, being unsure of how long it would be before she could leave.

'Hello, little girl.' Maria scooped her up into her arms and buried her head in her fur. 'I bet it's been a long day for you, too. Come on, let's get you settled again. It's just you and me tonight.'

It was nearly midnight. Jim had finally managed to get a bed on a ward, and she'd felt better knowing he could get some rest in a quieter area. She couldn't complain due to its nature, but it had been so noisy in the emergency department.

In the kitchen, she poured a large whisky and knocked it back in one go. She needed something to help her sleep. To stop the thoughts of life without Jim invading her thoughts. So far, things hadn't been as bad as she'd feared but, nonetheless, her mind kept running through the worst scenarios.

Keeping her mobile close, she scrolled through photos of him and the family. With Clara and Lucy; with Ellie and Saskia. Messing around with Aaron, Alex, and Tyler.

Jim was always sending her silly selfies when he was at work. When she thought about it, he was more the centre of the family than she was, so precious to everyone.

Her mind unable to settle, she made a slice of toast. But one bite in, she couldn't eat it, so went upstairs. Too weary to shower, she put on her pyjamas and slipped under the duvet. She didn't mind one iota that Delilah followed her and curled up on the landing outside her door. Maria knew she'd no doubt go back to her basket of her own accord.

She turned on her side and stared at the place where Jim should have been lying. It was then that it really hit her. What she would do to have him shove his cold feet on her calves right now.

She reached for his pillow and pulled it close to her chest, burying her face in it as more tears fell. How was she going to cope without him if something more serious were to happen?

No, she wouldn't think of that. Jim was fine – he *was* going to be fine. He had to be.

But, during the long evening, it had made her stop and think about life again, the busyness that running two businesses entailed.

Jim was fifty-one this year. They both had less years left to enjoy before age really caught up with them. This was a wake-up call, they had to slow down. They'd worked long hours for the past thirty years, they didn't need to do it all the time now. That's what they hired staff for.

Maria blamed herself for being a workaholic and control freak. She never came home after a day in the office and switched off until the next morning. She would inevitably be writing up details for a house she'd valued, ready to put it online first thing.

She'd be checking other websites to see what was coming up on the market, seeing if any of her properties needed a price drop to secure a sale.

She'd be thinking about budgets and forward planning. Only last week, she'd been wondering whether to open a second office in Hedworth and give Clara her own branch.

Had her obsessive ways rubbed off on Jim, causing him stress? Had he chosen to work during the evenings because she was? Had she forced her own nervous tension onto him unintentionally? She couldn't have, could she?

She must have dropped off because the next thing she knew, her phone was ringing. The time displayed read 5.30 a.m., but the caller's name was far more important to her.

'Jim, are you okay?' she asked immediately.

'Yes, I'm sorry. I just wanted to hear your voice. Did I wake you?'

'I didn't think I'd sleep as I felt so wired but I went out like a light. It's weird without you here, though.'

'I miss your snoring.'

'I do not snore!' His laughter made her smile. 'How are you feeling now? You were sleeping when I left you.'

'My head is hurting, and my wrist is aching, but I feel as if I've got over the worst.'

'You've barely been there long enough to know that.' She huffed: she couldn't help it.

'Believe me, the pain in my head was excruciating at the time. Now it feels like I've had a heavy night out.' There was a pause down the line before he spoke again. 'I was so scared, love. What would have happened if—'

'Stop.' She held up her hand, even though he couldn't see her. 'Everything is fine.'

'I know, but what if it wasn't? What if it *isn't?*'

'Well, it is, and I don't want to think of any alternative because it's all I did last night.'

'Everyone at work did an amazing job of looking after me until the ambulance came. I must do something to thank them.'

'We will, in time. You're not lifting a finger when you get home, and you're not going to work any day soon either, so don't make any plans. Paul will see to things for now.'

'Yes, Mum.' Jim chuckled.

It was so good to hear him joke that she had a lump in her throat. 'Now get some rest. I'll call you around nine to see what's happening today. Hopefully I can pick you up and bring you home soon.'

'I love you, Maria.'

'I love you, too.' The words choked her up after their recent argument. They were a tactile couple, showing affection but not always putting what they felt into words, so it meant everything to her to hear it now.

They ended the call, and she tried to sleep once more. But she was awake now, her mind restless. The house didn't seem like a home without Jim.

She sighed, pulling back the duvet and slipping her feet into her slippers. She might as well get up and do some cleaning. That would give her mind a rest.

CHAPTER FORTY

At nine a.m. as planned, Maria had called Jim. He was still being monitored, but there was a chance he might be released later that day. Once the consultant had done his rounds that afternoon, he'd find out more.

Having cleaned the house from top to bottom, there was nothing else for her to do. She decided to go into work, try and wrap up as much as she could.

Clara gave her a hug as soon as she stepped into the office, quickly followed by Lucy. Both of them had rung her that morning, so they knew she was coming in.

When Regan arrived shortly afterwards, the three Wilshaw women sat in Maria's office to discuss what was going to happen.

'I'll be taking the rest of this week off, and most probably the next, too,' Maria said. 'I need to give your dad my undivided attention to make sure he doesn't do too much. You know what he's like.' She rolled her eyes comically.

'Yes, we do,' Clara taunted. '*You* won't sit down for longer than ten minutes either.'

Their laughter was light, and Maria knew things had to

change, but for now she wanted to get through the next few days.

'Clara and I have been talking,' Lucy said, 'and if you need us to do anything more, even after Dad is well again, we're here for you.'

Maria smiled. 'What did I do to deserve you two?'

'I can do extra hours,' she volunteered. 'I'm sure Aaron will collect Ellie from school so I can stay until closing time?'

'Oh, would you? That would be a great help. I'll be at the end of the phone in case you need to speak to me.' She looked at Clara. 'And can you do the viewings? Run any valuations that you're not sure about past me?'

Clara nodded. 'I was going to suggest that.'

'Great. I'm sure you'll be fine. Regan will be here for the most part, and Sal is at hand. She said she'd come and work here, but I reckon you two can handle it on your own.'

For the next few hours, Maria cleared her desk of everything she could. She'd probably do some work from home, but she intended to do as little as possible. Her top priority was looking after Jim, getting him back to tip-top condition, and making sure he didn't do anything strenuous.

Finally, late afternoon, Jim called to say they were keeping him in for another night. Maria had remained upbeat, slapping on a brave face, especially when all the family descended on him, two by two, during visiting hours.

That night she hadn't been able to sleep, her insomnia returning. But the next morning, Jim called to say he was being discharged.

He was sitting on the end of his bed when she arrived and walked over as soon as he spotted her.

'I've missed you so much,' he said.

'You've only been here for two nights.'

'It felt like a lifetime!'

Maria pointed to her overnight case. 'I've brought you a change of clothes.'

'Never mind that.' He gave her a hospital bag with his possessions in it. 'Pop this inside it and get me out of here.'

She grinned. Jim sounded like his usual self, trying to make her laugh. She hoped it wasn't all an act because he wanted to go.

Jim said his thank yous as he left the ward and, half an hour later, they were home. After fussing Delilah who was so excited to see him, they went into the kitchen.

'Honestly, it feels like I've been away for weeks,' Jim said.

'I'm just glad to have you back. I'll mark your appointments on the calendar.' Jim was to have his stitches out in ten days. He also had to visit their local surgery for a check-up. 'And I'm making your favourite tea.'

'I've missed your cooking.'

She pushed him towards the settee in the conservatory. 'Sit,' she demanded.

He did as he was told, Delilah jumping up on his lap.

'Now, stay there. I don't want you moving.'

'I've been sitting around for ages!'

'I don't care. The paperwork from the hospital says you need to take it easy for the next fortnight. You're to do nothing that can tax your brain or give you eye strain. You're to rest completely, and no work for you, at all. Concussion can cause lots of symptoms that you want to avoid if you can.'

'I feel much better now I'm at home.'

'We'll take it day by day, but for now, you don't move. Do you hear me?'

'You're the boss.'

Maria took Jim's bag upstairs. In the bathroom, she pulled out the jumper he'd been wearing the day of the accident. There were patches and drops of blood all over it, and it had been cut along the inside of the arm and down the side, so they could get at him while causing minimum harm to his wrist.

She held it to her nose, breathing in the familiar scent of him, squeezing her eyes tight as thoughts of losing him flooded back. There would be more tests, but for now they'd had a reprieve.

While Jim would be off, she'd asked Paul to be in charge of the day-to-day operations. He was more than capable of running the business. She also knew Paul would look out for Jim, watch over him when he returned to work.

A few minutes later, Jim found her sitting in the bedroom gazing out of the window.

'You were told to stay put.' Her tone was stern but light.

'I wanted to see you.' He sat next to her, the dip in the bed pushing them closer together.

She reached up to touch his face. Despite her efforts, she couldn't stop the tears falling again.

'I thought I might lose you,' she said softly.

'I'm not going anywhere.' He drew her into his arms, kissing the top of her head.

'Things will need to change.'

'I know.'

'You're going to be a nightmare.'

He sniggered. 'I know.'

Carefully, they lay back on the bed, and Maria ran a finger along the cast on his wrist. 'Does it hurt?'

'It's aching, nothing more.'

'You'll have to put a bag over it when you shower.'

'That's going to be fun.' He sighed. 'I wish I knew if it was going to happen again, if there is anything I can do to stop it.'

'There is. You can rest, and then maybe slow down a little.'

Jim paused. 'You do realise we'll have to do that last date now?'

'I think that's the least we can do.' Maria smiled. 'If I'm forgiven for being so nasty to you the other day?'

'Well, you did seem rather fetching with a muddy arse.'

She slapped him playfully on the chest, then winced. 'Sorry.'

'I won't break.'

'You'd better not.'

Maria yawned, exhaustion getting the better of her. The past couple of days had knocked her for six, but Jim was home now. The danger was over, the recuperation just beginning. She wondered if there was anything she could do for him.

The most brilliant idea popped into her head. She'd need some help from Lucy and Clara. For now, though, all she wanted to do was sleep.

CHAPTER FORTY-ONE

Aaron had been fine with Lucy working a few extra hours but, today, he was finishing too late to change his plans. Lucy had collected Ellie from school. After a quick visit to see Jim, seeming surprisingly good after his accident, they hadn't been in long when the doorbell went. She wondered if Saskia had forgotten her key.

The woman standing on the path in front of the house wasn't anyone Lucy recognised, but she did look vaguely familiar. At a guess, she was a few years older than her, extremely thin with short brown hair, and dressed all in black. Her make-up was slight but didn't cover the darkness beneath her wary eyes.

'Is Aaron in?' the woman asked.

'He's at work at the moment.'

'Saskia?'

'May I help at all?' Lucy's curiosity was definitely piqued now.

'No, thanks. I'll try again later.'

'Shall I tell Aaron who called?'

'I'm Melissa, his ex-wife. I'll be in touch.'

The woman walked away, and Lucy didn't know what to do, afraid of what she would want, after all this time.

If she let her go, it would seem callous.

If she let her in, and Aaron got home to find her there and wasn't happy about it, she'd have made things worse.

By the time Lucy had run those thoughts through her mind, Melissa was out of hearing distance anyway. She closed the door and went to find her phone. At least she could give Aaron forewarning that life was about to get difficult.

'Did she say when she was coming back?' he said after a few expletives.

'No. Obviously I didn't recognise her, and then she was walking away before I had time to react after she told me her name.'

'You weren't going to invite her in?'

She paused. 'Did you want me to?'

'No!'

'Ah, that's good, because I hadn't a clue what to do.'

There was silence down the line. Lucy assumed Aaron was digesting her words, the clarity of what it could mean if Melissa was back on the scene. It was the first time Lucy had met her, and what about Saskia? How would she react after her mum had walked out and left her several years ago, and hadn't been in touch since?

'I'll be home soon,' Aaron said. 'We can talk about it then.'

'What do I do if she calls again?'

'Take her number, and I'll ring her.'

'Sorry, I should have asked for that earlier.'

'She walked off, didn't she?'

'Yes, but—'

'Don't worry. We'll take it as it comes. I can't say it hasn't given me a punch in the stomach, Luce. After all this time.'

'I'm worried about what it will do to Saskia. We don't want her to spiral out of control.'

'What do you mean by that?'

'Well, if her mum comes on the scene and then disappears again, she's going to be really upset.'

'It'll be no more than Ellie with her silly tantrums and strops.'

'Ellie is bound to have them, she's five years old.'

'Saskia has only just turned thirteen.'

'Well, she can be a bit lippy.'

'Oh, here we go. Let's pit your daughter against mine in the contest of popularity.'

'Aaron!' Lucy gasped. 'I wasn't doing that. I was merely saying.'

'Then don't. Never mind, I'll see you later.'

'Aaron?' She took the phone from her ear to see the call had been disconnected. She groaned. Melissa turning up unannounced had thrown a spanner in the works, that was for sure. Now she'd be on tenterhooks until she knew what she was after.

Saskia got in from school ten minutes before Aaron was due home. Lucy and Ellie were in the kitchen when she came in. She closed the door behind her with a sheepish look on her face.

'Don't shout,' she said. 'But my mum was waiting for me at the end of the road and—'

'I've already seen her. She came here first,' Lucy told her. 'What did she say to you?'

'She gave me a hug and said she was sorry for leaving me here with Dad. She says she wants to talk to me and him.'

Does she now?

Lucy tried to act as if she was cool with the idea. 'He'll be home soon, and I'm sure he'll want to talk to you as well.'

'I-I brought her back with me. She's in the hall.'

Lucy's eyes widened. 'You could have checked with me first,' she whispered.

'I don't have to ask you anything. You're not related to me.'

'I know but—'

'I said she could wait here until Dad gets home. I'm sure you won't mind. After all, it is his house.'

Tears pricked Lucy's eyes as Saskia glared at her coldly. It cut her to the core. Despite not seeing her mum in years, the teenager had sided with her already. There were going to be fireworks this evening. And she had Ellie to think about, always her top priority.

'You can please yourself,' she replied. 'As soon as your dad gets home, I'll take Ellie out. You can have the *house* to yourself this evening, play happy families all you like.'

'Great!'

'Great!' Lucy parroted. She turned away from Saskia before her tears fell. She wasn't sure if it was pregnancy hormones or general tears of upset that were threatening to flow. How had the day turned out so bad? And how was it going to end? Taking Ellie out was only safeguarding herself from the hurt until she returned.

But, with Aaron having a go at her about Ellie, and now Saskia turning up with Melissa and inviting her in, she only hoped she could hold it together so that it didn't upset her own daughter too much.

One thing was certain. Life wasn't going to be the same for a long time if Melissa was planning to stick around. Lucy prayed it was a flying visit to see Saskia that she wanted, and nothing of her old life back. She couldn't bear it if she tried to split their family up, not when everything had been going so well.

CHAPTER FORTY-TWO

Lucy was waiting at the door when Aaron came home. She'd messaged him to tell him what to expect. His demeanour was that of a man up for a battle, his face full of anguish at what was to come.

'Is she still here?' he asked, stepping into the hall.

Lucy nodded. 'She's in the front room with Saskia.'

He frowned. 'Why do you have your coat on?'

'Because I'm not staying why she's in there.' She hadn't meant it to come out as a whine. '*You* have to talk to her, I don't.'

He took her hand. 'I didn't mean to snap at you earlier.'

Lucy lowered her voice, the tension in it clear. 'I'll take Ellie to see my mum and dad for an hour.'

'I don't want Melissa causing an atmosphere.' Aaron reached for her arm. 'If she wants to talk to me, she can do it somewhere else.'

'Just get her to leave. It hasn't been pleasant feeling like a guest in my own home.'

'It used to be my home.'

They turned to see Melissa standing in the doorway,

Saskia behind her. Ellie had come to stand in the kitchen doorway.

'Ellie, why don't you show Saskia your new book?' Lucy suggested. 'I'm sure I saw it in your bedroom.' Ellie went to fetch it, and Lucy nodded towards the stairs, hoping Saskia would follow.

But Saskia shook her head.

Aaron rounded on Melissa.

'You have some nerve, coming here after so long.'

'I wanted to see her, Dad,' Saskia said.

'You stay out of this,' he snapped. 'You had *no* right to invite her in.'

'She has every right,' Melissa cried. 'She's my daughter.'

'How convenient of you to remember that after all these years.'

'I was ill. But I'm better now.'

'Oh, I bet you are.' Aaron grabbed her arm. 'I don't know what your game is, but you're not welcome in this house. I want you to leave.'

'Dad, stop!' Saskia protested, trying to pull him away.

'Leave this with me, Saskia.' Aaron opened the front door and marched outside with Melissa.

Saskia followed behind. 'Dad, you can't throw her out. She's only just got here! Dad!'

'Get inside, Saskia.'

'No, I—'

'I said get inside!'

Lucy's heart thundered as she watched from the step. Saskia's bottom lip trembled, but she turned and pushed past her.

'Saskia.' Lucy reached for her.

'Go away, I hate you. This is all your fault.'

'See what you've done?' Aaron snarled at Melissa. 'But I guess that was your intention anyway.'

'I want to see my daughter, and you can't stop me.'

'I can, and I will.'

'She wants to see me!'

'Then I suggest you give me the details of where you're staying, and we can talk this through another day.'

'On your terms, as usual.'

Lucy could see Aaron was losing his temper. Mostly, he chose not to engage in an argument with her. He'd said many times that he'd rowed enough with Melissa to last him a lifetime.

Melissa pulled her arm away from his grip.

Lucy didn't want this to go on longer than necessary. 'You might as well talk now.' She turned back to Saskia, who was sitting at the bottom of the stairs. 'Will you go and sit with Ellie, please?'

Saskia's eyes widened, as if she wasn't sure what to do.

'It's okay,' Aaron said. 'We won't be long.'

Saskia dashed upstairs, and Melissa stepped inside again. Lucy gave Aaron's arm a quick squeeze before they followed her into the living room. She motioned towards the table. Melissa sat across from them.

'Why now, after all this time?' Aaron spoke first.

'I wanted to see Saskia,' Melissa said.

'And now what, after you've caused chaos in the little time you've been back in Somerley?'

'I'd like to be in her life.' She raised a hand as Aaron was about to speak. 'From a distance, that's all. I won't take her away from you. I just want to see her, catch up on what I've missed.'

'And whose fault was that? You walked out, choosing alcohol over us. Saskia needed you. *I* needed you.'

Lucy bristled, trying to keep her emotions in check.

'Looks like you managed quite well on your own,' Melissa spat. 'Oh, wait, you're not on your own.'

'I was back then. And don't you dare bring Lucy into this. She's worth ten of you.'

'I think you two should calm down and lower your voices.' Lucy found herself playing mediator again. 'This is about Saskia really, not your past relationship.'

'Our marriage.' Melissa emphasised the word.

'If you could call it that,' Aaron muttered.

A silence dropped on the room, although the pressure seemed to have eased.

'I'm sorry,' Melissa said. 'I wish things could have been different, but at least it's under control now.'

'I don't want you getting to know her and then disappearing again,' Aaron replied. 'It will break her, and we'll have to then pick up the pieces. She's more fragile than ever at this age.'

'I'm moving to Australia.'

Lucy's eyes widened: she hadn't been expecting that. It seemed neither had Aaron as he didn't know what to say.

'I'm getting married there in autumn,' Melissa continued. 'Steve's from Perth. And no, he's not a recovering alcoholic. He keeps me on the straight and narrow. He taught me what life could be like without a drink.'

'I could have done that, if you'd let me.'

Lucy wanted to reach across and give his hand a squeeze. Although she was trying not to take anything personally, she could feel the hurt from his words. Aaron had moved on, and yet he still felt betrayed.

'No, you couldn't,' Melissa said. 'You are a sweet and caring person, and I hurt you too much. I got worse for a few years when I left but then I started going to a great AA group, made some friends who understood what I was going through, who could help when it was getting too rough for me. And then I met Steve, on a night out.'

'Do you have any children?'

'After I let Saskia down?' She shook her head. 'I couldn't. But I would like to see her, even if it's only a few times while I'm here. Perhaps then we could keep in touch online.' She looked at Lucy pointedly. 'I don't want to step back in and be Mum.'

'You'd have a hard job. Saskia adores Lucy.'

'He really does love you.' Melissa smiled at her.

Lucy's skin reddened.

'Which is why I don't want you spoiling anything,' Aaron reiterated.

'I haven't come to cause trouble. I just want to explain to Saskia why I left, and to say I'm sorry. And wish her well, to be honest. She's turned into a beautiful young girl.'

'No thanks to you.'

'Oh, I think you'll find there is. I walked away because I knew I'd ruin her life the longer I stayed.'

Aaron paused. 'Yes, I think you're right.'

'So you'll let me see her? I could take her for coffee, or something to eat after school.'

'I don't think I'd be able to stop you. She has your stubborn streak, more's the pity.' Aaron was half smiling.

'Thank you.'

Lucy's shoulders dropped at last, feeling all the tension leaving the room. If she was true to her word, Melissa didn't seem to be a threat to them, to her family, thank goodness. Perhaps things would go back to normal once she and Saskia had met, and Melissa had gone to Australia.

CHAPTER FORTY-THREE

It had been four days since Jim's accident, and it was nearly the weekend. Maria had enjoyed spending time with him, surprised how easy it was to switch off from work.

After his first full day back at home, they'd agreed for now that they would work for one hour each morning, speaking to Paul and Clara to check on what was happening. Once they'd done that, they switched off, knowing everything was working okay without them.

It had been fun taking Jim's mobile phone and iPad away from him, with the promise he could use them again next week, once he was fully rested. And actually, as she had done the same, it had given them both a good break, and time to relax.

Jim had slept a lot during that first day, mostly dozing on the settee. Maria loved any chance to mother him, making sure he didn't exert himself. Clara had popped in yesterday with Tyler, and Lucy had brought Ellie that afternoon. Sal was coming round later that evening. It was lovely to see everyone.

Now, she and Jim were sitting at the kitchen table,

halfway through a jigsaw puzzle she'd bought him from the charity shop on the high street. She'd passed the window last week and spotted it, the photo of an old tractor on a farm catching her eye, so she'd nipped in to buy it, glad to see it still there.

Jim had laughed when he'd seen it, but, for the past two afternoons, they'd shared pots of tea and good conversation as they pieced the image together.

'You're wandering away from me again,' Jim said, waving a hand in front of her face.

'What? Oh, sorry, I was miles away.'

'Which of the girls were you thinking about this time?'

She smiled: she couldn't help it. She'd never be able to hide anything from him.

'Both.'

'Why doesn't that surprise me?'

She slapped his hand playfully before leaning on her elbow. It had been awful to receive a call from Clara yesterday to say the owners of the cottage she was going to buy had decided not to sell after all. Maria had been about to console her, but it seemed she was staying upbeat, already on the case trying to find something else. In the meantime, she was going to lodge with Tyler.

'I wish Clara would come and stay with us,' she said.

'She'll have fun with him rather than us fuddy-duddies.'

'What are you insinuating?' Maria feigned hurt.

'It would probably feel like failing coming back home to live with us, even temporarily.'

'I suppose.'

'She'll miss all your mollycoddling, though.'

Maria tutted.

'I'm glad Clara *is* staying with Tyler.' Jim's face was deadpan. 'I don't think I could bear two women in the house again.'

'You'll be sleeping outside in the shed, if you're not careful.'

'What about Lucy? You haven't mentioned her for over half an hour.'

Maria's shoulders dropped. 'Am I that bad?'

'You worry too much.'

'I can't help myself, can I?'

'No, but I'm not sure I'd want you any other way.' Jim got up and went over to the larder.

She heard him moving things around and strained her neck to see. 'What are you doing in there?'

He came back holding a purple jewellery box. He handed it to her, sitting down again.

'This is the gift I had for you when we went to Sapphire Lake.'

'Oh, Jim, I don't deserve anything after—'

'Open it.'

Inside was a silver bangle with a flattened oval area, embedded with three sapphire stones in a row. Maria gasped. It was so understated, delicate. It was so... her.

'Do you like it?' Jim's voice held a note of anticipation, as if he was desperate to please her.

'I don't know what to say, Mr Wilshaw. Apart from thank you, of course.' She took the bangle out of the box and pushed it onto her wrist. 'It's beautiful.'

'It's delicate, just like you. Now, about this last date. Shall we keep it a secret from the girls that you know what it is?'

Jim had told Lucy to book lunch for the following weekend. Maria was going to open the envelope tomorrow, even though she knew what was inside it.

'Yes, I think that's a good idea.'

'Don't wear the bracelet until then.'

'I won't.' She paused. 'I'll just practise my surprise face.'

CHAPTER FORTY-FOUR

It was Saturday evening, and after the week she'd had worrying about her dad, Clara was on a rare night out with a friend. She'd bumped into Megan in Somerley Stores when she'd fetched her lunch earlier in the week, and she'd invited her to join her and a few others for a drink.

Megan was two years younger than Clara and hadn't settled down with anyone yet. Clara wondered if it was because Megan's parents were divorced, her mother leaving her father after being a victim of domestic abuse. Perhaps she didn't trust men to stick around, so she didn't put much pressure on herself to get involved with one who might not treat her well enough.

Or maybe it was Clara who was old-fashioned and not moving with the times? Her parents were still in love after all those years together. They were the proverbial two peas in a pod, and it was what Clara had hoped she'd have with Alex.

Who was right, though? Clara, who had married and was now looking at divorce? Or Megan without a thought in her head that she wanted to settle down and start a family? Each to their own, she pondered.

They'd caught a taxi into Hedworth and were now in their third pub. For some reason, Clara wasn't in the mood for drinking. Already, she felt herself slipping into a bout of self-pity. There were couples everywhere. It reminded her of what she hadn't got anymore, in spite of being over Alex's departure.

In the fourth bar, which she couldn't remember the name of because they all seemed similar, a man waved to get her attention. It was someone she'd known from school.

'Hi, Clara!'

'Phil! Hi, how are you?'

'I'm good, thanks. You?'

'Not so bad.'

'On your own?'

'Out with friends.'

'Have you left the old man at home?'

Clara's heart plummeted. She supposed she'd better get used to telling people who hadn't heard about her marriage breaking down. It still stung, though.

'We've separated.'

'Oh!' He smiled, then faltered. 'I mean, oh, sorry. That's sad to hear.'

'Not for me. I found out he'd been having an affair.'

'That's terrible, the creep.'

'I know. How about you?'

'Single.' He pointed to the bar. 'Can I get you a drink? I'm out with some guys you'll know. Want to come and say hello?'

'Yes, thanks. I'll have a Bacardi and Coke, please.' She smiled, noting how nice-looking he was up close. His hair was dark and wavy, with a fringe that kept flopping over his deep-set blue eyes. He sported a neat goatee beard and smelled divine. His T-shirt was on the verge of being tight enough to show off a workout-with-weights physique.

Had he been like that at school, or was it the alcohol that was playing tricks with her eyes?

An hour passed, and Clara was still with Phil and his friends, of which she knew all but one. They'd had a laugh reminiscing about old times. None of them knew Alex, so it had been good not to hear his name, making her forget her woes for a while.

Megan and her friends had left for the next pub. Clara had promised to catch her up, seeing a way she could slope off early rather than going on to a club. By midnight, she was ready for home. She stifled a yawn.

'I'm going to head off now,' she said to Phil.

'Let me walk you to the taxi rank.'

'It's no problem. It's only the next street.'

'Maybe, but I'd prefer to see you are safe.' He reached for her hand.

'Well, if you insist.'

They weaved through the crowd and into the street.

'Wow, I hadn't realised how hot it was in there,' Phil said, wiping at his brow. 'I'm melting.'

'Me, too. I bet I stink.'

'You smell amazing.' Phil gazed at her. 'Gorgeous, in fact, just like you.'

She laughed, then realised he was being serious. And just like that, their lips met, and they kissed in the middle of the pavement as if there was no one else around.

'Do you want to share a taxi?' he asked. 'We can drop you off first, if you prefer?'

'Yeah, let's do that.'

They clambered in the back seat of the car. Clara told the driver her address, and before he had moved away, she and Phil were kissing again.

It felt so good to be in a man's arms. Phil was gentle with her, pressing her to him, running his hands through her hair.

Murmuring into her ear. She couldn't help but giggle at one point, and he laughed once they drew apart.

'Well, this night ended up a little different than I'd expected,' he said. 'Do you fancy meeting up again one night?'

Clara wasn't quite sure about that but, for once in her life, she was going to take a risk. 'You could always come in for a coffee once we get to mine?'

The smile he gave her was worth her heart skipping a beat at her courage. He nodded, and they sat together, lips apart, for the rest of the journey.

Once at her home, she led him into the kitchen.

'Coffee?' She held up the kettle, putting off the moment. Now she was back, she wasn't sure whether she was doing the right thing.

'Please.' He pointed to the hallway. 'What's with all the boxes?'

'The house is sold, and I'm moving out soon. I was supposed to be buying a cottage, but the sale fell through this week, so I have to stay with a friend for a couple of months while I find something else. I don't want to stop my sale from happening.'

In the kitchen, they chatted some more before moving into the living room.

'Great place you have here,' he said, glancing around. 'Have you been here long?'

'Ever since we... about six years.' Clara sat down on the settee quickly before she started getting sentimental again. Now that she was home, something had definitely changed. This clearly wasn't the good idea it had seemed.

Phil came to sit next to her and, seconds later, almost pounced on her in his will to get close again.

'Sorry.' He grinned. 'Nerves. Just a bit keen. I've always liked you from afar.'

She wondered if it was a compliment that he'd almost bashed her teeth out with his own, but she laughed with him.

'And I'm not long out of a relationship, too.'

Ah, now she understood. Was she *his* idea of getting over an ex, like he was hers? Stuff it, she thought. It would do them both the world of good.

They kissed so long that the experience itself almost had her losing her breath with giddiness. But twenty minutes later, they were still on the sofa, hands all over each other, clothes dishevelled, yet neither of them keen to move things on.

Eventually, they broke apart.

'It's not going to happen, is it?' he said, a gentle smile playing on his lips as he tucked his shirt back into his jeans.

'I don't think it is.' She pulled the straps up on her top. 'I'm sorry, it's too soon.'

'We've known each other for years,' he teased.

'I mean too soon after my... my break-up. I'm not ready for this.'

'Neither am I, to be honest. I'll call a cab.'

'There's a spare room you can use, if you like? I could drive you home in the morning.'

He shook his head. 'Perhaps another time?'

She picked up the coffee mugs to avoid his eye. She groaned inwardly while she rinsed them out, anything to stop going back into him.

Did she think by sleeping with someone else that she would forget Alex? That it would be easier to move on? Instead, she'd made a fool of herself, and she'd probably annoyed Phil, too.

Inevitably, there was an agonising wait for a taxi and, twenty-five minutes later, she had never been so thrilled to say goodbye to someone once it arrived.

This time, Phil kissed her on the cheek. It wasn't chaste, just a friendly goodbye.

'See you again soon?' he asked.

She nodded, but she didn't get her phone out to share her number with him. Neither did he ask for it. Perhaps in the morning, he'd realise how close they'd come to making a mistake, too.

After closing the door, she raced upstairs and threw herself onto the bed.

'Idiot!' she shouted, and then she laughed at the absurdity of the evening. Wait until she told Lucy and Tyler about her escapades. A one-night stand that hadn't even been for one night.

She turned over and drew her knees close to her chest. The only company she needed right now was her own.

CHAPTER FORTY-FIVE

Dear Mum

It's the final date, number five!

On Sunday, you're going to have lunch with the family. But don't worry, this time you won't have to cook! Get your glad rags on. We're taking you to The Moorland Hotel. Not so much of a nostalgic date, but a celebration of the past and a look towards the future.

After all, Mum, you taught us that family is everything, and we love ours so much.

'Now this sounds right up my street.' Maria clapped in glee. 'Lunch brought to me on a plate.'

'What else did you expect it to be brought to you on?' Jim quipped.

'Oh, ha ha.' She flicked the tea towel at him. 'I mean that I don't have to buy, prepare, and serve.'

'I thought you enjoyed doing that?'

'I do, I really do. But it's still such a treat when we go out for lunch, too.'

'We should do it more often then, and maybe just the two of us.'

'I would love that.'

They smiled at each other. It was becoming quite cheesy at times, but since the accident, it was almost as if they didn't want to spend time apart. They'd have their arguments again soon, and of course they were still bickering, but since the trip to the emergency department, things had been much calmer between them.

The days since Jim had got back had been almost like getting to know each other again. They'd taken a few short walks and made an effort not to talk about work too much. And she was really enjoying not being glued to her phone. It was like being in the nineties again, living life in the here and now. Present at all times, peaceful, good for the soul.

Jim checked his watch. 'Better get a move on. Sal will be here soon, once she's collected Tyler. She's offered to give us a lift so we can both celebrate.'

'I can drive.' Maria shook her head. 'I don't mind.'

'It's all arranged.'

Maria smiled. Jim was wearing a short-sleeved shirt, the only smart thing he could get the cast on his wrist through, and a tie she'd bought him many moons ago. Jim wasn't a tie man, so she appreciated his effort, especially having to fasten it for him.

Maria had bought a floral dress and felt like a million dollars. They were probably going to be overdressed, but she didn't care. This was a special occasion. She had news, too. Her plan was about to be revealed.

Gently, she ran a finger over the gash to the side of Jim's head. He was due to have his stitches out later that week, but for now, it remained uncovered, getting air to it. Luckily, it was slightly less prominent and angry looking.

'My poor man,' she said.

'Hey. That's my gangsta rapper scar,' he told her, laughing as she giggled.

As usual, the venue was jovial and the food delicious. The family had been coming to dine at The Moorland Hotel for quite some years: for birthdays and anniversaries, when Clara graduated from university and Lucy had become a mum. When Maria completed the qualifications she needed to go it alone as an estate agent; for when Clara and Lucy had come to work in the business, too.

Recently, it had been refurbished and a large orangery built on the back that took in the view of Sapphire Lake. They were seated at a table by the doors, the weather warm enough to have them open so they could enjoy the fresh air wafting in.

While Saskia and Ellie went to the play area, they continued to chat.

'Are you glad you did the final date, Mum?' Lucy asked.

'I am, and thank you so much for all your effort. It really was perfect.'

'Who knew when me and Lucy thought of the idea, that I'd be separated from Alex by the time you finished them?' Clara raised her glass in a toast. 'Good riddance, I say!'

No one noticed Maria and Jim exchanging surreptitious glances, trying hard not to smirk and give the game away.

'Hear, hear!' Tyler chanted.

Everyone laughed.

'Don't you miss Alex a teeny bit?' Lucy teased.

'I'm more surprised as to how much I *don't* miss him. You have to admit, the atmosphere is a tad lighter today without him here.'

They all nodded in agreement, and Clara raised her glass again. 'Here's to me finding a new home! I'm sad to lose the cottage, but onwards and upwards.'

'Here's to new beginnings all round,' Tyler added.

Maria glanced at Lucy. Her smile was there but weak. It had been a tough few days for her and Aaron. Saskia had met Melissa, and the two of them had been out to dinner. It seemed to go well, but when Melissa left, promising to keep in touch with Saskia online, Saskia had withdrawn from the family.

Lucy was worried about the long-term impact on Saskia, seeing her mum after so long only for her to leave soon after. So far, there had been no tantrums. But Saskia had been really quiet over lunch, not her usual bubbly self.

Maria gave her eldest daughter a smile, glad to see it returned. But she could see the strain behind it. Hopefully, things would blow over soon.

Jim cleared his throat loudly. 'I have an announcement to make.' He signalled. 'Actually, it's more of a confession.' He took Maria's hand in his own. 'It was my idea to do the dates.'

'I knew it,' Maria cried, hoping she wouldn't blush as she lied.

'You did?' Jim's eyes widened. Only she could see that extra twinkle in them.

'Well, I had an idea. There were so many memories and anecdotes that you shared with me—'

'Most that you had forgotten about,' he teased.

'—that I *knew* it had to have been orchestrated by you.' Maria turned her attention first to Clara, and then Lucy.

'He told us to say it was from us because he didn't think you'd go on them!' Clara acknowledged.

'Jim!' Maria pretended to be distressed, while inside cringing at the way she had stropped off when she'd fallen in the mud. 'How could you think that?'

'You have to admit that you didn't like them all.'

'It was the thought that counted.' She smiled at her daughters. 'Thank you for helping your dad to set them all up. And now... I have a confession, too.'

'Uh-oh,' Sal cried. 'What have you been up to?'

Maria pulled five envelopes from her bag and passed them to Jim. 'I have some dates of my own set up for us, starting from next weekend.'

'So this is what you've all been planning?' Jim tapped the side of his nose twice. 'You weren't quite as discreet as I was.'

Maria slapped his arm playfully. 'I did have help from your favourite daughters.'

Jim picked up an envelope. 'I suppose I can't open any of them, to see what's in store?'

'Not until tomorrow,' Maria replied.

'Spoilsport.'

'Yeah, spoilsport,' Tyler joined in. 'We want to see what it is, too.'

To chants of "open it, open it," Maria gave in before the whole restaurant was looking at them.

'Okay, okay! Mind you, after your dishonesty about the first lot, you're lucky I'm going with you at all.'

Jim kissed Maria gently on the nose. 'I don't suppose one of them is roller skating?'

CHAPTER FORTY-SIX

Maria glanced out of the kitchen window, hoping the rain would stop soon. For her, seaside towns were better in sunny weather, and this was April. The least it could do was stay dry.

Jim finished his toast. 'Are you going to buy a *Kiss Me Quick* hat?'

'For you or me?' Maria teased. 'Come on, we don't want to get caught in too much traffic.'

'It should take an hour, tops. It's a pity we can't plan the weather, too. It's going to be horrendous on the seafront if it doesn't calm down before we get there.'

'It'll be fine. You'll see.'

Maria set the alarm, shouting her goodbyes to Delilah who would probably be glad she had the house to herself for a few hours. They'd thought about taking her with them but had decided against it. Besides, Maria swore she could see Delilah smiling at the thought of being left alone, peace at last.

'Blackpool was our first weekend away together, wasn't it?'

Maria said, a giggle escaping her as she thought about it. 'Well, us and four others.'

'And what a weekend, apart from the poxy B and B.'

'It was a bit disgusting.'

'I remember everyone crying with laughter over breakfast before we went home. Either that, or we'd have cried real tears of sorrow.'

'We couldn't get away quick enough. *Fawlty Towers* had nothing on it.'

'Paul kept shouting for Manuel.' Jim laughed. 'The landlady hadn't been very amused.'

'Serves her right. Everything about the place was rank. I'm surprised we didn't come home with nits or bed bugs or something just as nasty.' Maria gasped, remembering something. 'You were so drunk on Saturday night that I caught you peeing out of the window.'

Jim's laughter became raucous. 'I'd forgotten that! I'm surprised I got it all out.'

'I don't think you did, to be fair. When you got up in the morning, you said it had been raining in the room. Until I told you not to put your hand in it!'

'I was so hungover I didn't care.' Jim smirked. 'What was the nightclub we ended up in?'

'The Flagship.'

'That's the one. It was more of a working men's club, from what I can remember. It had everything but bingo.'

'We spent most of Sunday there after Saturday night.'

'Those were the days when no matter how much you drank, you didn't really suffer from a hangover.'

'It was such a laugh.' Maria changed lanes to get past a lorry up ahead.

'I remember you and Diane nipping off to the shops and coming back with clothes from the sale,' Jim recalled.

'It was a bank holiday!' she objected. 'We had to do something with our time while you were in the pub.'

They continued their conversation, reminiscing about the weekend and, in no time at all, they were almost at their destination.

'There's the sea!' Maria cried.

'I saw it ages ago,' Jim replied. 'I let you see it first.'

'Fibber.' She pointed ahead. 'There's a car park somewhere here – I Googled it before I started out. I'm sure there'll be plenty of spaces today.'

The rain had stopped, but the wind hadn't died down at all. They got out of their car, almost blown away with the force of it. Jim reached for her hand, and they pushed towards the sea front. It wasn't cold, but it took their breath away, and they could barely hear each other speak.

Maria patted Jim on the arm as they rushed past two amusement arcades and a candy floss stand. She pointed towards a café up ahead.

'Let's grab a coffee in there!' she yelled. 'We can have a hot drink and order some food to go.'

'You're sure you want to venture nearer the sea?'

'I'm sure!'

'We can sit in one of the shelters. It will be... fun.'

'It'll be wet.'

Inside the café, they found a table and gave the waitress their order. Maria rummaged in her bag and then handed him an envelope.

'What's this?' he asked.

'I rooted out some photos of the Blackpool weekend.'

Jim raised his eyebrows. 'Did I have lots of hair?'

'You did.'

The first one was with the six friends, all standing up with their arms in the air. In front of them was a table full of bottles and empty glasses.

'Blimey, we could get through some booze in those days.' He laughed. 'Was that really one night?'

'Yes, I remember the hangover very well.' She pointed to the man at the end of the photo. 'I miss him.'

Adam Craddock had died in a car accident five years after the photo had been taken. He'd been their best man, and it was only now that they could look at images of him without getting upset.

Adam was the brother they both never had. He'd taken Maria under his wing like a sister when she and Jim got together. Then he met Diane, Paul fell in love with Sonia, and the Somerley Six had been created.

It had torn a hole in the group on hearing of his death. They'd kept in touch with Diane for a few months afterwards, but eventually she'd moved away. Now it was the four of them who met up, down to Paul working for Jim.

'I miss him, too.' Jim sighed. 'He was a big part of our lives.'

'I think he changed the course of it in a way.'

'What do you mean?'

'You and he had plans to travel. That all stopped when he died.'

'It was just talk.' Jim popped the photos in the envelope.

'I don't believe that. You always wanted to see the world.'

'I did, but then I bought a house with a beautiful young woman. I never wanted to leave that – well, the feeling of home. I don't feel I've missed out by staying put.'

'I think I have something in my eye.' Maria wiped at her tears welling up.

Jim leaned across the table and kissed her. 'You're home to me, Maria. Wherever you are is good enough for me.'

'Stop it, you big mush!'

They drank their coffee and then took their takeaway food out with them, braving the elements once more.

'It's like being in a wind tunnel,' Maria shouted.

'Let's make a run for it.' Jim took her hand again. 'Three, two, one, go!'

They raced across the road, mindful of the traffic. Maria couldn't get her breath for laughing so much.

When they arrived at the first shelter, there were too many people inside, having the same idea as them. Another one farther along was home to two pigeons, so they sat down to eat.

'I miss fish and chips not being wrapped in newspaper, and the print coming off all over your hands.' Maria opened her biodegradable cardboard box. She sniffed as the vinegar wafted under her nose, sighing with content. 'Bliss.'

Jim popped a chip in his mouth then blew out air. 'Hot, hot, hot.'

''Course they are, you numpty. They're delicious, though. I thought they'd be too greasy.'

'I can't remember the last time we called at the chippy. We should treat the grandkids more often to these.'

'They'd probably prefer a Nando's or a Maccy Ds.'

'Young 'uns.' Jim rolled his eyes. 'They don't know they're born.'

'Mr Wilshaw, you sound like a grumpy old man,' Maria chided.

'Better than sounding like you. The only reason we never have fish and chips is because you're on a permanent diet, and I've told you over and over that you're lovely as you are.'

She was about to snap at him – she wasn't always on a diet. Never at the weekend as they always began on a Monday. But he was right. Why couldn't she eat what she wanted without feeling guilty, worrying about where the pounds might pile on? She should rip up the diet sheets forever.

After they'd eaten their meal, they sat chatting for ages, looking out to sea. The waves were high, crashing into one another. Dark clouds were looming, and Maria spotted them first.

She pointed upwards. 'I think we'd better make a move if we're to have a stroll along the prom.'

Jim nodded. They wrapped up their rubbish and popped it into the bin.

As they passed the rows of amusement arcades and shops selling all kinds of beach paraphernalia, Maria pulled Jim into a shop selling rock and grabbed several sticks in different flavours and colours. She spied a Kiss Me Quick hat and placed it on Jim's head, mindful of his wound. Then she moved closer.

'Have to do what the hat says.'

CHAPTER FORTY-SEVEN

Clara gave a dramatic sigh as she picked up yet another box in her arms. Tyler had given up his Sunday to help her with the removal of her belongings.

'Not many more to go,' she cried cheerily when she saw him rolling his eyes.

'How many pairs of shoes do you have?' Tyler picked up a clearly labelled box and popped it into the van they'd hired for the day. 'Seriously, this must be the fifth lot I've carried.'

'A woman can never have too many!'

'You can only wear one pair at a time.' Tyler reached for another box, labelled kitchen. 'And mugs. You have a *lot* of mugs.'

'I like collecting them.'

'You like collecting tat.'

Clara looked on sheepishly. 'Even I have to admit I have a bit of a problem.'

'You're not kidding. I don't know where they'll all go in the new place.'

'I suppose it will give me the chance to have a good clear out.'

'Weren't you supposed to do that *before* you moved?'

'I did.' Clara chuckled at the expression on Tyler's face. 'At least it's mostly going into storage until I find a new home.'

'Thank goodness. We wouldn't be able to move around with it in my flat.'

She nudged him with her elbow, and he almost lost his footing.

'Careful of the merchandise,' he chastised. 'I work hard to get this six-pack.'

'More like a two-pack. Actually, not even that.' Clara roared with laughter. 'Come on, less chatter or else we'll be here until midnight. And I can hear a takeaway calling us.'

'You drive a hard bargain, Miss Clara.'

'Less gassing and more action!'

'Yes, boss!' Tyler saluted her.

Two hours later, everything Clara wanted to take was packed in the van. There were a few items that a local charity were coming to clear, and some that Alex was going to collect.

It was weird seeing the house empty as she took one more look around. Bare floors and carpets, no curtains and knick-knacks. Memories flooded back with each room she entered.

Sharing a bath and always being relegated to the tap end until they'd refitted the bathroom and she'd chosen taps in the middle of the new one.

A surprise breakfast in bed, and then spoiling the moment because she spilled coffee everywhere.

In summer, sitting out in the garden until the sun went down, drinking wine with music playing low. Hot chocolate in winter, wrapped up in coats, hats and gloves when it was snowing.

Clara couldn't help but smile. There had been some really good times, and yet she didn't feel sad that her relationship with Alex was over. She didn't *feel* anything for him, which was a good sign moving forward.

Laurence Place was somewhere she used to live now. She was going to be in another home soon, leaving the past behind. Starting again with fresh hopes and dreams for the future.

Tyler found her in the kitchen, staring out of the window.

'You'll be much better once you've closed the door on the past – literally,' he said.

'I'm not sad. I'm excited.'

'But first you have to live with me!' Tyler grimaced. 'I might be too much of a clean-freak for you.'

'Are you saying I'm a slob?' She growled at him. 'You're quite obsessive about cleaning, though.'

'I am not!' Tyler was indignant for all of a few seconds before nodding profusely. 'Actually, I am. It drives me mad at times, to be honest.'

'So maybe I can teach you some of my bad habits.'

'Do you have many?'

'I don't have any, I'll have you know! But I can create some, especially for you.'

They went out to the van, and Clara took one last glance behind. It was going to be weird not coming back. But equally, it was going to be good moving on.

CHAPTER FORTY-EIGHT

Pleased to be back in the swing of getting out and about again, Maria was almost late for her first viewing of the morning. She arrived just as Vicky and Luke Westleigh were getting out of their car. Being late made her all of a fluster. She grabbed her bag, house file and keys, and rushed over to them.

'Good morning,' she greeted in a singsong voice. 'I see you've brought wonderful weather with you. All the better for spotting the sunny parts of the garden. Come on in, I think you'll love this property.'

The couple were older than Maria, in their late fifties, perhaps. The house they were moving from was on their books, too, and was a splendid four-bedroom detached with a large garden. Vicky and Luke wanted something a little smaller now that their children had left home.

'I knew it would have a wonderful feel to it,' Vicky exclaimed the minute she set foot inside the property. She turned to Maria, her skin flushed. 'I know you're not supposed to be enthusiastic about something you might want to make an offer on, but really, nowadays, when you've scoured photos online, the only thing left is whether it feels like a home.'

'I know exactly what you mean,' Maria replied. 'I've felt all sorts of vibes from properties I've visited. This one has been loved. It's over a hundred years old and yet it's only had two previous owners. It was obviously a wonderful place to raise a family.'

'Yes, we had that, too.' Vicky's eyes brimmed with tears. 'We've done all we can for our boys to start them off well.'

'Thank goodness.' Luke chuckled. 'They bled us dry over the years.'

'They still do.' Vicky nudged him playfully. 'Of course, we get to see them and our grandchildren often, but we don't need so many rooms now, and the garden is a part-time job every week for Luke. I can't wait to get started on a small project for summer.'

'You're supposed to be taking it easy,' Luke protested.

'I'm recovering from cancer,' Vicky explained.

'Oh.' Maria's shoulders drooped momentarily, but then she stood upright again and smiled. 'I hope you continue to have good health.'

'Thanks. I've fought it three times already. The damn thing won't leave me alone, but I've had a clean bill of health for a year now. Near on destroyed me at times, though. Some of the treatments were brutal.' She turned to Luke. 'But I got through it with the love of a good man and a family who rallied around me.'

Maria didn't know what to say, thoughts of losing Jim after his accident rushing to her mind. She swallowed her despair and fixed her smile back in place. If Vicky and Luke noticed, they didn't say anything.

As they were still in the living room, Maria pointed to the kitchen. 'Let's see the rest of the property, and then I'll give you time alone to—'

'We don't need to see it all to know it's what we want.' Vicky pointed to her heart. 'I know.'

Maria had seen a lot of people fall in love with properties as they'd viewed them, but never one so certain as Vicky. It was almost as if she was coming home, excuse the pun. Maria knew without a doubt that the couple would be happy here. She only hoped she could get them, and the seller, the best price to make it happen.

They walked on, and Maria took a moment to discreetly wipe at her eyes. It had brought back thoughts of what had happened to her own family over the past few months. The worries of Jim after his accident; Lucy's problems with Melissa showing up unannounced; Clara and Alex splitting up. No matter what happened to them, their family home was their refuge.

Their place for conversation and advice over a mug of coffee.

Their place for a get together over lunch.

Their place to let off steam, sometimes ending in disagreements where she and Jim became referees.

Suddenly she was filled with a burst of love for their home in Lilac Grove. Maybe she could settle in it now. Jim had never been keen on moving again since they'd found that one.

Like this property, they had landscaped their gardens so there was minimum maintenance as they were both out at work. There were four bedrooms, ample for when the girls stayed over, and everything they had wanted doing to it had been done. Maria employed a cleaner once a week to do the bigger jobs but did the rest herself. Unless they had to move due to illness, it had everything they needed.

Maria didn't need another house, another project. It *was* their forever home.

What was it Jim had said to her? All you change by moving is your address. The problems you had before would still follow you, no matter what. And her worries were small in comparison to a woman who had battled cancer not once, but three times.

It was what Vicky Westleigh was saying to her. Vicky had found her forever home, too, right here. And Maria was happy to have helped.

FIFTEEN YEARS AGO - 4 GROSVENOR PLACE

'I'm not sure about this purple, Maria,' Jim said as he removed the lid from the tin of paint. 'It seems a little, er, bright.'

'It's what Clara wanted.' Maria came over and peered at it. 'Hmm, I see what you mean. Perhaps you can lighten it up by adding white emulsion. She'll never know. And it is only for the main wall.'

'Thank goodness. With the scatter cushions she chose, there's going to be all the colours in a bag of Jelly Babies!'

Maria smirked. 'We did say they could choose their own colour schemes.'

It had been ten days since they'd moved into Grosvenor Place. Lucy was fourteen now, Clara twelve, and even though they had their own rooms at their last home, they needed larger ones now. The house in Somerley High Street had three bedrooms, but the smallest was a box room. So when Maria had spotted house number four on the market, she had swooped in.

'I'd love to be an estate agent, showing people around

properties all day, making dreams come true.' She ran the brush along the wood. 'It must be so much fun.'

'You certainly have experience of selling, packing, and moving. I hope this is our last stop.'

'What? Absolutely not.' She reached for a rag to wipe a dollop of gloss paint from her hand. 'Where's the fun in that?'

Jim added the white to the purple, stirring it afterwards. 'I'm glad Lucy has gone with pastels. It's much easier on the eyes.'

'Do you think this will be our last move, Jim?' Maria was back on her knees, painting the skirting boards. 'It has a lovely feel to it and yet...'

'We've been here less than a fortnight!'

'You know I get a sense of belonging and I—'

'We're staying put for at least five years. If you don't like it then, we'll move.'

'You might not like it.'

'I don't get as attached as you.'

Maria was about to snap at him but closed her mouth instead. Jim was right. She was still trying to find the right house – the right home – for them all. But with this having four bedrooms, two separate living areas as well as a huge kitchen, a garden to die for and a double garage with a long driveway, it had all they needed. Their family wasn't going to expand anymore, not until they had grandchildren.

'You might be a granddad if we move again,' she teased.

'And you'll be a granny!'

'I'm looking forward to it.'

'Well, I never. That's the first time I haven't heard you moaning about growing old.'

'There has to be some perks, I suppose.' She stood up, stretching her lower back that had begun to ache, and put down her brush. 'I think it's time for a cuppa. I bought a cake from Somerley Stores.'

'Excellent.'

'But first, you need to finish that wall.'

'You drive a hard bargain.'

Maria headed downstairs, almost skipping into the kitchen. She still smiled when she saw it. Business was good with the builders merchants, and finally, they could afford to buy homes already done to their specification. It had taken a long time to find this house, waiting for something that had everything on her new list of requirements.

She could tell they would be very happy here. Until the next move, of course.

CHAPTER FORTY-NINE

Lucy groaned as Saskia stormed out of the front door, leaving it to bang behind her.

Lucy had been feeling under the weather with a bout of morning sickness, so the last thing she'd needed was Saskia pushing her luck. Saskia had come downstairs wearing make-up. It was a school day, and yet she wouldn't be allowed to wear that much even at the weekend.

She wished Saskia would let her show her how to apply it properly, to look as if she hadn't trowelled it on. But since Melissa had arrived and then left again in the blink of an eye, it was as if all communication between them had broken down.

Lucy had sent Saskia swiftly back to the bathroom, insisting she wipe it all off. Saskia had backchatted, and then stropped around over breakfast. She said it wasn't fair and that all the girls at school wore at least a bit of lipstick.

Lucy would never let her do any of the things that some of the girls Saskia's age were doing to make themselves look older. Saskia didn't have false nails; no sculpted eyebrows or lashes. Lucy couldn't stop her pouting her lips on photos, but she tried her best to keep an eye on her, seeing as Saskia was only thirteen.

Having said that, she could imagine how hard it must be to grow up in today's social-media-influenced times, having to make yourself better by enhancing everything, using all kinds of crap and dangerous concoctions.

And there were so many predators online. Lucy hoped they could keep Saskia safe from harm. She worried about her every day.

'Can I take my new book to school, Mummy?' Ellie broke into her thoughts.

'Of course you can, angel.' Lucy popped it into her rucksack, making a mental note to call into The Book Stop to pick up two more she'd ordered for her the week before. 'Are you ready to go now?'

'Yes!'

Lucy closed the front door, hoping to leave all thoughts of the home situation behind, but they followed her to work. Her mum noticed and collared her in the staff kitchen.

'How's the morning sickness? I must admit, you seem drained today.'

'It's been really bad this week. I'm glad I don't get it all the time like some women.' She sighed. 'But it's Saskia who's causing problems. She's really turned against me, and I don't know what to do. I'm not even sure if it's Melissa showing up or the baby she doesn't like the idea of.'

'It's not the baby.' Maria shook her head. 'I heard her talking to Ellie, and it sounds as if she can't wait to be a big sister to the bump.'

'Oh, that's one less thing to worry about. I just want things to go back to how they were before Melissa turned up for her whirlwind trip.' She paused. 'I'm scared I'm not a good enough mum.'

'That's poppycock.' Maria shook her head. 'She's just finding it hard to readjust, that's all.'

'But what if it doesn't work out for Melissa in Australia and she comes back and wants to claim Saskia as her own again? The way Saskia feels about me now, I fear I'll lose her. I don't want to share Saskia with her mum.'

'But Saskia has to share Aaron with you, Ellie, and the bump.'

Lucy frowned. 'Do you think I push her away?'

'No, not at all. But why don't you encourage her to keep in touch with Melissa?'

Lucy didn't understand.

'Saskia won't expect that. She'll think you're dead set against her having any contact. Melissa will be in Australia. It isn't as if Saskia can threaten to walk out and live with her. It's a bit far to go on the bus.'

Lucy smiled at her mum's attempt to cheer her up.

'You're threatened by a ghost. Melissa is in the past. It's all about you and Aaron now.'

When Maria got home that evening, she couldn't get Lucy from her mind. Over dinner, she told Jim what had happened.

'Everything seems to be going wrong this year,' she said.

'Life will never be perfect, no matter how hard you try,' Jim remarked, trying to cut his meat and giving up with a sigh. His plaster cast would be on for another month at least.

Maria helped him with it, instantly being taken back to when she did it for the girls, and passed him back his plate.

'Thanks, love.' He tucked in again.

'I want everyone to be happy, but I don't know how to stop the family from falling apart,' she went on.

'Things have a habit of sorting themselves out. I'm sure the two of them will be fine eventually.'

'Perhaps—'

'Stop worrying!'

She paused for a moment before answering. 'I think I should give a helping hand.'

'Or a shove.' Jim shook his head in jest. 'I wouldn't even try to stop you.'

'Good, because I have a plan. Let's have a barbecue this weekend.'

CHAPTER FIFTY

Dear Jim,

This Friday, we are going to the fair! I had to change this date when I saw it had arrived in Hedworth for a few nights.

I remember it was one of the first places we were alone together. You weren't perturbed when I said I couldn't see you in the week, so we'd arranged to meet for a date a couple of nights later. I was going to sneak out, no matter what.

But like most kids, when the fair came to town, everyone who was everyone went to hang out there. I mentioned it to my mum, and as she was feeling okay, she let me go. I couldn't get out of the house quick enough.

I was with Sal and yet I couldn't take my eyes off the crowd as we walked around. I was hoping to see you. I went round the outside of the waltzers, and there you were, with Paul and Adam on your racer bikes.

Can you remember those bikes? That was your mode of transport at sixteen. We stayed in a group until you suggested we had a little time alone. You left your bike with the boys, and I told Sal I'd be about ten minutes.

It was summer, so the evening was light. We sat on the

grass behind the fair and talked, getting to know each other even more. I do recall there was more kissing, that we forgot the time, and that ten minutes turned into forty before we returned to the fair.

Sal was furious. At that age, you didn't abandon your best friend for a boy, no sirree. (I think she was more annoyed that Paul didn't want to date her after he'd walked her home on Saturday, and then being left with him that evening.) I would have felt the same if it had happened to me, to be honest.

Sal stormed off while I trailed behind her, pleading for forgiveness. I don't think she spoke to me for two days afterwards and I was even at one point wondering if our friendship was over!

But good friends, as well as husbands, stick around through thick and thin. I got to keep both of you close. I am so very grateful for that.

Love, Maria x

'Do you think Sal will forgive you for not bringing her to the fair, too?' Jim asked as they walked across the field towards it.

Ahead, rides were in full motion, lights were glaring, and loud music was in competition with the noise coming from the many generators. Smoke filled Maria's nostrils, quickly followed by the sickly smell of candy floss and doughnuts.

'She wouldn't want to play gooseberry again,' Maria said.

'I can remember her being annoyed with me that night and I had no idea what I'd done to deserve it. I just thought she hated me.'

'Oh, she *really* hated you.'

'She will once again when we tell her we've been on the waltzers.'

'What?' Maria glanced at Jim's face. It was lit up like an excited child. 'No way. I'm not going on them.'

'Yes you are.'

Before she could protest, he took her hand, and they raced up the metal steps. The ride was slowing, so they waited for it to stop and then slid into the nearest car. Undercover, the music was deafening, colourful flashing lights making her feel disorientated. Jim patted her hand, which was gripping the rail as if it were a matter of life and death.

The operator made sure the safety bar was in place, and the ride began. They slid from side to side, their bodies pushed against the back of the seats, and spun until she was sure she didn't know where she began and where she ended.

It was the longest three minutes of her life.

Finally, it was over, and they scrambled out in a fit of giggles.

'I feel so sick!' Maria's wobbly legs struggled to get down the steps onto the grass. 'Did we really enjoy going on those time after time, on the same night, when we were young?'

'I can't understand the attraction now.' Jim helped her, and they made it to the ground. 'My insides are still going round and round.'

'The operator thought it was hilarious when he kept spinning us. He wouldn't have laughed so much if I'd thrown up all over the seat.' She put a hand to her head. 'Ugh. Please don't tell me it will take longer to recover now we're older.'

'I have just the thing to stop you thinking about it.'

Jim grabbed her hand and walked with her towards the Ghost Train. Maria pulled away.

'I'm not going on that.' She shook her head. 'I'm a wimp, remember?'

'I'll keep my arm around you and protect you. You said I'm your knight in shining armour.'

'That excludes fairs!' Maria was laughing again, the night turning out to be much better than she'd anticipated. She'd thought they might have a wander round, throw a few darts, and shoot a few bullets to try and win a teddy bear. Perhaps walk through the hall of mirrors, and there would definitely be candy floss to try again. But this was way more fun.

They paid their money and climbed into the car. The operator pushed the safety bar towards them, ensured they were secure in their seats, and they set off when the siren went.

The machinery was so old that it seemed to stall before moving off, almost giving them whiplash as it pressed forward. They crashed through the doors into the dark.

Maria screamed when she felt something on her shoulder and batted her hand at it. She hid her face in Jim's chest when someone – or some*thing* – ran out in front of them. She winced when they rode through sprays of mist made to resemble fog, where gravestones and zombies were painted on the walls.

But how she laughed, too. Maria thought she might wet herself, and her sides were aching so much. She had tears running down her face once they emerged outside again.

All of a sudden, she was back to being sixteen, with so much teenage lust for Jim, and wondering if he would be part of her future. He'd been the first person to show her real affection. He *had* become her knight in shining armour. Her younger self would be proud.

'Oh, that was so much fun,' she exclaimed as they rejoined the crowds. 'What's next?'

'Nothing for a while – I need a break!'

'But it's made me feel alive.' She looked up at the lights, flashing every colour of the rainbow now the evening was turning into night. 'There's so much more to do.'

Jim paused. 'How about a hot dog?'

'Is that a euphemism?' she asked coyly, running her tongue over her top lip lasciviously.

'It definitely could be.'

For once, when they got home that evening, Maria didn't care about her body when they went to bed. She left the light on so they could see each other, and she didn't cover herself up under the duvet.

And even though they took it easy so she didn't get bashed with the cast on Jim's wrist, she still felt young again.

She wanted to be close to him. Her usual inhibitions, her self-conscious mannerisms, and her shyness, had gone completely.

For tonight anyway.

CHAPTER FIFTY-ONE

As luck would have it, Maria had chosen the right weekend for a barbecue. The weather was dry, the sky exceptionally clear blue for early May.

The family were in the garden. Ellie and Saskia were sprawled out on a picnic blanket, Ellie reading a book, and Saskia flicking through a magazine.

Jim was in charge of the barbecue. He wore a baseball cap to protect his scar from the sun, and a frilly pinny that he got out especially for the occasion each year. He was deep in conversation with Aaron, his spatula pointing this way and that.

The Wilshaw women, along with Sal, were seated around the patio table, underneath the awning. Wine was flowing as Tyler came to join them. Clara was telling them about a date she had lined up.

'Half of me wishes I hadn't bumped into Megan at Somerley Stores, yet the other part enjoys her company,' she said. 'But she has this obsession about fixing me up again. She seems to think I'm heartbroken and so needs to pair me up with someone. She wanted me to go on a double date with her and her new man, can you believe that? I told her I'm twenty-seven, not twelve.'

'She's only trying to help,' Lucy said.

'She was ecstatic about it,' Clara went on. 'It's as if she's come up with the perfect solution.'

'So what are you going to do?'

Clara leaned forward. 'She's been talking to this guy at work and says I'll—'

'You're going on a blind date?' Maria asked.

'Not exactly because I've seen a photo of him.'

'Ooh, let's see.' Sal held out a hand for Clara's phone.

'I'm not showing you lot!' Clara laughed. 'You'll take the piss.'

'We can vet him for you,' Sal insisted, her hand still out.

Clara sighed, searched out an image, and gave it to her. 'His name is Christian. He's thirty-two, divorced, and has no children.'

Lucy, Tyler, and Maria crowded around Sal to coo over the photo. Clara had to admit that Christian was quite dishy. His smile instantly drew you towards him. His dark hair was thinning, but he had enough to pull off a spiky style that suited him, and he had a shaped goatee. Clara had a thing about beards. She didn't like them too long and fluffy, but she did like stubble when she felt it against her skin.

'He's a dish,' Lucy said.

'Indeed,' Sal added. 'I wouldn't throw him out of my bed.'

'Sal!' Maria admonished.

'A woman can dream. Although, unless he's into the *older* woman, I don't stand a chance.' She pointed at Clara. 'But you should go for it.'

'I don't know,' Clara mused, but she was still looking at her phone.

'I've said I'll keep in touch with her via WhatsApp, in case she needs to bail,' Tyler said before sitting down.

'That makes me feel better,' Maria admitted. 'You never know these days. Please be careful, love.'

'If we do meet, I'll suggest the cinema, and afterwards, I'll stay in public with him. But he is Megan's friend, and she's known him for years.' Clara could almost think she was talking herself into a date with Christian, she was so quick to defend him. 'Besides, if I have to play the dating game again, I might as well try and have a little fun. And Tyler will be at the ready, to bail me out if necessary.'

'We had nothing like WhatsApp in our day,' Sal said. 'Which would have been handy for the blind date I went on. Can you remember, Maria?'

'That's right, with Dean Trent!' Maria's laughter was infectious.

'Tell us more,' Lucy said, Tyler and Clara nodding profusely.

'I went to a club with a friend, King's it was called, known locally as grab-a-granny night. It's gone now, though.'

'It was at the back of Somerley Square, near to the estate,' Maria added, reaching forward to top up drinks. 'It was such a dive, but it was all we had at the time. I didn't go out much, so Sal often went with a group of friends.'

'I was waiting with Natalie for her date, and mine, to arrive. I must have been, what, seventeen at the time?' Sal glanced at Maria who nodded.

'Yes, about that.'

'We were waiting by the bar, and then Natalie said, oh, here they come now. I hadn't met her new fella yet, so as these two men walked over, I thought, okay, he's not too bad. But—'

'That was Natalie's man?' Clara enquired with a smirk.

'You're right! My blind date, Dean, was behind him. Honestly, anyone would have to be *blind* to go out with him.'

They all roared hysterically.

'I saw his neck first,' Sal went on. 'It was like a swan, but that wasn't the worst of it. He was five foot five at a push, and I had heels on to make things worse.'

'What did you do?' Lucy leaned forward, eager to learn more, then immediately sat back when her bump wouldn't allow her to do it comfortably.

'Well, I was polite.'

'Yeah, right.' Maria smirked. 'She did her own thing all night while he followed her around like a puppy.'

'I couldn't get rid of him!' Sal shrieked. 'In the end, I started dancing with someone else, and he got the message. Natalie wasn't bothered as she was snogging the face off Mr Okay.'

Tears were pouring down Maria's cheeks as they all chortled.

'I'm not really ready to date yet,' Clara added afterwards. 'It's nice of Megan to look out for me, though.'

'You should definitely give Christian a try,' Sal told her. 'He can't be any worse than Dean!'

Their frivolity brought Jim and Aaron over.

'What's so funny?' Aaron wanted to know.

'We're reminiscing. Talking about a blind date I went on.'

'Now, now, Sal,' Jim teased. 'Not every ugly man will want to date you. You might find a prince one day.'

'I don't want a prince. I want a king!'

Maria spotted Saskia sitting on the grass, deep in thought and, if she wasn't mistaken, close to tears. She stood quickly.

'I think we need more drinks. Saskia, how about you give me a hand?'

CHAPTER FIFTY-TWO

'It's a lovely day out there,' Maria said to Saskia as she reached bottles out of the fridge. 'Are you enjoying yourself?'

Saskia nodded, but Maria saw her bottom lip wobbling.

'Oh, love, what's wrong?' She took her in her arms and held her.

'Nothing, really.'

'Are you sure? Because you should tell me before Ellie rushes in to interrupt us. That girl can't half pick her moments.'

Saskia drew away from her and leaned on the worktop. 'I-I don't feel like I belong in this family anymore.'

Maria's heart almost broke. The poor girl's world had been rocked when her mum had visited. She'd been as surprised as Lucy when she'd heard what had happened. In a way, she understood Melissa wanting to make amends for what she'd done, and also her need to see Saskia before she emigrated. Alcoholism was a terrible disease, and it was quite brave of Melissa to face up to her mistakes.

Sadly, it seemed to have left Saskia with a conundrum.

One Maria thought might be solved with a chat with someone who knew what it was like to lose a parent.

'Is it because of the baby coming along?' Maria knew it wasn't but wanted to start off on mutual territory.

'Not really. I don't know how it's going to fit into our house, but I suppose it's okay.'

Maria smiled. 'So this is about your mum, then?'

Saskia clammed up.

'I never felt as if I belonged when I was growing up either.'

That had Saskia's attention.

'Do you know what a manic depressive is?'

Saskia shrugged. 'It's someone who is up and down with their moods.'

'Kind of. My mum was like that. My dad left when I was five, and I muddled along with her. Sometimes she'd be fun to be with, but mostly she would be low. I'd come home from school to find her still in bed from the morning, the house untidy and hardly any food in. By the time I was fourteen, I was doing most of the shopping, the cleaning, and cooking. I barely had a life of my own.'

'Oh, that's sad.'

'I know. I don't talk about it now.'

Maria tried not to think about her past too much either. She knew it was the reason for her obsession with perfection. Back in her teens, she'd thought that if the house was always tidy, her mum might be happy, but that hadn't happened. It had changed in adulthood, to becoming everything needing to be just so or else she feared her world would fall apart.

'Some people are simply not cut out to be a parent,' she continued. 'Our house always had a black cloud hanging over it.'

'What do you mean?'

'I never felt happy when I was there because I didn't

know what mood my mum would be in when I got back. I used to enjoy myself at school and then dread going home. It shouldn't be like that.'

'Do you keep in touch?'

Maria paused. She might be on sticky ground now, but Saskia was old enough to understand mental health issues.

'She took her own life, just before I got married.'

Saskia looked shocked. 'That must have been hard.'

'It was.'

Back then, Maria had often struggled to find time for her and Jim to get together because she had to keep an eye on her mum, Eve. On numerous occasions, Jim would come round to her house, and they'd watch TV together because Eve hadn't wanted to be left alone. It was one of the reasons Maria had pushed Jim away when they were younger, thinking it wasn't fair on him. Thankfully, they'd reconnected.

Two weeks before the wedding, Maria had gone out with friends. She hadn't wanted a hen party, but the women at work had insisted they went out for a meal. She'd had such a laugh, arriving home a little worse for wear.

But she'd sobered up pretty sharpish when she'd found Eve lying on the settee, unconscious with drool running from her mouth. An empty bottle of whisky lay where she'd dropped it, alongside blister packs of tablets that were all gone, and a note that had broken Maria's heart.

Eve wrote to say she didn't want to be a burden once Maria was married; she wanted Maria to have a chance of happiness without her to worry about.

Jim had wanted to postpone the wedding, but Maria had decided to go ahead with it. She had to move on somehow.

And from that moment on, she had always felt loved and protected by Jim, but with the extra fear of being abandoned. It was the reason why she panicked if everything wasn't just so, why her demons never left her.

'Do you ever see your dad?' Saskia asked.

'No. From the day he left, I never saw him again. I don't even know where he lives.' *Or even if he's still alive.* 'I don't mind so much now, though. I've blanked him from my mind and realised it had nothing to do with me. Families are complicated things.'

They stood in silence for a moment, the only noise coming from the garden. Ellie was giggling as Tyler was giving her a piggy-back.

'Let me tell you something,' Maria added. 'Belonging in a family is all up to the individual. It doesn't have much to do with blood. You can choose to stay on the sidelines and be unhappy, or you can join in and be with people who love you, who get to see you every day, who will *never* leave you, but will give you all the support you need. Your mum left for a good reason, but she did what was best for you. That doesn't mean she won't think of you every day of her life.' Maria pointed to her chest. 'You'll always have a special place in her heart.'

A smile formed on Saskia's lips. 'We're going to keep in touch on FaceTime.'

'That's great! And when you're older, you'll be able to go out and visit her.'

Saskia shook her head at that.

Maria frowned in confusion.

'I don't want to see her again. She saw me to say she was sorry, and that's okay. But I don't love her like I love... Lucy.' Her eyes brimmed with tears. 'And I think I've upset her now.'

Maria was filled with love for the mixed-up girl standing in front of her. She reached for her hand. 'I think Lucy would be so pleased to hear what you've just told me.'

'Really? I feel like I'm a nuisance.'

'Of course you're not. Lucy loves you like you're her own daughter. She's always telling me how proud of you she is.'

Saskia beamed.

'Would you like me to mention it to her, so she'll come and talk to you about it? I think you'll both be happier then. Because Lucy is really sad about upsetting you.'

Saskia seemed to give it some thought and then shook her head.

'No, I'm going to talk to her.'

Maria almost burst with pride. What a brave young girl she was.

Before they went back outside, she gave Saskia another hug.

'I'm really pleased you're part of our family now,' she said, her voice a little choked.

'Me, too. I'm glad I met you, and everyone else.'

They went out into the garden. Maria went to stand with Jim who was back at the helm of the barbecue, flipping burgers and looking important.

'Everything okay?' he spoke quietly.

'Yes, I think so.'

They watched Saskia go over to Lucy. As she turned to glance her way, Maria gave her an encouraging thumbs-up.

The exchange between them was magical. Obviously, she couldn't hear what they were saying, and neither did she want to, but Saskia spoke first, then Lucy. Saskia threw her arms around Lucy's waist. Lucy's face was a mixture of emotion before she hugged her, kissing her on the top of her head.

Jim nudged Maria. 'Your plan worked, I see.'

She smiled at him. 'Yes, everything is perfect again. For a little while, at least.'

CHAPTER FIFTY-THREE

Clara was walking along the high street on her way to Tyler's flat when her phone rang. She moved nearer towards the buildings, wondering whether to answer the call or not.

It was Alex. She hadn't heard from him in a while, and she didn't really want to talk to him now. But curiosity got the better of her.

'Hi, Clara. How are you?'

'Well, I'm surprised to be hearing from you. Is everything okay?' She pressed the phone closer to her ear to drown out the traffic.

'Yes, everything is fine. Can we meet? I'd like to talk to you?'

'What about?'

'I'd rather say it face to face. Where are you?'

'In the high street.'

'Can I pick you up? Take you out for something to eat?'

'I don't think that's a good idea.' It was one thing to suggest meeting, but Clara wondered what her heart would think about having to spend a couple of hours in the company of her ex.

'Please. I'm only a few minutes away. We could go to The Caramel Leaf.'

Clara wasn't keen on going there. The restaurant was amazing, but it was more for a special occasion.

'Or maybe grab a pub meal?' Alex added.

She paused, the lights from the crossing ahead beeping while she thought about it. A gaggle of schoolkids crossed the road and walked along the pavement towards her. 'Okay. I'm outside Somerley Stores. Shall I wait here for you?'

'Great. See you in five.'

Clara disconnected the call. Once the kids had gone past and there was more room, she took out her compact mirror. Quickly, she wiped away rogue mascara from under her eyes and reapplied her lipstick. Running her hands through her hair, she felt respectable enough to meet her ex.

Alex's car approached, and she waved, stepping forwards so he could see her. She slid in the passenger seat, immediately feeling out of place and a sense of déjà vu at the same time.

'Hi.' Alex's smile was shy.

'Hi.'

He pulled away, and they made small talk until they were seated in The White Lion, a couple of miles away, perusing the menu. It was a weeknight, so the venue was quiet but busy enough to have a welcoming atmosphere.

'Have whatever you like. It's my treat.' Alex grinned. 'Although I know you'll want the gammon and egg?'

Her smile was false. It seemed really weird sitting across from him after all this time. Like they were strangers, and yet they had been a couple for almost seven years. How could she not feel anything for him now?

Or did she?

'How's work?' he asked, to fill the gap once their orders had been taken.

'It's good, really busy with the summer months coming up.' She took a sip of water that had been brought to them. 'Lucy is pregnant, so we'll be after a temp soon.'

'Wow, that's good to hear. Please send my congratulations.'

Clara nodded, laughing inwardly at what response she'd get from Lucy if she did. He wasn't her favourite person.

They ate a main course, conversation verging on the safe and boring, to say the least. Lucy put down her cutlery and wiped her mouth.

'When we spoke on the phone, you said you wanted to talk to me about something?'

'I did, but I-I don't know where to start.'

'The beginning would help.'

Alex put his cutlery down, too.

'I made a terrible mistake leaving you for Kirstie.'

Clara flinched when he said her name.

'We've split up.'

'Oh!' That was a surprise.

'Apparently, she got fed up with me comparing her to you all the time. "When me and Clara did this, Clara and I used to do that." I guess I never realised until then how much I still think of you, how I'd like you back in my life again.'

Her jaw dropped.

'Could we try?' He reached across the table for her hand. 'I miss you, every single day. I long to be with you.'

'But we've just sold our house!'

'We could buy another. It would be a fresh start.'

Clara couldn't comprehend what she was hearing.

'Have you told Kirstie yet?'

'Well, not until I'd spoken to you.'

It was then she clicked in. 'And if I said no, you'd stay with her until someone better came along?'

'No, it's not like that.'

'So you still love me?' She pulled away her hand. 'Is that what you're saying?'

He stared at her.

'This is self-preservation, Alex. You don't want to be with Kirstie, so good old Clara will do until you find someone else. You know I'm staying with Tyler at the moment?' She watched his brow furrow as he worked out the logistics. 'You thought I had a place of my own.'

'Don't you?'

'The sale of the one I wanted fell through at the last minute. But, really, that shouldn't make a difference. You should want to come back because you love me. You only seem to have enough of that for yourself.

'You're a self-centred shit, who I spent far too much time with, and spilled way too many tears over when you left me for Kirstie. But do you know what? Every minute was worth it, because I am free of you.' She removed her jacket from the back of the chair, reached for her bag, and stood. 'Thanks for the meal, but I'll find my own way home.'

'Wait, Clara!' Alex grabbed her hand as she marched past.

She stopped for a moment, enjoying the feeling of looking down at him.

'Please, think about it. We were good together and we can find that magic again.'

'Really? You only get one chance to make a fool of me. I won't give you the opportunity again. The answer is categorically no, and it will always be no. Please don't call me. Ever.' She pulled away her hand and continued walking.

'Clara. Clara!' Alex cried.

His voice died down the more distance she put between them. At the exit, she made a detour into the bathroom, where she took a few deep breaths before getting out her phone.

'Tyler, are you busy?'

'Why?'

'I need a favour?'

'Sure, what's up? Are you okay?'

She briefly told him what had happened.

'Wait there for me.'

After she'd spoken to him, Clara glanced at herself in the mirror above the sinks. The reflection was of a woman who was proud of herself. She wasn't going to be used, especially not by Alex. He'd had his chance and blown it.

Seeing him tonight had cemented everything for her. Despite him invading her thoughts with different scenarios and what-ifs every now and again, she realised there was nothing left.

She really had moved on.

CHAPTER FIFTY-FOUR

On Friday, we're going to London on the train, Jim! We have a reservation on the 09.02, getting us there for eleven. We'll walk around Westminster before heading back to Trafalgar Square for lunch.

After some great food, we'll continue with our sightseeing, our feet taking us wherever we want to go. Then we'll catch the last train home, getting back to Somerley for eleven.

Maria had been thinking of ideas for the nostalgic dates for some time. There were many memories she could recall, but only so many places in the UK where she and Jim had been when they were younger. She'd talked to the girls about her worries.

'What about doing something completely different?' Clara had proposed.

'I wanted it to be nostalgic.'

'There are no rules. You can do what you like really, as long as you spend time together.'

Maria had thought about the things on her bucket list. She'd always wanted to visit The Shard in London, go on a water taxi along the Thames, and visit a pub with a quirky name. Scrolling through the tourist information site for London's finest things to do, she had planned out an itinerary and booked train tickets that evening. It wasn't somewhere they'd visited in their teens, but it was something she knew Jim would enjoy.

'First-class tickets to London!' he said after he'd read the note, giving her a hug.

She smiled at his excitement, glad she had made the decision to go. 'And we're going to drink champagne at the top of The Shard.'

'Are you saying that afternoon tea at The Coffee Stop wasn't good enough?' he teased.

'Of course not. But I wanted to do something different, taking us out of Somerley for the day.'

The next morning at the station, they chatted for a few minutes while they waited on the platform for the train.

'I suppose you have lots of sweets in your bag?' Jim asked in anticipation.

'You're worse than Saskia and Ellie,' she chastised. 'I have mints and a few chocolate bars, that's all.'

'Dark chocolate?'

'Of course.'

'Ooh, give me one now.'

'Behave. You've only just had your breakfast!'

'I'm a growing boy.'

'You'll still have to wait.'

'Spoilsport.' Jim pointed at the train coming in. 'Here we go.'

They boarded their carriage, got comfortable in their seats, and settled for the journey. Maria took out her Kindle while Jim read the morning's newspaper.

Over coffee, and then tea, they chatted about where they wanted to go, what they'd like to see, and before long they were pulling into Euston Station.

'How alien does riding on a Tube feel when you're not used to it?' Jim shouted above the rattle of the train as it raced through another tunnel towards Charing Cross.

Coming out onto Trafalgar Square, the buzz of the traffic, people everywhere, was intoxicating. They dodged the crowds walking down The Mall, marvelled at Buckingham Palace, and came back through Horse Guard Parade.

They crossed The Strand and walked a few more streets until they were outside The Sherlock Holmes pub. Lunch was fish and chips washed down with a local ale.

Then, it was back on the Tube and over to London Bridge. They found the entrance to The Shard, and then the lift. Maria gasped, an overwhelming feeling of leaving her stomach in the lobby as they flew up. She squeezed Jim's hand, but it was over in seconds.

They were shown to a balcony with an incredible view of London. They could see for miles, and the people below were so tiny.

'Wow, just wow,' Jim said. 'This is mind-blowing!'

'I know it's not a nostalgic date,' Maria said. 'But it is a date, and that's what counts.'

Jim kissed her gently on the lips. 'It's perfect. Do we have time to go on the wheel?'

'We do.'

The afternoon and evening were spent racing around the capital, taking in as much as they could. The taxi boat was a rush, taking them down to Tower Bridge, and then they caught an Uber to Oxford Street and hit the shops. They bought gifts for Ellie and Saskia, and London Bus fridge magnets for themselves, and the girls.

Another meal, in an Italian restaurant this time, a glass of wine apiece while they rested their feet, and then, it seemed in no time at all, they were back on the train, settling into their seats for the journey home.

Now, Jim was dozing as Maria reflected on the day. It had been tiring but so much fun. She hoped Jim hadn't been telling white lies when she kept asking him if it was too much. But the look on his face, the excitement in his eyes, and the permanent smile, told her all she needed to know.

It had been good to do something just for the two of them, a surprise for Jim and something Maria had wanted to do for a long time. Already she'd decided to bring the whole family on the same trip. If Lucy became too tired, she could always plonk herself at a pub table with her old mum, leaving everyone else to do the full tour.

Half an hour from home, Jim woke up and flashed her a smile.

'You tired me out,' he said.

'It was worth it, though, wasn't it?'

'It was the best day we've had in years.'

'This is what making memories is all about.' She laced her fingers with his. 'Taking time out to enjoy it with the person you love the most in your life.'

'And a lesson learned.'

'Hmm?' She didn't understand.

'We need to spend more time together, just you and I.' He smiled. 'We should definitely do this more often.'

Maria smiled back. She couldn't remember feeling this happy for years. Realising what was most important in her life these past three months had been a godsend. She'd taken Jim for granted, putting too much emphasis on her work to fill her hours rather than enjoy life with him.

His fall could have been far more serious, so she was glad they'd had the opportunity to reconnect even though she'd have preferred something a little less drastic.

From that moment on, she would see to it that she never, ever, forgot the little things.

CHAPTER FIFTY-FIVE

Somerley Heights was a retirement complex for the over sixties and, although all the properties were privately owned, there was a warden on site twenty-four hours and assisted living if needed. Maria had moved several people there over the years, some couples, some singles. She loved the idea of your own space but with company or help if required. The place had a lovely vibe to it. Home from home, with added extras.

She stepped into the reception area, all welcoming pale blues and cream, and smiled at the woman behind the desk.

'Morning, Julie, what a gorgeous one it is, too. How are you?'

'I'm fine, thanks. Busy, busy, as usual. How's Jim doing?'

'He's getting along fine now, thanks.' Maria smiled to herself about how gossip travelled around Somerley. She didn't mind, though. It was nice to be a part of it and to hear her concern. 'How are those twins of yours? I bet they're into everything now.'

'*Everything*!' Julie rolled her eyes in jest. 'I thought it would be good to have two babies together when I found out

I was expecting them, but now it's all amplified! And having boys – I never have a minute to myself.'

Maria laughed, seeing the weary woman before her with such love in her eyes for her children. 'I remember going through it all twice. I'm not sure which way is best, to be honest. It's all hard work, no matter what.'

Julie pointed towards the main corridor. 'I'll let you find your own way and then I'll send Mr and Mrs Redfern to you when they get here.'

'You're a diamond, thanks.'

Maria pushed the door into the main hallway. She stopped at number seventeen, unlocked the door, and let herself in. The flat had a long hallway, doors opening into two bedrooms and a bathroom on the right, and a kitchen and living room on the left. It had been recently decorated, new carpets, too. The smell of fresh paint lingered.

She went through to the living room, which had a picture window, and a door to a private garden.

Shortly afterwards, there was a knock on the door, and she went to meet her clients.

Elsie and Bill Redfern were in their eighties. Elsie was a small woman, stooped over and using a stick. Her grey hair was thin, but styled and neat, her dress a riot of colours. Bill was wearing a suit and tie. He gave Elsie a helping hand as they shuffled in.

'Welcome to Somerley Heights,' Maria greeted. 'It has the best of both worlds. Your own private property, but with the option of care and companionship, now or in the future, on site, too.' She pointed through the window. 'The complex is surrounded by countryside. The roof of the local pub is visible above the hedges, there's a small shop within walking distance, and a bus stop right outside the main entrance.'

'We didn't want to leave our home,' Elsie said quietly to Maria. 'But we wanted to maintain our independence for as long as we could. Even so, we're lucky we have family to look after us. Some people don't. We have three daughters and a son. Do you have children?'

'Two girls, and two granddaughters, thirteen and five, and a bump on the way!'

'How wonderful.' Elsie's eyes twinkled beneath hooded lids. 'And do you see them often?'

'Yes, my daughters work at the agency with me. We get on really well. It's nice.'

'Elsie, don't be so nosy.' Bill's tone was good-natured.

'It's fine,' Maria assured him. 'I love talking about them.'

'We've had our fair share of ups and downs, but they all seem to be settled for now.' Bill patted his wife's hand. 'But I wouldn't swap any of it, especially not this one. She's the love of my life. I've been such a lucky man to share my years with her.'

'Oh, get off with you, Billy.' Elsie tittered, a slight blush appearing on her cheeks.

Maria thought it was lovely to see. 'Let me show you two lovebirds the rest of the property,' she said.

Half an hour later, Maria reckoned the deal was done. Mr and Mrs Redfern had already sold their home and had been living with their daughter until they found somewhere suitable. It meant a quick sale with no chain, the ones Maria liked best.

'So what do you think?' Maria asked, even though she'd sensed their answer.

'We think it's perfect, don't we, Bill?' Elsie said.

'Yes, we do.' Bill nodded. 'Our daughter and son-in-law who live nearby will need to see it, too, if you don't mind? They want to make sure it's right for us.'

'Of course. Get them to ring me, and I can pop back anytime.'

'That sounds wonderful.' Elsie beamed, Bill smiling as he patted her hand.

Maria turned away from its intimacy. She could see so much of her and Jim in Mr and Mrs Redfern. The couple were so happy – still so much in love – and that was all she wanted, too. Which was what she should concentrate on. What she had, not what she assumed she needed.

With thoughts running through her mind of the final date she'd set up for Jim, Maria realised there was something much better that she could do for the two of them.

And that she needed her daughters' help again.

SEVEN YEARS AGO - 6 LILAC GROVE

Maria couldn't contain her excitement as Jim parked in the showhome car park. They were coming to see their potential new home. Jim had heard there was a development being planned and had been straight in there finding out the details. Lilac Grove was going to be a small cul-de-sac of individually designed homes, each with their own plots, in a prime location, but only minutes from Somerley High Street.

'This is what we've been working towards, Maria,' he'd told her when he brought home the brochure. 'We can have something we want exactly to our spec, without having to do it ourselves, or rip things apart to change it to suit once we move in.'

They walked towards the show house, construction work taking place all round, and into the portacabin that was being used as an office. A woman in her twenties was sitting behind the desk. She rose when she saw them.

'Hi again, Jim. And you must be Maria. I'm Becky.' She offered her hand to them both. 'I'm so excited to show you around Lilac Grove. Have you chosen which plot you'd like?'

'Two actually.' Jim nodded. 'I'm hoping today we can figure out which one.'

'Great.' Becky pointed to her desk where there were three yellow hard hats. 'They're not good for the hair,' she joked with Maria. 'But nevertheless, we'll need to use them for safety purposes. But first, the house!'

Maria was blown away as they were shown around the show house. She had to keep closing her mouth, her jaw hanging down when she entered every room. Of course show houses were there to sell the others, so had to be immaculate, but these were rich and elegant. Everything was beyond anything they'd had before.

It suddenly made all those long hours at work and putting things off to earn more money to save for their next venture worthwhile when she imagined herself living in something like that.

And if seeing the house itself wasn't enough, both plots were amazing. They were up to the first level, holes for windows and doors, scaffolding up.

Becky took them inside, showing them the views so far. It was hard to decide, so they'd gone away to think about it.

Once they were back in the car, Jim turned to her. 'What do you think?'

'It's gorgeous, Jim,' Maria beamed. 'Beyond my wildest dreams. What we've worked towards, I suppose.'

'What I mean is, will you settle there? This is somewhere no one else has lived. It could be a way of making everything perfect for you.'

Maria sighed. 'I don't know, Jim.' Then she grinned. 'But it will certainly be a wonderful place to try.'

He roared with laughter and started the engine. 'You crack me up.'

'As long as I can still make you smile.'

'So, it's a yes?'
'It's a yes!'

CHAPTER FIFTY-SIX

Clara had decided at last to meet Christian. They'd messaged a few times to arrange things, and she'd sent him a photo, so he knew what she looked like. They were going to watch a film. At least if she didn't like him much, she could slip out to the ladies and never come back. And, of course, Tyler was on standby.

She chastised herself; she should give Christian a chance. She didn't have to arrange to meet him, after all. She could have left things as they were. But a part of her was curious to go on a date, too. See how it would feel to be with someone other than Alex. She had disregarded her encounter with Phil as a mistake that, luckily, hadn't gone too far.

Christian was waiting for her at the entrance to the cinema, looking suave in jeans, a shirt, and a casual jacket.

His face lit up as she approached him. 'Hi. Clara, it's lovely to meet you.'

'Likewise.'

He leaned forward and kissed her gently on the cheek, his aftershave lingering in the air. Musky, scents of white oak and vanilla.

'Shall we go in?' He threw out an arm. 'What do you fancy watching?'

'I don't mind, really, although perhaps nothing too violent?'

He ushered her into the foyer and Clara felt a flurry of anticipation in her stomach. On first impression, he seemed really nice.

They chose a comedy action film and settled down to enjoy it. But, after half an hour of trying to laugh in the right places, she glanced across at Christian who caught her eye.

'Are you enjoying it?' he whispered.

'Yes.'

'Really?'

'Well, it is a bit cheesy,' she admitted.

'I agree.' He paused. 'Do you fancy ditching it and grabbing a drink instead?'

'That sounds like a good idea!'

They quietly made their way out. Once in the fresh air, with his hand wrapped around hers, they walked across to the first of several bars. There was a good crowd standing around, and lots of people sitting at tables on the edge of the room.

'What can I get you?' Christian asked.

'A Coke, please. I'm driving.'

'Ah, I got a taxi here. Do you mind if I have a pint?'

'Of course not.' She looked around, spotting an empty table. 'I'll grab some seats.'

Twenty minutes later, they were laughing as if they'd known each other for ages. Christian was a natural-born storyteller, regaling her with some of the horrors of online dating he'd heard on the Facebook group he'd joined. He rattled off so many funny anecdotes that she had to wipe tears from her eyes at times.

'So you can see why I gave up.' He chuckled.

She nodded fervently. It felt wonderful to be out enjoying

herself. Christian was good company, time flew by, and the next thing she knew, it was nearing eleven. Despite the last film finishing half an hour ago, the bar was thinning out.

'I'd best be making a move.' Christian glanced at his watch. 'I've really enjoyed your company this evening,' he said. 'Would you be interested in meeting again, perhaps for dinner?'

Clara nodded. 'Yes, I'd like that, but to be honest with you, I'm not ready for anything more. If I'd met you in a few months' time, this would have been even better.'

'We don't have to rush into anything.'

'I wanted to be straight with you – in case you fancy trying the dating apps for yourself.' Clara raised her eyebrows in jest.

'Not likely.' Christian shuddered. 'Let's see how we get on as friends first then? I've really enjoyed your company, so I'm happy to get to know you gradually if necessary.'

'Great!'

He took her hand as they got outside and walked her to the car park. Surprisingly, conversation was still flowing. It felt really natural being with him.

She stopped at her car. 'This is me. Would you like a lift home? I wouldn't usually offer, but as we have a mutual friend in Megan...'

He gave her another of those smiles. 'If you don't mind. I only live a few minutes away.'

'It's fine. Hop in.'

In no time at all she was pulling up outside a small, detached house on the edge of a new-build estate.

'This looks lovely,' she said. 'I've admired these homes from afar for quite some time, seeing as stalking streets online is part of my job.'

'They're quite cosy,' he said. 'Which is another word for tiny.'

'Home is a feeling, as my mum always says.'

He turned to her then. 'I've had a really wonderful evening. I really would like to do this again when you're ready.'

'Sure.' Clara gave an inward sigh of relief he wasn't expecting anything else from her. It was all well and good thinking of one-night stands when you were in your twenties, and even then she hadn't had any. But, nowadays, when it came to sex, she wanted to sleep with someone and have it mean something, rather than be a notch on a bedpost.

'Well, I guess this is goodnight, then.' Christian's hand went around the back of her neck as he kissed her on the lips. It was a gentle but passionate kiss, lasting long enough for it to be promising, but equally fulfilling.

'I hope it won't be too long until the next time,' he added before getting out of the car.

Clara waved and then drove off, grinning like the proverbial Cheshire Cat.

Tyler was still up when she got back to his flat. Clara flopped down on the settee next to him and gave a deep sigh of satisfaction.

'Well?' Tyler probed.

'I had the *best* evening.'

'Ooh, tell me more. I was actually expecting you to message me for a get out. What was he like?'

'Really nice. The film was a bit naff, so we went for a drink.'

'Sounds good. Are you seeing him again?'

'Maybe, but not for a while. He made me realise I don't want to date anyone yet.'

'I said you weren't ready.'

'I know, don't gloat! I was curious, that's all.'

'You'll know when you are. Perhaps you could meet Christian a few more times and see.'

'I do like him, but I'm a bit more mindful after seeing Alex the other evening. I longed for him to ask to come back, and when it happened, it wasn't what I wanted anymore.'

'You were missing him but only as being part of a couple.'

'Yes, exactly.'

'I suppose you did well getting him to stay with you for so long really. You drive me bananas at times, and I'm not even married to you.'

Clara threw a cushion at him. 'Being with someone all the time is hard work. I suppose a long-term relationship has to be worked at.' She paused. 'Do you think I gave in too easily?'

'I think Alex did, and once that happens, it's hard to work at something again. I know I wouldn't want to. That seed of doubt would always be there.'

'I thought Mum was the wise one, but you've just stolen her crown. Don't tell her I said that.' She laughed. 'How was your evening?'

'I have a date of my own lined up for tomorrow.'

Clara raised her eyebrows. 'With Kelsey?'

'How do you know?'

'Because you haven't shut up about her in days!'

'Have I been that obvious?'

'Yes, that and your skin turning the colour of beetroot every time you dropped her name into conversation.'

'You know me too well.'

'I hope she'll be okay with our fake marriage.' She grinned. 'I'm so lucky to have you, even though I know I'll have to share you one day.'

'Maybe.' He tapped her leg. 'But until then, it's your turn to make a cuppa!'

CHAPTER FIFTY-SEVEN

Since meeting Elsie and Bill Redfern a fortnight ago, Maria had been planning something extra special for Jim. She had thought of taking him bowling, one of the things they'd enjoyed during their earlier years together. But seeing Elsie and Bill so happy, she wanted to make a wonderful memory of her own. She and Jim were moving on to the next stage of their lives together. She needed to shed some demons before she could do that.

Jim popped an overnight bag in the boot of the car. 'Are you going to tell me where we're off to yet?'

Maria hadn't let him open the envelope until they were ready to leave. She gave it to him now.

'Sapphire Lake?' A small grin appeared. 'That was the last place I thought you'd say.'

'I wanted to make a better memory for us after the last, ahem, mishap.'

'What will we be doing?'

'Wait and see.'

The journey took less than fifteen minutes. Maria pulled into the main car park and continued down a track towards the lake. Jim turned to her with an inquisitive look, but she said nothing.

Moments later, she stopped outside a log cabin, the first of four in a row. There was ample space between them for privacy and decking around two sides.

'Tada,' she cried.

'I didn't realise these were open yet.'

'They're not. I spied the press release and charmed them into letting us try one out beforehand. I'm going to do a write up about our visit, and Clara's offered to help with some PR pieces.'

Jim raised his eyebrows. 'I'm impressed.'

'Wait until you see inside.'

The cabins were new to the village of Moorland. Their planned opening in spring had been delayed until summer as the owner had wanted to get a road dug out to make things easier.

They stepped onto the decking and took in the view first, the lake looking as splendid as ever. Then Maria unlocked the door. She couldn't wait to see inside.

'Wow.' Jim put their bag on the settee. 'This really is something.'

'Isn't it just?'

The cabin was all on one level, with a living space and a kitchen combined. To their right, there was a large bedroom and bathroom. Everything was high end, the colour schemes of blue, grey, and pale lemon pleasantly flowing through. The art on the wall had been painted by a local artist, all available for sale.

'Let's unpack and take a walk,' she said, eager to erase the memories of their last visit. 'Then we can grab a bite to eat.'

'Sounds good to me.'

This time, she walked around Sapphire Lake, her hand nestled inside Jim's, with a sense of contentment.

'Do you want to go to the top of the hill?' she asked, a hint of humour in her voice.

'Naw.' He smirked. 'I have all I want down here.'

'We're so lucky, Jim. What we have, and what we've done. I don't want my age to drag me down so that I can't enjoy the years that are left. It's time for me to change now, look forward rather than back all the time. I *don't* want to feel invisible anymore, and I *don't* want to constantly watch what I eat in case I add on another kilo or two. I want to embrace being *me*. I'm different now.'

'We both are, even though I hate to admit to feeling my age at times.'

'It's not a competition, but I think it's harder for me. When I see Clara and Lucy, I constantly see younger versions of myself. How did we make such beautiful girls?'

'I enjoyed the making part, so I expect that was down to me,' Jim teased.

'I'm trying to be serious, you big sap!' Maria glanced across the lake for a moment. 'I still want to have fun as well as work on the businesses. But I want work to start coming second rather than first. We have enough.'

She told him then about Elsie and Bill; enjoyed how he laughed at their antics. Even now she could see her and Jim both together like that, all old and wrinkly. Their bodies were never going to be free of aches and pains. In fact, they would get worse over the years. But true love would never fade, it changed and deepened.

It was all about acceptance now, not dwelling on how much had gone compared to what was left. All those things she'd thought about, put off until later, she was going to do. There was no time like the present. No one was guaranteed a tomorrow.

They had so much to look forward to, and who knows, in time, they could have great-grandchildren like Elsie and Bill.

Later, after a long lunch by the waterside, they spent the afternoon browsing the craft cabins, and then enjoying a glass of wine at The Moorland Hotel. Maria glanced at Jim. He was the best she'd seen him in a good while. She faked a yawn.

'I feel a nanna nap coming on. Want to join me?'

Jim reached across to squeeze her hand. 'Sounds good to me.'

Things had been going well with Lucy and Saskia since their talk at the barbecue. A calm had fallen on the house – well, as much as could be expected with a family of two girls.

Lucy had basked in it. For the first time ever, she felt settled, happy with life, and excited about the future. The latest scan had shown everything was fine with the baby, and in herself, she was feeling good.

Last night, Aaron had mentioned the job he was working on would finish earlier than expected, so he'd be home for the afternoon. He'd suggested collecting the girls from school together and taking them out for tea.

'Can I have fish fingers and chips, please?' Ellie asked as soon as she'd sat at a table for four in The White Lion.

'You don't want to see the new menu?' Aaron questioned, pushing the chair in for her. 'I think they might have dinosaur eggs on it.'

'Do they really?' Ellie's eyes widened.

'Dinosaurs are extinct,' Saskia told her. 'Stop teasing her, Dad.'

'Yeah, silly Daddy.' Ellie laughed along with Aaron as he tickled her.

Lucy smiled. She was glad Ellie wasn't put out, as for some reason, Saskia had sat next to her, taking her daughter's usual seat.

Aaron and Ellie were now discussing Velociraptors and their claws.

'What are you having?' Lucy asked Saskia as she studied the menu. 'I think I'll go for a chicken burger.'

'I might go for that, too.' Saskia turned to her, a shy smile. 'Could I ask you something?'

'Sure.'

'You know that Ellie calls Aaron, Dad?'

'Hmm-hmm.' Lucy froze while she waited to see what Saskia said next. Please let it be what she hoped.

'Well, could I call you Mum?'

'Oh, Saskia, nothing would make me prouder.' Lucy flung her arms around the young girl.

'What's all this, then?' Aaron wanted to know. 'Is it women's stuff, or can anyone join in?'

'I've just asked Lucy if I can call her Mum,' Saskia said, this time her voice assured.

Lucy smirked when Aaron tried to hide the look of astonishment before grinning like a loon. It had been hard for her to hide that, too. Elated with what Saskia was saying, she hadn't wanted it to seem as if she wasn't pleased.

'Well, here's to our family,' Aaron said.

'To our family.' Lucy placed a hand on her tummy.

CHAPTER FIFTY-EIGHT

It was seven p.m., and Maria was getting ready for the evening ahead. She smoothed down the material on her dress, smiling at her reflection in the wardrobe mirror. She may not be as slim as she'd like, but even she had to admit that the blue in the dress made her come alive. There was a radiance about her.

Or maybe that was because of the time she was spending with Jim.

'Wow,' Jim exclaimed as she rejoined him in the living area. 'You look incredible.'

'You don't look so bad yourself.'

He was wearing navy trousers and a short-sleeved checked shirt. Maria's heart gave a flutter when he winked at her.

'You do remember what I said about blue dresses?' He pulled her into his arms. 'I'd rather see it off than on.'

'We can save that for later.' She heard herself giggle like a teenager and laughed even more. Because that's exactly how she felt.

She realised that the dates they'd been on had accumulated to create this feeling. She was in love again, unsure how it had happened but enjoying every minute of it. Reminiscing about Blackpool, playing board games again, watching movies, even the trip halfway up the hill, had brought them closer together.

Then there were the ones she'd organised. Laughing at the fair, getting blown away at the seaside, the trip to London. Through them all, she had found herself again, and in doing so had reconnected with Jim, making him happy, too. Their relationship had strengthened, and there was nothing that would stop them getting old and grey together.

'What are you thinking?' Jim asked, his voice inquisitive.

'That I don't want this day to end.'

'Ah, but the night is young.' They drew apart, and he held out his arm for her to slip a hand through. 'Are you ready to go?'

Maria shook her head. 'I'm waiting.'

'For what?'

'You'll see.'

A couple of minutes later, there was a knock on the door. Maria opened it to find three teenage boys. They were ladened down with straw hampers and food bags. One had a cooler box.

'Room service,' the nearest one said.

Maria beckoned the boys in.

Jim nodded his approval and moved to one side. 'Oh, this is top-notch.'

Maria beamed. Everything seemed to be going to plan.

The table was laid for two, the puddings and extra wine popped into the fridge. Maria gave them a handsome tip, and they left in a flurry of thank yous.

Once they were alone again, Jim pulled out a chair for Maria, and she sat down. He poured wine as she got out her phone, locating what she needed. Songs from the year they'd met.

They ate the meal, laughing and chattering in between bites. The summer evening turned dark eventually, the lights shining across the lake a display in their own right.

Afterwards, they took their coffee outside and sat on the veranda, cuddled up close.

'This has been a wonderful day, Maria.' Jim ran a finger lazily over her arm. 'I can't believe you went to so much trouble for me.'

'I changed my mind again about the last date. It was seeing Elsie and Bill that made me want to do something special, for us both. I'd planned for us to go bowling.'

'Oh, that's a shame.'

She smiled, hearing the joy in his voice, but then he became all serious.

'I've been doing some thinking and I want to run something past you. How would you feel if I promoted Paul to general manager? That way I could take a day off during the week, perhaps Wednesdays? It would be nice to have a break in the middle of the week to spend with you.'

It was just what Maria had hoped he'd say. She nodded.

'I've already been chatting to the girls about the same thing. Lucy won't be able to do any additional hours, and we'll have to hire someone to cover her maternity leave. But Clara is up for taking on more responsibility, and I'll always be on the end of the phone if there's a problem. I'm also going to employ Regan full time at the end of her apprenticeship. She's such a hard worker, and I think she'll grow with the business.

'Great, that's settled then.' Jim clinked his coffee mug with hers. 'Here's to new beginnings.'

'New beginnings.' She stopped. 'I tried to write you a poem, but I'm afraid I was useless at it.'

His eyes widened. 'Can you remember any of it?'

'It sounded so childish.'

'Go on.'

'Well, it had something about loving you, warts and all.'

'I don't have any warts!'

'You know what I mean.' Maria thought back to her words. 'I wrote that I loved this about you, and that about you, and that I loved you more now than I did when I first met you, and that I don't want us to change, and something about here's to the next thirty years.'

Her words came out in one long, awkward sentence.

'You *are* a soppy sod.' He kissed her forehead. 'But you're right. I feel like a teenager again.'

'So do I, but I've also realised that getting older doesn't have to stop us from having fun.'

'I've realised something, too.' He paused, a look of embarrassment flashing across his face before he continued. 'Sometimes when I see you, I want to say I love you, but because I don't say it so often, it always feels forced, as if I shouldn't have to tell you because you already know how much. So I put it off. I'm going to put a stop to that and just come out with it. These dates have shown me how much I love you, Maria, more and more each day.'

'I love you, too, Jim.' And she did, with all her heart. But she couldn't say anything else due to the lump in her throat.

'What do you have planned for the final date?' Jim lightened the mood. 'I think you should tell me, seeing as I told you.'

'You spat it out in anger,' she objected.

'Which was your fault, if you recall.'

'I'm still not telling you.' She laughed. 'I have one more thing lined up, and then that's it. Unless you'd like to continue with them? It would be your turn to choose the next one if so.'

'We don't really need anymore, but they have been fun.'

'Maybe it could become a new family tradition. We could take it in turns to choose.'

'Okay. Can I go first?'

'Do you have something in mind?'

'I may have something planned.'

'You do?'

'You'll have to wait and see.'

CHAPTER FIFTY-NINE

It was Sunday morning. Lucy was in the car with Aaron. They'd dropped Saskia and Ellie off at her parents' home. Aaron was being all secretive about somewhere he wanted to take her without them being there.

'Where are we going?' she asked as they drove along Somerley High Street.

'You'll see in a few minutes, it's not far.'

'So, why all the secrecy?'

'I'm learning that from your mum and dad. All those dates, and doing things for each other? Well, call me a mush, but I wanted to do something for you, too.'

'Oh!'

'For all of us, really. You me, the girls, and the ever-growing bump.'

Lucy automatically placed a hand on her tummy. Now that she was past the sickness stage, she was beginning to look forward to the arrival of a new baby. There were months to go yet, but it was still exciting.

'So what is it?'

'Wait and see!'

Aaron turned into Roman Avenue, and Lucy gasped.

'Number fourteen!' She held her breath for a moment, her eyes wide in anticipation. Yesterday, her mum had shown her a house being sold by another estate agent. In the office, they'd all oohed and ahhed over the photos of each room and the gardens outside. Lucy had even said she wanted to live in something like that in the future.

'What's the one thing I've been saying to you for months now?' Aaron questioned.

'We need a bigger house.'

'That's right. I know it must be hard for you to live in the home where I started with Melissa, especially after she turned up out of the blue.'

'At least that's sorted now. I'm still staggered – but really pleased – that Saskia wants to call me Mum.'

'Well, this is the icing on the cake.'

Lucy beamed. 'Are you sure we can afford it?'

'Yes, I've sorted out a mortgage in principle. And if you don't like this house, we can look for another. My – our house – is going up online tomorrow, if you're happy to move?'

'I am!'

'Your mum reckons she has a few people who will be interested in it straightaway.'

'Oh, I bet she has. Good old Wilshaw Estate Agents.' Lucy clapped. 'Oh, Aaron, do you really think we could?'

'I'm certain.'

They pulled up outside the property, and Aaron took out a bunch of keys.

'The perks of knowing an estate agent is that I get to show you around myself.' He took her hand. 'Your mum wangled the keys for the weekend as it's empty. Come on, let's go inside.'

Aaron opened the front door, and they stepped into a

hallway, a staircase leading off it with doors to the living room and a kitchen at the far end.

'I think you should do the spiel on me,' he said. 'Oh, wait, perhaps I know someone who will do it for you.'

Lucy followed him into the kitchen to find her mum there. She squealed, running into her arms for a hug. 'What are you doing here? I've just left you at home!'

'It's why I took the scenic route,' Aaron explained.

'Are you arranging things for all of us now?' Lucy wanted to know.

'As much as it's giving me pleasure, this is all down to Aaron. I just helped you along by showing you both some houses online.' Maria threw an arm across the room. 'What do you think of the size of the kitchen?'

'I love it, Mum. Perfect for all the family get-togethers.'

'I think you'll all be very happy here. Your dad and I wanted to give you this, too.' Maria handed a cheque to them.

'Oh, Mum.' Lucy's mouth dropped open when she saw it was for ten thousand pounds. 'Are you sure? I mean, thank you, but it's a lot of money.'

'It's a gift for your future. We're giving Clara the same.'

'Wow, thanks, Maria.' Aaron kissed her on the cheek. 'I don't know what to say.'

Maria glanced at her watch. 'I'm going to leave you to have a nosy around on your own. I've borrowed the keys until tomorrow. But don't be too long. I'll see you later for lunch.'

As Lucy took another tour with Aaron, she reflected on how much her life had changed since Christmas. Not only was she going to be moving into the house of her dreams, with a baby on the way, but she was deliriously happy. There was only one more thing that would make things perfect.

'I think Saskia will love this room,' she said, going into the second largest bedroom. 'She'll have her own space again. And just look at that garden!'

'So will I.' Aaron came up beside her and reached for her hand. 'I've always wanted somewhere I can have a man cave to hide in. Away from all the women until the bump comes along.'

'Cheeky.' Lucy rested her hand on her stomach. She was dying to know what they were having but was mindful that Aaron wanted it to be a surprise.

'Yes,' Aaron whispered into her ear.

'Yes, what.'

'Let's find out what we're having at your next scan.'

'Yes!'

'If it's a boy, I think Albie would be cool,' he said after a moment.

Lucy paused. Albie Foxley. She rolled the name around her mouth. Then she laughed. She'd automatically given her unborn child Aaron's surname. Well, there was only one thing left to do.

She gazed into the eyes of the man who meant everything to her. So what if they were an eclectic family. They had their moments, and there would be lots more of them, but she was very fortunate. It was what her mum had been telling her for years.

Love. When you always have someone there to support you, stand by you, most things come good in the end because of it.

'What?' Aaron said, his eyes narrowing.

She placed her hand on the side of his face. 'Aaron Foxley, will you marry me?'

He broke out into a grin, nodding profusely. 'There is nothing I'd love more.'

Lucy didn't want the moment to end. She wanted to stay here, in this house, make it into a home for her family and her man. Her fiancé. Wow, what a day.

'Wait until we tell your mum that she was right,' Aaron said.

'What do you mean?'

'She said if you saw this place, you'd ask to be my wife.'

'She never!' Lucy grinned. 'It seems that mums are always right.'

CHAPTER SIXTY

Maria was finally back at home in the kitchen, her family and friends spread out in the dining area and conservatory. She was trying not to join in with the banter and good-natured bickering, concentrating on dishing up. Sunday dinner was all about precise timing.

As soon as the food was on the plates, she passed them to Clara and Saskia, who were helping her.

'That's your dad's.' Maria pointed. 'He has extra roast potatoes.'

'But that's not fair,' Clara protested. 'I like them, too.'

'Have one of mine,' Tyler shouted over.

Clara smiled coyly at her mum, pinching one from his plate and popping it onto her own.

Maria picked up the last two plates and walked over to the table with them. She gave one to Lucy and one to Aaron.

'I want to sit next to Granddad,' Ellie shouted.

'You're fine where you are, little miss,' Lucy chided. 'Granddad can't cut your meat because of his arm.'

'Oh, yes!' Ellie covered her mouth and giggled. 'I'll sit by you then, Mummy.'

Everyone tucked in, sighs of appreciation all around the room.

'This beef is delicious, Maria.' Jim waved his cast in the air. 'Only one more week and I'll be able to cut it myself again.'

Maria smiled. Jim was healing well. There had been no more episodes, and once the cast was removed, the only reminder would be the scar that was luckily hidden by his hair. Maria would still worry about him until he'd been checked out by specialists, but it was all good for now.

She took a moment to watch everyone enjoying their food. This was her family, her brood, and she loved every one of them. Sal and Tyler, too. Sal was her sister from another mister; Tyler the son she'd shared since his birth. They'd earned their place at the family lunches. Things would inevitably change in the future, but for now, it wouldn't seem complete without them.

Maria caught Jim looking at her and smiled. How had she thought that all this was never enough? She cursed herself inwardly for being such a fool. Family was love, and love was family. She'd been lucky enough to be blessed with both. Not a lot of people could say that.

Tyler was spouting off a story from his postal deliveries that week. Already everyone was amused at his antics. It was good to see Clara laughing so heartily. Maria had been pleased to hear she was meeting Christian again next week, glad she was taking things slowly, too. Who knew, maybe in the future, he'd be sitting around the table with them.

She watched as Lucy gazed at Aaron in adoration, the same thing she had seen between Elsie and Bill. Lucy's tiny bump was getting bigger by the week, and Maria couldn't wait to meet another little one and welcome them into their family.

She had been so excited to hear their news. Their engagement would be imminent, and for now, she and Jim had been sworn to secrecy. Lucy hadn't wanted to overshadow their last date. It was a nice gesture, but equally, it needed to be shared.

At the far end of the table, Jim was still staring at her. She crossed her eyes and flicked out her tongue, relishing hearing his laughter, her smile then matching his. But then he hushed everyone and raised a glass.

'Here's to family.'

'To family!' The words rang out around the room.

'I love that you include me and Tyler in that,' Sal said, wiping rogue tears from her face.

'Ah, me ma has come over all emotional,' Tyler said. 'But actually, I feel the same way.'

'If you let me finish,' Jim continued. 'There are two further things I want to say. Well, three actually.'

Everyone groaned, good-natured backchat erupting.

'Three things!'

'Typical Dad needing to have the last word.'

'He never can keep his mouth shut for long.'

'I wonder what crap he'll come out with now.'

'If you don't mind.' Jim cleared his throat. 'Firstly, I want to say something to Lucy.'

They all turned to stare at her. Lucy coloured in an instant.

'What, Dad?' she asked.

'Please let that be a grandson in there. I can't take any more girls!'

'Well, I can't promise that!' Lucy laughed, everyone joining in. 'But we have decided to find out, so you'll all be the first to know.'

A cheer went up.

'Is there anything else you'd like to share?' Jim urged.

'Jim, behave!' Maria admonished, even though she was in with what he was going to do next.

'Well, if it's a day of celebration...' Aaron glanced at Lucy. Lucy nodded.

'Lucy and I are getting married.'

This time there was a lot of clapping and whooping amidst congratulations.

'And finally.' Jim disappeared for a moment and came back with a box which he gave to Maria. 'This is for my lovely wife.'

Maria's eyes widened. 'What on earth is it?'

'Open it and see.'

'Is it a new pair of shoes?'

'Not exactly.'

Maria ripped off the wrapping, opened the plain box, and snapped the lid shut again. She burst into raucous laughter. Then she glanced across at Jim. He had the most childish grin on his face. She opened the lid again and held up her gift.

'Roller skates!'

Maria was relaxing in the conservatory as Jim finished loading the last of the dishes. The tribe had gone moments ago, Delilah was already in her basket catching up on her sleep, and the house was silent.

Bliss.

The garden was looking lovely at this time of year. But winter was her favourite season in the house, and she couldn't wait to get to it, especially with a new grandchild due around the same time.

Maria hadn't told Jim about her thoughts after meeting Mr and Mrs Westfield. She wanted to be certain her emotions weren't running away with her because of finding out that Vicky was in remission from cancer.

But, ever since that day, every time she came home to

Lilac Grove, it was just that. A sense of belonging flooded her. She knew she could be happier here now.

She understood that her life was about going forward rather than constantly wanting to go back in time. She couldn't change her past, but she could dictate her future. She and Jim may not be love's young dream anymore, but what they had was precious and had stood the test of time.

'Maria?' Jim walked towards her, snapping his fingers to get her attention. 'You're miles away.'

'I was just thinking about the family. We did a terrific job raising our daughters.'

'We sure did.' He sat beside her. 'I suppose with Lucy and Clara on the move, you'll be wanting to put our house up for sale soon?'

It was almost as if he'd been reading her mind. She doubted he knew what she was about to say next, though.

'For a long time in my life, I've felt as if something was missing. Now I realise, I don't care where I live as long as I have you, and all my girls. I've accepted that I'm fifty and fabulous, that I am doing okay, and that this is where I want to be.'

'So we're staying put?'

She nodded, delighted at the elation in his voice. 'Yes, because, for me, home is wherever you are.'

A LETTER FROM MARCIE

First of all, I want to say a huge thank you for choosing to read Moving On. I hope you enjoyed my fourth outing to the market town of Somerley, and getting to know Maria, Lucy and Clara as much as I did. This was a dream book to write – family, love and nostalgia, some of my favourite things.

If you did enjoy Moving On I would be grateful if you

would write a small review. I'd love to hear what you think, and it can also help other readers to discover one of my books for the first time. Maybe you can recommend it to your friends and family.

Many thanks to anyone who has emailed me, messaged me, chatted to me on Facebook or Twitter and told me how much they have enjoyed reading my books. I've been genuinely blown away with all kinds of niceness and support from you all. A writer's job is often a lonely one but I feel I truly have friends everywhere.

Why not join my readers VIP club? I'll send you a free ebook, Coffee with Marcie, with stories you can read on a break. I'll keep you up to date with when the next book will be out, as well as run regular competitions to win books and goodies, and talk about other books I've read and enjoyed.

I'd love to keep in touch,
Marcie x

WHAT'S NEXT?

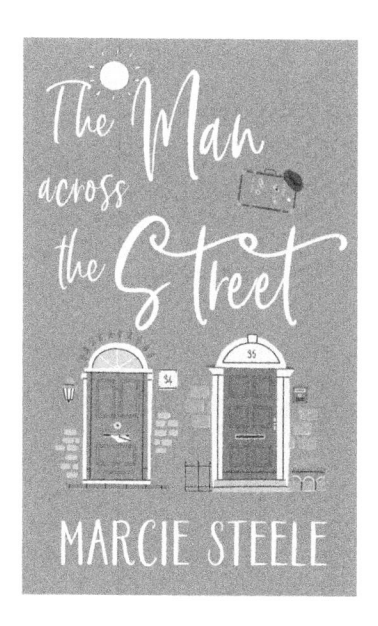

Welcome to Hope Street. It's full of warm people, loving relationships, and charming friends - well, most of the time.

Hannah has been her mum's sole carer since she was eighteen. Now alone after Martha's death, she's coming up to her fortieth birthday and wondering what her purpose in life is. When a letter left by her mum reveals a family secret, it shocks her to the core. Hannah's sister left over twenty years ago – could this be the reason why?

Doug is a workaholic, but a mild heart attack gives him a wake-up call. Now on the mend, he needs to de-stress his life and focus on living it, to make sure it doesn't happen again. He moves to Hope Street, number 35. Hannah lives directly opposite him. From the moment they meet, there's a spark.

But just as things start to look up for Hannah, she finds out that Doug has a secret too, and this one threatens to destroy everything. Will she ever get the happy ending she yearns for? Or will the path of true love stop at the cobblestones?

Find out more here

ALSO BY MARCIE STEELE

The Somerley Collection
Stirred with Love
Secrets, Lies and Love
Second Chances at Love
The Man Across the Street
Coming Home to Hope Street
Moving On
One Letter

ACKNOWLEDGMENTS

To my friends Alison Niebierszczanski, Caroline Mitchell, Imogen Clark, Louise Ross, Talli Roland and Sharon Sant. Thanks for all the coffee, cake and chats!

Many thanks also to anyone who has emailed me, messaged me, chatted to me on Facebook or Twitter and told me how much they have enjoyed reading this book. I've been genuinely blown away with all kinds of niceness and support from you all. A writer's job is often a lonely one but I feel I truly have friends everywhere.

ABOUT THE AUTHOR

Marcie Steele is a pen name. I'm Mel Sherratt and ever since I can remember, I've been a meddler of words. Born and raised in Stoke-on-Trent, Staffordshire, I used the city as a backdrop for my first novel, Taunting the Dead, and it went on to be a Kindle number one bestseller and the overall number eight UK Kindle bestselling book of 2012. Since then, I've written twenty-six books and sold over two million copies.

As Mel, I like writing about fear and emotion – the cause and effect of crime – what makes a character do something. Working as a housing officer for eight years also gave me the background to create a fictional estate full of good and bad characters (think *Brassic* meets *Coronation Street*.)

But I'm a romantic at heart and have always wanted to write about characters that are not necessarily involved in the darker side of life. I like to write about love, romance, friendship, family, secrets and lies in everyday life - feel good factor with humour and heart.

Coffee, cakes and friends are three of my favourite things, hence writing under the name of Marcie Steele too. I can often be found sitting in a coffee shop, sipping a cappuccino and eating a chocolate chip cookie, either catching up with friends or writing on my laptop.

Copyright © Marcie Steele 2023

All rights reserved.

The right of Marcie Steele to be identified as the author of this work has been asserted in accordance with the Copyright, Designs and Patents Act 1988. All rights reserved in all media.

No part of this publication may be reproduced, stored in or transmitted into any retrieval system, in any form, or by any means (electronic, mechanical, photocopying, recording or otherwise) without the prior written permission of the publisher. Any person who does any unauthorised act in relation to this publication may be liable to criminal prosecution and civil claims for damages.

This is a work of fiction. Names, characters, businesses, places, events and incidents are either the products of the author's imagination or used in a fictitious manner. Any resemblance to actual persons, living or dead, or actual events is purely coincidental.

Cover design copyright © Marcie Steele

Printed in Great Britain
by Amazon